FUTURE WEAPONS OF WAR

edited by
Joe Haldeman &
Martin H. Greenberg

FUTURE WEAPONS OF WAR

edited by
Joe Haldeman &
Martin H. Greenberg

FUTURE WEAPONS OF WAR

A Baen Books Original

Baen Publishing Enterprises
P.O. Box 1403
Riverdale, NY 10471
www.baen.com

ISBN 10: 1-4165-2112-7
ISBN 13: 978-1-4165-2112-9

Cover art by David Mattingly

First printing, March 2007

Distributed by Simon & Schuster
1230 Avenue of the Americas
New York, NY 10020

Library of Congress Cataloging-in-Publication Data:

Future weapons of war / edited by Joe Haldeman & Martin H. Greenberg.
p. cm.
"A Baen Books Original"—T.p. verso.
ISBN 1-4165-2112-7
1. Science fiction, American. 2. Imaginary wars and battles—Fiction. 3. Weapons—Fiction. 4. Soldiers—Fiction. I. Haldeman, Joe W. II. Greenberg, Martin Harry.
PS648.S3F93 2007
813'.54—dc22

2006100468

Printed in the United States of America

10 9 8 7 6 5 4 3 2 1

Table of Contents

INTRODUCTION

Joe Haldeman

When John Helfers and Marty Greenberg asked me to edit this anthology, I have to admit that the title was irresistible. I'm not a nut about weapons, future or present, but I've carried them when, technically, my life depended on them—lugging them around 24/7, eating and sleeping with them, cleaning them incessantly and keeping ammunition close to hand.

Which has been the soldier's lot for a long time, of course. What will the future hold? Self-cleaning weapons that make their own ammo? Somehow I don't think so.

Like most soldiers, I had a love/hate relationship with the weapons I carried: they can protect or save your life, but they also make you a target. And sometimes they don't work as advertised, or even turn on their owners.

In Vietnam, a couple of hours before I was to get on the helicopter that would take me out of the base camp and into war, I had an interesting colloquy with the company

armorer, a chain-smoking sergeant who was obviously glad to be staying behind. He set four hand grenades in front of me and I had to tell him about raking leaves.

In Basic Training, which was a world away but only a few months before, we had practiced grenade throwing with one-pound, grenade-shaped lumps of iron. I was no good at it. As a kid, I could never throw a ball, and after six years of college had long since stopped trying.

You were supposed to be able to throw this little anvil forty meters; I couldn't even get it forty *feet*. That was well inside the thing's fifteen-meter radius of wounding. There was no way they were going to let me throw a real one. So when the time came for practice with live grenades, they arranged for me to go rake leaves in front of the officers' living quarters. Everybody thought that was funny, the college boy draftee raking leaves because he couldn't handle balls, but I guess I felt a little relieved, hearing a grenade go off every minute or so, glad to be humiliating myself by raking leaves rather than by losing an arm or an eye.

I'd never even seen a live grenade, and here I was in Vietnam with four of them sitting in front of me. I explained to the sergeant about raking leaves, and he applied the universal U.S. Army solution: Green Tape.

Green Tape is actually duct tape in camouflage, and is just as handy as its civilian counterpart. In this case, you wrap it around each grenade a couple of times, so that even if the pin is dislodged, the thing won't go off, because the arming lever won't spring away. He advised me that I did have to carry them, regulations, but I could put them in the bottom of my rucksack and forget about them.

Then I got my assault rifle, the legendary M-16, that looked so cool from a distance. Mine had a dent in the plastic stock, which was gray with oxidation, and the barrel sported speckles of rust. Like many of them, its stock was defaced with scratched graffiti, in my case the

disturbing observation THIS MACHINE DOESN'T WORK. I asked the sergeant about that, and he shrugged it off. The rifle had come from the brigade armory; there was nothing wrong with it. I asked whether there was someplace I could take it and try it out, and he was as shocked as a stateside pawnshop clerk would be. Hell, no, where do you think you are? Wait till you get out in the field.

Of course, when I got out in the field, they had a similar "where do you think you are?" attitude, with more justification. You don't just go shoot a weapon in combat. Somebody might think you were shooting *at* something. Even them.

My job description didn't involve shooting, anyhow. I was a combat engineer (Pioneer), which meant I got to blow up stuff while other people carried rifles to protect me.

I went through some months of combat without ever having to shoot, which was typical for engineers. They stay in the middle, with the officers and other technical folk, and only shoot when everybody else has been overrun, which fortunately didn't happen to us.

I finally did try out the M-16—we had the occasional "mad minute" when everybody just faces outwards and blasts away, getting rid of old ammunition and inhibitions—and I could see that the message on the stock was inaccurate. It should have said THIS MACHINE WORKS AFTER A FASHION, BUT YOU BETTER HIT YOUR TARGET WITH THE FIRST ROUND. Because the second round in the clip came up sideways and jammed. I tried it again and it did it again. I had the only single-shot weapon in a fully automatic war.

I complained to my sergeant and lieutenant, and they said I'd have a replacement right away. I guess the request went to the same armorer who'd given it to me in the first place, though. Nothing ever happened, but then I'd never really wanted to shoot anybody, except maybe that armorer.

I did get to throw one hand grenade. It was probably one of the most expensive hand grenades ever thrown.

We were in a tense situation. A large North Vietnamese force was headed for Saigon, and we were in the way. We were on high alert, with "sound and light" discipline at night, no lights or noises. When we were on guard at night, two hours on and two hours off, under no circumstances were we to fire our M-16s at the enemy. The muzzle flashes would give away our position. Throw grenades instead.

I tried to unwrap the tape on my grenades, but months of jungle heat and moisture had turned the Green Tape to a solid mass. I was able to cut free the arming levers with my Swiss army knife scissors, though, and I lined up the four instruments of destruction on the lip of my foxhole, so I could find them by touch in the dark.

And it *was* dark, dark as the inside of a black hole. Raining, though. We strained our ears, in case the enemy wasn't constrained by sound discipline. And I heard something.

Someone was coming toward me through the woods. He wasn't sneaking, either.

I did what I'd been told, whispering into the radio, "Tiger-one, this is Tiger-seven. I have movement."

The answer threaded back: "Chuck a grenade at 'im."

I didn't have time to explain about raking leaves and all. Before long, the guy was going to be close enough so that even I could hit him. I worked the pin out of the grenade and pointed my left hand out into the darkness, as I recalled having done with the one-pound dummies, and heaved the little bomb with all my might.

Straight up, approximately. Or so it felt.

I yelled "Fire in the hole!"—engineer-speak for "Big noise coming!"—and heard lots of people crashing around, getting into their respective holes (or probably just the nearest one), and, about three seconds later, the grenade exploded, very loud, though not as close to being in our laps as I had feared.

(Note: An actual grenade is not at all like the ones they have on television, which make a big orange flame and throw cars around. They really make a little puff-cloud of gray smoke and a small flash, with dangerous bits of metal singing and whirring through the air.)

Somebody yelled "Incoming!" and all hell broke loose. We had about a hundred and fifty guys in our circle, armed to the teeth, and they now thought somebody was shooting at them. Well, maybe somebody was. In a couple of minutes, a nearby artillery base joined in, pounding the woods around us with high explosive and white phosphorous. Then a couple of gunships came throbbing up and added their guns and rockets to the show.

It seemed to go on for a long time, but it was probably only about 45 minutes. Then eerie quiet, illumination rounds falling under parachutes, their magnesium flares hissing and crackling. Call it $150,000 worth of ordnance, in 1968 dollars.

At least no one was hurt by my feeble grenade toss, least of all the person I threw it at, who was probably some drunken farmer trying to find his way home.

That's not a future weapons story, but suppose I put it on another planet, gave the drunken farmer eight legs, and made the grenade one that worked by tweaking the weak interaction force in transuranium elements?

It still wouldn't be a future weapons story, of course—it would be the monstrosity that James Blish dubbed "Call a rabbit a smeerp": an otherwise ordinary story that takes place on a planet that has cuddly long-eared things called smeerps.

Military science fiction does provide fertile ground for that kind of story, but you won't find one here.

There is vivid imagination in these stories; there is cleverness and intelligence and occasional wisdom. Violence on the cosmic scale and the molecular, and violence up close and personal. Sometimes the avoidance of violence altogether.

There are aliens who seem human here, no surprise, and humans who seem alien. Soldiers who are animals or machines or abstract entities.

They all speak to the human condition, though, of which war has been an aspect for as long as there have been divisions of humanity on the basis of geography, citizenship, race, or religion. Perhaps we'll evolve out of it before it destroys us.

For that, Albert Einstein may have had the final word on the future of weapons:

"I don't know with what weapons World War III will be fought, but World War IV will be fought with sticks and stones."

CRATERS

Kristine Kathryn Rusch

What they don't tell you when you sign up is that the work takes a certain amount of trust. The driver, head covered by a half-assed turban, smiles a little too much, and when he yes ma'ams you and no ma'ams you, you can be lulled into thinking he actually works for you.

Then he opens the side door of his rusted jeep and nods at the dirt-covered seat. You don't even hesitate as you slide in, backpack filled with water bottles and purifying pills, vitamins and six day's dry rations.

You sit in that jeep, and you're grateful, because you never allow yourself to think that he could be one of them, taking you to some roadside bunker, getting paid an advance cut of the ransom they anticipate. Or worse, getting paid to leave you there so that they can all take turns until you're bleeding and catatonic and don't care when they put the fifty-year-old pistol to your head.

You can't think about the risks, not as you're getting in that jeep, or letting some so-called civilian lead you down sunlit streets that have seen war for centuries almost non-stop.

You trust, because if you don't you can't do your job.

You trust, and hope you get away from this place before your luck runs out.

I still have luck. I know it because today we pull into the camp. This camp's just like all the others I've seen in my twenty-year career. The ass-end of nowhere, damn near unbearable heat. Barbed wire, older than God, fences in everything, and at the front, soldiers with some kind of high tech rifle, some sort of programmable thing I don't understand.

My driver pulls into a long line of oil-burning cars, their engines only partly modified to hydrogen. The air stinks of gasoline, a smell I associate with my childhood, not with now.

We sit in the heat. Sweat pours down my face. I nurse the bottle of water I brought from the Green Zone—a misnomer we've applied to the American base in every "war" since Iraq. The Green Zone doesn't have a lick of green in it. It just has buildings that are theoretically protected from bombs and suicide attacks.

Finally, we pull up to the checkpoint. I clutch my bag against my lap, even though the canvas is heavy and hot.

My driver knows the soldiers. "Reporter lady," he tells them in English. The English is for my benefit, to prove once again that he is my friend. I haven't let him know that I know parts (the dirty parts mostly) of two dozen languages. "Very famous. She blog, she do vid, you see her on CNN, no?"

The soldiers lean in. They have young faces covered in sand and mud and three-day-old beards. The same faces I've been seeing for years—skin an indeterminate color, thanks to the sun and the dirt, eyes black or brown or covered with shades, expressions flat—the youth visible only in the body shape, the lack of wrinkles and sunlines, the leftover curiosity undimmed by too much death over too much time.

I lean forward so they can see my face. They don't recognize me. CNN pays me, just like the *New York Times News Service*, just like the Voice of the European Union. But none of them broadcast or replicate my image.

The woman everyone thinks of as me is a hired face, whose features get digitized over mine before anything goes out into public. Too many murdered journalists. Too many famous targets.

The military brass, they know to scan my wrist, send the code into the Reporter Registry, and get the retinal download that they can double-check against my eye. But foot soldiers, here on crap duty, they don't know for nothing.

So they eyeball me, expecting a pretty face—all the studio hires are skinny and gorgeous—and instead, getting my shoe-leather skin, my dishwater blond going on steel gray hair, and my seen-too-much eyes. They take in the sweat and the khakis and the pinkie jacks that look like plastic fingernails.

I wait.

They don't even confer. The guy in charge waves the jeep forward, figuring, I guess, that I clean up startlingly well. Before I can say anything, the jeep roars through the barbed wire into a wide flat street filled with people.

Most cultures call them refugees, but I think of them as the dregs—unwanted and unlucky, thrown from country to country, or locked away in undesirable land, waiting for a bit of charity, a change of political fortune, waiting for an understanding that will never, ever come.

✧ ✧ ✧

The smell hits you first: raw sewage combined with vomit and dysentery. Then the bugs, bugs like you've never seen, moving in swarms, sensing fresh meat.

After your first time with those swarms, you slather illegal bug spray on your arms, not caring that developed countries banned DDT as a poison/nerve toxin long ago. Anything to keep those creatures off you, anything to keep yourself alive.

You get out of your jeep, and immediately, the children who aren't dying surround you. They don't want sweets—what a quaint old idea that is—they want to know what kind of tech you have, what's buried in your skin, what you carry under your eyes, what you record from that hollow under your chin. You give them short answers, wrong answers, answers you'll regret in the quiet of your hotel room days later, after you know you've made it out to report once more. You remember them, wonder how they'll do, hope that they won't become the ones you see farther into the camp, sprawled outside thin government-issue tents, those bug swarms covering their faces, their stomachs distended, their limbs pieces of scrap so thin that they don't even look like useful sticks.

Then you set the memories—the knowledge—aside. You're good at setting things aside. That's a skill you acquire in this job, if you didn't already have it when you came in. The I'll-think-about-it-later skill, a promise to the self that is never fulfilled.

Because if you do think about it later, you get overwhelmed. You figure out pretty damn quickly that if you do think about all the things you've seen—all the broken bodies, all the dying children—you'll break, and if you break you won't be able to work, and if you can't work, you can no longer be.

After a while, work is all that's left to you. Between the misplaced trust and the sights no human should have to bear, you stand, reporting, because you believe someone will care, someone stronger will Do Something.

Even though, deep down, you know, there is no one stronger, and nothing ever gets done.

5:15 PM Upload: **Suicide Squadron Part I** by Martha Trumante

General Amanda Pedersen tells the story as if it happened two days ago instead of twenty years ago. She's sitting in one of the many cafeterias in the Louvre, this one just beneath the glass pyramid where the tourists enter. She's an American soldier on leave, spending a week with her student boyfriend at the Sorbonne. He has classes. She's seeing the sights.

She's just resting her feet, propping them up—American-style—on the plastic chair across from her. From her vantage, she can't see the first round of security in the pyramid itself, but she can see the second set of metal detectors, the ones installed after the simultaneous attacks of '19 that leveled half the Prado in Madrid and the Tate in London.

She likes watching security systems—that's what got her to enlist in the first place, guaranteeing a sense of security in an insecure world—and she likes watching people go through them.

The little boy and his mother are alone on the escalator coming down. They reach the security desk, the woman opening her palm to reveal the number embedded under the skin, her son—maybe four, maybe five—bouncing with excitement beside her.

A guard approaches him, says something, and the boy extends his arms—European, clearly, used to high levels of security. The guard runs his wand up the boy's legs, over his crotch, in front of his chest—

And the world collapses.

That's how she describes it. The world collapses. The air smells of blood and smoke and falling plaster. Her skin is covered in dust and goo and she has to pull some kind of stone off her legs. Miraculously, they're not broken, but as the day progresses, part of her wishes they were, so she wouldn't be carrying dead through the ruins of the Roman area, up the back stairs, and into the thin Paris sunlight.

She can't go to the rebuilt pyramid, even now, nor to the Touleries Garden or even look at the Seine without thinking of that little boy, the smile on his face as he bounces, anticipating a day in the museum, a day with his mother, a day without cares, like five-year-olds are supposed to have.

Were supposed to have.

Before everything changed.

The driver has left me. He will be back in two days, he says, waiting for me near the checkpoint, but I do not believe him. My trust only goes so far, and I will not pay him in advance for the privilege of ferrying me out of this place. So he will forget, or die, or think I have forgotten, or died, whatever eases his conscience if a shred of his conscience still remains.

I walk deep into the camp, my pack slung over my shoulder. My easy walk, my relatively clean clothing, and my pack mark me as a newcomer, as someone who doesn't belong.

The heat is oppressive. There's no place out of the sun except the tents the Red Cross and its relative out here, the Red Crescent, have put up. People sit outside those tents, some clutching babies, other supervising children who dig in the dirt.

Rivulets of mud run across the path. Judging by the flies and the smell, the mud isn't made by water. It's overflowing sewage, or maybe it's urine from the lack of a good latrine system or maybe it's blood.

There's a lot of blood here.

I do no filming, record no images. The Western world has seen these places before, countless times. When I was a child, late-night television had infomercials featuring cheerful men who walked through such places with a single well-dressed child, selling some religious charity that purported to help people.

Charities don't help people here. They merely stem the tide, stop the preventable deaths, keep the worst diseases at bay. But they don't find real homes for these people, don't do job training, don't offer language lessons, and more importantly, don't settle the political crises or the wars that cause the problems in the first place.

The aide worker has a harder job than I do, because the aide worker—the real aide worker—goes from country to country from camp to camp from crisis to crisis, knowing that for each life saved a thousand more will be lost.

I prefer my work, focused as it can be.

I have been on this assignment for six months now. Writing side pieces. Blogging about the bigger events. Uploading pieces that give no hint of my actual purpose.

My editors fear it will make me a target.

I know that I already am.

Whoever called these places camps had a gift for euphemism. These are villages, small towns with a complete and evolved social system.

You learn that early, in your first camp, when you ask the wrong person the wrong question. Yes, violence is common here—it's common in any human enclave—but it is also a means of crowd control.

Usually you have nothing to do with the extended social system. Usually you speak to the camp leaders—not the official leaders, assigned by the occupying power (whoever that may be), but the de facto leaders, the ones who ask for extra water, who discipline the teenagers who steal hydrogen from truck tanks, who kill the occasional criminal (as an example, always as an example).

You speak to these leaders, and then you leave, returning to the dumpy hotel in the dumpy (and often bombed-out) city, and lie on the shallow mattress behind the thin wooden door, and thank whatever god you know that you have a job, that your employer pays the maximum amount to ensure your safety, that you are not the people you visited that afternoon.

But sometimes, you must venture deep into the enclave, negotiate the social strata without any kind of assistance. You guess which tents are the tents of the privileged (the ones up front, nearest the food?), which tents are the tents of the hopelessly impoverished (in the middle, where the mud runs deep and the smells overwhelm?), and which tents belong to the outcasts, the ones no one speaks to, the ones that make you unclean when you speak to them.

Never assume they're the tents farthest away from the entrance. Never assume they're the ones nearest the collapsing latrines.

Never assume.

Watch, instead. Watch to see which areas the adults avoid, which parts the parents grab their children away from in complete and utter panic.

Watch.

It is the only way you'll survive.

The people I have come to see live in a row near the back of the medical tent. The medical tent has open sides to welcome easy cases, and a smaller, air-conditioned tent further inside the main one for difficult cases. There is no marking on the main tent—no garish red cross or scythe-like red crescent. No initials for Doctors Without Borders, no flag from some sympathetic and neutral country.

Just a medical tent, which leads me to believe this camp is so unimportant that only representatives from the various charitable organizations come here. Only a few people even know how bad things are here, are willing to see what I can see.

Even though I will not report it.

I'm here for this group within the camp, an enclave within the enclave. I must visit them and leave. I have, maybe, eight hours here—seven hours of talk, and one hour to get away.

I'm aware that when I'm through, I may not be able to find a ride close to the camp. I must trust again or I must walk.

Neither is a good option.

The tents in this enclave are surprisingly clean. I suspect these people take what they need and no one argues with them. No children lie outside the flaps covered in bugs. No children have distended stomachs or too thin limbs.

But the parents have that hollow-eyed look. The one that comes when the illusions are gone, the one that comes to people who have decided their god has either asked too much of them or has abandoned them.

I stand outside the tent, my questions suddenly gone. I haven't felt real fear for twenty years. It takes a moment to recognize it.

Once I go inside one of these tents, I cannot go back. My interest—my story—gets revealed.

Once revealed, I am through here. I cannot stay in this camp, in this country, in this region. I might even have to go stateside—some place I haven't been in years—and even then I might not be safe.

When I came here, I was hoping to speak a truth.

Now I'm not even sure I can.

6:15 PM Upload: **Suicide Squadron Part 2** by Martha Trumante

Two other devastating explosions occurred in Paris that day: One hundred fifty people died as the elevator going up

the Eiffel Tower exploded; and another twenty died when a bomb went off in one of the spires near the top of Notre Dame Cathedral.

France went into an unofficial panic. The country had just updated all its security systems in all public buildings. The systems, required by the European Union, were state-of-the-art. No explosives could get into any building undetected—or so the creators of the various systems claimed.

Armand de Monteverde had supervised the tests. He is a systems analyst and security expert with fifteen years' experience in the most volatile areas—Iraq, Russia, and Saudi Arabia. The United States hired him to establish security at its borders with Mexico and Canada, as well as oversee security at the various harbors along the East, West, and Gulf coasts.

He consulted with the French, went in as a spoiler—someone who tried to break the system—and declared the new process temporarily flawless.

"Why temporarily?" some British tabloid reporter asked him.

"Because," Monteverde said, "systems can always be beat."

But not usually so quickly, and not without detection. What bothered Monteverde as he pored over the data from all three Paris explosions was that he couldn't find, even then, the holes in the system.

He couldn't find who had brought the explosives in, how they'd been set off, or even what type they were.

No one else had those answers either, and they should have.

Until the Paris bombings, explosives left traces—some kind of fingerprints or signature. Until the Paris bombings, explosives were easy to understand.

I slip into the third tent to my left. It's cool inside, not just from the lack of sun, but also because some tiny computerized system runs air conditioning out of mesh covering the canvas. It's a rich person's tent, installed at great expense.

The tent has furniture, which surprises me. Chairs, blanket-covered beds, two small tables for meals. A woman, sitting cross-legged on a rug near the back, wears western clothing—a thin black blouse and black pants—her black hair cut in a stylish wedge. An eleven-year-old boy, clearly her son, sits beside her. He glances at me, his eyes dark and empty, then goes back to staring straight ahead.

I know he has no internal downloads. The camp doesn't allow any kind of net coverage, even if he has the personal chips. There's some kind of blocking technology that surrounds everything including the medical tent. International agreements allow medical facilities to have net links at all times, but these camps often exist outside an established international perimeter. Even though it straddles the borders of three separate countries, it is in none or all of them, depending on which international law the people in charge of the camp are trying to avoid.

I introduce myself. The woman gives me the look of disbelief that the soldiers should have given me. I slid her my plastic ID, since we have no systems to log onto here.

She stares at it, then turns it over, sees the hologram of the woman who plays me on the vids, and sighs.

"They warned me," she says, and I do not ask who they are. They are the people who arranged our meeting, the ones who use dozens of intermediaries, and who probably, even now, believe they are using me for some nefarious purpose. "They warned me you would not be what I expect."

A shiver runs through me. Even though I am impersonated on purpose so that the "bad guys," as our president calls them, do not know who I am, someone out there does. Maybe many someones. Maybe many someones connected to the "bad guys."

We go through preliminaries, she and I. I sit across from her, slightly out of range of her child's empty eyes. She offers tea, which I take but do not intend to drink. The cup is small and dainty, trimmed with gold. She has not yet had to trade it for a meal.

Then she slides a chip to me. I press it. A smiling man wearing a western business suit, his head uncovered, his hair as stylishly cut as the woman's is, grins at me. He holds the hand of a young girl, maybe five, who is the image of her mother. The girl laughs, one of those floaty childish laughs that some people never outgrow. The sound fills the tent, and the boy, sitting across from me, flinches.

"That's her?" I ask.

"Them," she says. "He died too."

I made it a point to know the case. There are so many cases that sometimes the details are irrelevant to all except the people involved. He had just parked his car outside a café in Cairo. He had told his wife he was taking his daughter to a special class—and indeed, an English-language class for the children of businessmen who had dealings with the West, was meeting just a block away.

He opened his door and the car exploded, killing him, his daughter, and three people on the sidewalk. If they had made it to class as was the plan, over fifty children would have died.

"She's so beautiful," I say. Hard to believe, even now, that a child like that can carry a bomb inside her. Hard to believe she exists only to kill others, at a specified place, at her own designated time.

I have promised myself I will not ask the standard question—*how can you do this? How can you do this to your own child?*

Instead, I say, "Did you know?"

"None of us knew." Her gaze meets mine. It is fierce, defiant. She has answered this question a hundred times, and her answer has never varied. Like so many survivors, she cannot believe her husband doomed his own child.

But I have promised myself I will get the real story, the story no one else has told. I want to know what it's like to be part of a society where children are tools, not people to be loved. I want to know how these people believe so much in a cause—any cause—that it is worth not only their own lives, but their child's as well.

So I must take her initial answers at face value. Perhaps I will challenge them later, but for now, I will see where they lead.

"If neither you nor your husband knew . . . " I say.

"My son didn't know either." Just as fierce. Maybe fiercer. She puts her hand on her son's head. He closes his eyes, but doesn't acknowledge her in any other way.

"If none of you knew," I say, trying hard not to let my disbelief into my voice, "then how did this happen?"

"Like it always does," she snaps. "They put the chips in at the hospital. On the day she was born."

The job is strange. It cannot be work because you cannot leave at the end of the day. It becomes part of you and you become part of it. That's why you and your colleagues label it a calling, put it on par with other religions, other callings that deal with ethics.

You sit across from murderers and ask, what made you decide to kill? as if that's a valid question. You sit across from mass murderers and ask, what is it about your political philosophy that makes your methods so attractive to others? as if you care about the answer.

You think: we need to know, as if knowing's enough to make the problem go away. As if you did the right thing when you were granted the only meeting ever with some charismatic leader—this generation's Vlad the Impaler or

Hitler or Osama Bin Laden—and interviewed him as if he were a reasonable person. As if you did the right thing when you failed to grab a guard's old-fashioned pistol, and blow the charismatic leader away.

Later you discuss ethics as if they are an important concept.

You say: your job prevents you from judging other people.

You say: other reporters could not get interviews if we take such lethal sides.

You do not say: I lacked the courage to die for my beliefs.

And that is the bottom line. Behind the talk of ethics and jobs and callings lies a simple truth.

You can look. You can see.

But you cannot feel.

If you feel, you will see that your calling is simply a job, a dirty often disgusting one at that, and you realize there were times when you should have acted. When you could have saved one life or a dozen or maybe even a hundred, but you chose not to.

You chose not to—you say—for the greater good.

7:15 PM Upload: **Suicide Squadron Part 3** by Martha Trumante

Investigations always seem to hinge on luck. The Paris investigations are no different.

Three months into sorting the Louvre wreckage, the authorities find a chip, its information largely undamaged. Curiously, its technology was five years old, a detail that stumped the investigators more than anything else.

But not General Pedersen.

"I was watching the news that day," she says. "I don't know why. It's not something I normally do. I usually scan the relevant feeds. But that day, I was watching, and it hit me. I had seen the bomb come into the museum. I'd seen him

laugh and rock back and forth and smile in anticipation. I'd thought he was looking forward to his day when really, he was looking forward to his death."

At first, other security experts would not listen to Pedersen. In a world where suicide bombers had become commonplace—when child suicide bombers packed with explosives were part of the norm—no one could believe that a child could have had a chip implanted years before with enough high density explosives to destroy an entire building.

People could not plan ahead that far, the common wisdom went. People could not be that cruel.

But they were. That was the new truth—or maybe it was an old truth.

They were.

She shows me the documents the hospital had her sign. She shows me the diagrams, the little marking some doctor made on a chart of a newborn baby, showing where the chips would be—"chips that will enable her to live in the modern world," the doctors told her.

She shows me computer downloads, bank accounts her husband set up in her daughter's name, the college enrollment forms—required for a wealthy child of age four to get into some of Cairo's best private schools—the plans she and her husband had for her daughter's future, her son's future, *their* future.

The authorities, she tells me, believe her husband created all these accounts and family documents to protect her, to prove that she and her son had nothing to do with the family's patriotic explosion.

Only he is not political, she tells me. He never was, and no one believes her.

They believe her enough to send her here instead of killing her as so many other families have been killed in the past. They don't even try or imprison her. They just disown her, her and her son, make them people without a country, refugees in a world filled with refugees.

She can afford this tent on this sandy piece of land. She pays for the space closest to the medical tent. She hoped that someone would befriend her, that the medical personnel—the aide workers—would help her and her unjustly accused son.

Instead, they shun her like everyone else does. They shun her for failing to protect her daughter. They shun her for failing to participate in her husband's crime. They shun her for being naïve, for forcing the so-called patriots to ignore her husband and daughter's martyrdom, for failing to die with her family.

They shun her because they cannot understand her.

Or because they do not want to.

8:15 PM Upload: **Suicide Squadron Part 4** by Martha Trumante

Experts spend their entire career studying this new bombing phenomenon. Some experts who specialized in suicide bombing have moved to this new area of research.

One, Miguel Franq, wanted to know how three families decided to murder their five-year-olds in well-known Paris landmarks on the same day. Initially, he believed he would find a link that would lead him to a terror cell.

When he did not find the link, he worked with some of the scientists to see if the bomb-chips were set to activate on a certain day, then detonate when they were hit with X-rays, laser beams, or sonar equipment—all three being the main items used in security scans.

The intact chip revealed nothing like that. Only a detonator that was set to go off at a particular time on a particular day.

After much research, many hours of survivor interviews, and that inevitable lucky break, Franq found the link. Someone had given the families free tickets to each site. That

all three children did not end up at the same tourist attraction is another matter of luck, although what kind of luck no one can say.

Would it have been better to lose more of the Louvre? Or the Eiffel Tower? Or Notre Dame?

Would it have been better to lose one monument instead of damage three? Would more lives have been saved? Lost? Would more people have noticed? Or would less?

I speak to all the parents in this part of the enclave. All of them survivors—some male, some female—of a once-intact family. All of them claiming to be non-political, claiming they did not know—nor did their spouse—that their child was programmed to die.

I ask for proof. They give me similar documents. They give me bank accounts. But, tellingly—at least to me—the names of the hospitals vary, the names of the doctors vary.

"It is the nursing staff," one man says to me.

"It is an outpatient procedure," says another woman.

"Anyone could do it," says a second man. "Even you."

The rules of journalism have tightened in the past forty years. The scandals of fifty years ago, the tales of made-up sources, or badly researched material or political bias—true or not—nearly destroyed the profession.

When you were hired, you were reminded of those past scandals, told that any story with less than three *verifiable* sources (sources that have proof of their claims, sources that can be reinterviewed by the fact-checker—no listening to vids [which can be manipulated], no scanning of notes), any story with less than three will not be run. Any such stories appearing in blogs or personal writings will be considered the same as a published or viewed news piece.

Hire an editor for your own work, you're told. You will be watched.

We're all watched.

So you become an observer and a detective, a recorder of your facts and a disbeliever in someone else's. You need to verify and if you cannot, you risk losing your job.

You risk damaging the profession.

You risk losing your calling—because you might believe.

Finally, they take me to the person I had hoped to see. They take me into the medical tent to see a six-year-old girl.

She has her own air-conditioned section. It has a hospital bed, a holo-vid player (nothing new; only old downloads), several comfortable chairs, and a table covered with playing cards. Someone is teaching her poker, the international game.

An aide worker accompanies me. He whispers, "No one outside the family visits her. We're not supposed to say she's here."

Until now, she has existed primarily as a rumor.

You know, right, of the little girl? The one who lived?

Permanently blind, she is . . .

They pay her millions of Euros just to remain quiet . . .

She lives in a palace in Switzerland . . .

. . . in Baghdad . . .

. . . in Singapore . . .

She lives in a corner of a medical tent in a refugee camp. Her face is crisscrossed with scars and the shiny tissue of a dozen different plastic surgeries. She has only one arm. You don't realize until you come close, that half her torso is a kind of clear plastic, one designed for the medical interns to monitor the fake parts inside her, the miracles that keep her alive.

As I say hello, her eyes move toward me. She can see, then. She says hello in return, her accent upper-class British with a touch of India in it. She looks wary.

I don't blame her.

No parent watches over her. Her mother committed suicide—the real kind, the kind that's personal, and lonely, and takes no one else with it—when she heard the news. The blast killed her father.

She was an only child.

I sit next to her, on her right side so that I don't have to see that clear torso, the workings of her rebuilt interior, that missing—and soon-to-be-replaced—arm.

She is being rebuilt as if she were a machine. Someone is paying for this, real money that keeps this medical tent, and hence the people in the camp, alive.

Someone who, no matter how hard I investigate, manages to remain anonymous.

"Do you know who I am?" I ask.

"Reporter lady," she says, just like my driver, which makes me nervous. I will not stay here two days. I will leave tonight, maybe even on foot. There are too many connections, too many people who know what I'm doing. Not enough ways to make me safe.

"That's right," I say. "Reporter lady. Can I talk to you about your accident?"

She makes a face, but half of her skin does not move. "Not an accident," she says. "I sploded."

The words, said so flatly, as if it is a fact of life. And, if I think about it, it is. A fact of her life.

A fact of all the lives I've touched here today. Every single one of them knew someone who became a bomb.

"Do you know why you exploded?" I ask.

She nods, runs her remaining hand over her stomach. "Someone put something in me."

So flat. Like a child discussing rape.

"Did your daddy know about this?" I ask. Her father took her to an open-air market that day almost one year ago.

She shakes her head. Those bright, inquisitive eyes have moved away from me. Despite the flat tone, she hates talking about this. Or maybe hates talking about her father, the man who decided she was going to be a weapon.

"What did he say when he took you to the market?" I ask.

"Mommy wasn't feeling so good," she says. "We had to get her some medicine and a flower."

"Nothing else?" I ask.

She shrugs.

"Nothing about going to a better place?" I don't know what euphemism to use. I don't know enough about her or her past, being unable to research much of it. I don't know if she was raised Christian or Muslim or Jewish, since that open-air market catered to all three. I don't even know what nationality she is, something these camps like to keep as quiet as they can.

"No," she says.

"He didn't hug you extra hard? Tell you he loved you? Act strange in any way?"

"No," she says.

"Did your mom?"

"No!"

"Did they ever tell you that you were special?" I ask.

She looks at me again. A frown creases her brow, creating a line between the scars. "Yes."

My heart starts to pound. "What did they say?"

She shrugs.

"It's all right to tell me," I say.

She bites her lower lip. This is a question she clearly hasn't been asked much. "Special," she says, "because I'm the only one."

"The only one what?" I ask.

"The only one they ever wanted." Her voice shakes. "Everyone else, they have two, three, four."

I blink for a moment, trying to find the context.

She sees my confusion. Color runs up her cheeks, and I wonder if I've made her angry.

That fear returns—that odd sensation. Afraid twice in one day, after years without it. Afraid, of a damaged six-year-old girl.

"My daddy said I was so perfect, they only wanted me. Only me." Her voice rises, and she squeezes something in her hand.

The aide worker appears at the door. He looks sadly at me. I stand. My time is up.

As I walk out, he says, "She was an only child, in a culture that frowns on it. Her parents were trying to make her feel good about that."

"Is that what you think?" I ask.

"You're not the first she's told that to," he says. "Investigators, officials, everyone tries to find the two, three, and four others. You people never seem to remember that she's a lonely little girl, in a lot of pain, who can't understand why everyone thinks she's evil."

I look over my shoulder at her. Her lower lip trembles, but her eyes are dry.

I want to go back, ask her different questions, but the aide worker doesn't let me.

I am done here. I had hoped I would find my proof. Instead, I found a child whose parents told her she was special—because she was an only child? Or because they had planted a time-release bomb-chip in her?

Or both?

9:15 PM Upload: **Suicide Squadron Part 5** by Martha Trumante

The Paris bombings were the first and last time more than one child detonated in the same city on the same day. Ever since, these explosions have occurred at all times of the day, at hundreds of locations across the globe, at thousands of targets—some large, like the Eiffel Tower, and some small, like a deceptively normal home in a tiny suburban neighborhood.

The small bombings lend credence to the rumors that have plagued this weapon from the beginning: that these children and their parents are innocent victims of fanatics who have wormed their way into the medical establishment, that the true bombers aren't suicidal at all. Instead they are nurses, doctors, interns, who piggyback the detonator chip onto a relatively normal chipping procedure—giving a child an identity chip, for example, or the standard parental notification chip that must now be inserted into every newborn—a procedure that's a law in more than one hundred twenty countries.

Hospitals insist that medical personal are screened. Each chip brought into the building is scanned for foreign technology. Each chip has its own identification number so that it can be traced to its source.

None of the chips found at the thousands of bomb sites since the Paris bombings have had hospital identification. Yet the rumors persist.

Perhaps it is wishful thinking on the part of all involved. How much easier it is to blame a nameless faceless person hidden in the impersonal medical system than a parent who knowingly pays someone to place a bomb inside a child—a bomb that will not go off in days or even weeks, but years later, after that parent spends time feeding, clothing, and raising that child.

Bonding with that child.

Treating her as if she's normal.

Treating her as if she's loved.

One of the soldiers gives you a ride back to the Green Zone. You lean your head against the back of his modern, hydrogen-powered, air-conditioned behemoth—too big to even call a truck—and close your eyes.

The little girl has shaken you. Some stories do that—some interviews do that—and the key is to hold onto your professionalism, to remember what you can prove.

But in that space between wakefulness and sleep, you find yourself thinking that you live your life in three distinct ways: You have your everyday experiences, which are so different from most people's. How many people travel from war zone to war zone, from danger spot to danger spot, running toward the crisis instead of away from it? Such behavior is now second nature to you. You think of it only at odd moments, like this one, when you should be asleep.

You also live through your articles, your "live" reports, your blogs. People who see/read/hear those things believe they know the real you. They believe they have walked with you into the valley of the shadow of death, and they believe that they, like you, have survived some kind of evil.

Really, however, you live inside your head, in the things you're afraid to write down, afraid to record, afraid to even feel. You lied when you implied that fear hasn't been in your life in decades. Fear is in your every movement. But you speak truth when you say you haven't *felt* fear.

You haven't felt anything in a long, long time.

That's the most important thing they fail to tell you when you sign up for this job. Not that it could kill you or that you might even want it to kill you.

But that you can look at a little girl who has lost everything—her health, her family, her belief that someone once loved her—and you think she does not measure up to the rumor. She isn't the story that will save you, the news that will make you even more famous than you already are.

She doesn't even merit a mention in your long piece on suicide squads because she doesn't change anything. She is, to you, another body—another item—another fact in a lifetime of useless facts.

She is not a child, any more than you are a woman.
She is a weapon, and you are a reporter.
And that's all you'll ever be.

DAVID IN THE LION'S DEN

Geoffrey A. Landis

Monday 25 March, U.S.A.

David had both of his arms up in a glove box when Jake walked into the lab. He was concentrating on pipetting one drop of a cultured retrovirus into each of the sixteen tissue culture samples that his grad student Asim had carefully prepared and didn't notice Jake was there until he spoke.

"Have you heard the news yet?" asked Jake. His voice was grim.

"News?" David Kantrowicz sighed. "There's news? No, haven't heard it." He put down the sample, capped it off, and withdrew his arms from the glove box carefully.

He was a tall man, with dark curly hair and wire-rimmed glasses. Only a close friend or exceptionally keen observer would notice the slight hesitation in his step from where he'd stopped a small-caliber bullet long ago. "From your tone, though, I can guess that it's not good. They made the decision? It's Saud the younger?"

"It's him."

"Damn." After months of bitter infighting after the death of the king, the council of princes of Saudi Arabia had finally reached agreement. Aboud ibn Abd al-Saud would be king of Saudi Arabia, protector of Mecca and nominal leader of the Moslems. It had come at the worst possible time, when the Arab world was increasingly becoming disenchanted with the lack of any signs of resolution to the peace process. Al-Saud was a fanatic; he had made his pledge that he would not accept compromise with Israel of any sort, no matter how well crafted, or what the cost. And the cost was sure to be high. No matter who won. "As my grandfather would put it: *oy, vey,* such *tsuris* we need like we need holes in the head."

"Yeah?" Jake said. "Did your grandfather really talk like Woody Allen imitating a Poconos comedian?"

David shrugged. "How should I know? He died when I was a kid. To hear my father speak, he did. So anyway, we're ready?"

"We've talked about it enough. The question is, are *you* ready?" Jake asked.

"I guess so." David sighed again. He turned back to his glove box to start putting away his samples. "Although I'd rather not. War is for young fellows, not superannuated postdocs like me. But, last week I called Yosef in Tel Aviv. He said that they were pretty sure it would be Saud, and when it hits the fan he'd welcome having me back with him. I told him that if it comes down to it, I'll be there."

"You don't count as old until you get tenure, kid. I got the tickets. You fly out tonight at seven, arrive in Rome late morning, and get into Tel Aviv about two."

"So soon? I'd hoped for more time to prepare."

"Things are moving faster than we'd expected."

"So be it. How about your part? Are you ready?"

"Yes." Jake reached into his pocket and took out a finger-sized test tube, the end sealed with a wax plug. A small amount of dirty water was pooled in the bottom. He handed it to David. "We finished last night."

Dave looked at it skeptically. "Doesn't look like much, does it? This is enough?"

"Don't doubt. It's plenty."

He looked at it critically. "You know . . . that's some real work here. It's a pity we can't get something publishable out of this . . . maybe *Nature* . . ."

"Don't even think about it."

"I know." He paused. "I'd better be off, I guess."

"One more thing." Jake walked to one of the stainless-steel lab refrigerators and retrieved a sandwich in a Zip-loc bag from behind the rows of sample jars and tissue cultures. The refrigerator was labeled with a large red letters: LABORATORY USE ONLY. DON'T KEEP YOUR LUNCH HERE. "Here you go. Ham and swiss with bean sprouts. For your trip. *Shalom*, my friend. And *mazel tov*."

"Yeah, right." David looked back at his glove box. He thought about leaving a note for his grad student to clean it up and keep the cultures alive, but realized it wouldn't do any good. The virus he'd been working with wasn't dangerous; it had been engineered to infect guinea-pig livers, part of a study tracing enzyme expression. The work would wait. He'd much rather stick here, tracing protein variants through an unexceptional biochemical pathway, than fly across the world to a place where people would be killing each other, but they'd made their plans long ago, and now it was time to see what they could do.

He looked at the sandwich with distaste, then looked back at Jake. "And—by the way—you mean b'hatzlacha, not mazel tov. Mazel tov is for happy occasions." It figured. He hated bean sprouts.

Tuesday 26 March, Tel Aviv

The airport was crowded with people waiting to flee the country, grandmothers with paper bags full of possessions and arms full of children, business men with their laptops and cell phones, young mothers with infants sleeping over their shoulders, tourists whose vacations had been abruptly cut short. Foreigners, David noted; almost all foreigners. The Israelis weren't leaving.

Every few yards was a soldier in full battle gear, submachine gun at hand, restless eyes scanning the crowd. Disembarking from the planes were mostly students who had been studying abroad. What little conversation there was was muted and purposeful: What unit are you with? Think they're really serious, or are they just blowing hot air? Do you have a pickup? He could hear no idle chatter.

It reminded him of his own service, twenty years ago, doing the military duty he'd needed to put in to keep his dual citizenship. It had been fun, in its way. The old soldiers had talked endlessly about the Yom Kippur War, which back then hadn't been so far in the past. They had an attitude combining tough masculinity with self-deprecating humor. They themselves had taken their jobs seriously, but while David had served, they had faced nothing more than thrown epithets. And in his off time he and Yossi had wandered the streets of Jerusalem, finding beauty equally in the narrow stone streets of the old city and in the cafes and high-rise apartments of the new.

The airport was more modern than he'd remembered, but then, it had been more than twenty years since he'd left. He hadn't been back since.

From the airport he called Yosef, whom he'd known for years. Yossi was a companion from his military duty days—his best buddy, back then; Yossi had been smart, and athletic, and irreverent. "I'm a Jew by heritage, an atheist by choice," Yossi had declared, and the two of them had defiantly found every restaurant in the city that served (not on the menu, of course) ham. They'd gotten along fabulously. Yossi had stayed with the Israeli defense forces, while David had gone back to America, first to graduate school, and then staying on in a series of postdocs and eventually an untenured research professorship. They'd kept in touch, mostly by e-mail these days, and when things started looking like they would get bad, he had told Yossi that when his service was needed, he would be there, and Yossi had in turn promised that there would be a place for him.

When David called, he found Yosef was already in the Kiriya, where an emergency meeting of the defense command was under way.

David made arrangements to meet him at the Defense Ministry early the next day, and found a hotel room off Ibn Gvirol Street. On the short walk from the corner where the bus had dropped him, he found a crummy, run-down restaurant, Yin-Yang Chinese Villa. There was time to kill. Without bothering to look at the menu, he sat down and asked for moo goo char shu, forgetting for a moment that he was no longer in America, and, miracle of miracles, they even had it.

Wednesday 27 March, the Kiriya

The briefing room was small, spartan, and windowless. Stale smoke from half a dozen stubby, filterless cigarettes overpowered efforts of the tiny ventilation fan to clear the air. The men inside didn't notice the stale air. "So it's certain the Saudis are going to strike?" asked the prime minister.

"Yes."

The minister drummed his fingers against the table top. "And they are conducting their attack as we expected? From the staging area outside Aqaba?"

"Our agents have heard no indication of a change."

"And the rest of the Arabs?"

"Mobilizing, but so far staying out. Waiting to see, I'm sure. But the Saudis will be bad enough, I think."

The prime minister turned to another man at the meeting. "What about the Americans? Will they help?"

"No. This time, they're leaving us strictly alone. The Saudis have been long-standing allies of theirs; they're playing this one, as they say it, strictly hands-off. We can't count on any support at all. However, our own people in America stand behind us, as always."

"In that case, we have no choice but to implement plan Aleph. Preemptive retaliation. Hit them first, hit them hard. Destroy their attack before they start."

"I'll notify the task force immediately," said Yosef Abrahms. He had risen quite a way in the army since the day long ago when he and David had fought side by side. "What target date?"

"Sunday. We will make the final dry run Friday, get a day of rest, and hit them early Sunday morning."

"Roger."

Wednesday 27 March, Jauf, Saudi Arabia

"So the Zionists think to attack Sunday."

"That is what I have heard, my commander."

"Then you have served well, Asim. None other than you could have so well penetrated the secrecy of the Israelites. You have done very well, indeed. And you shall be fittingly rewarded."

"Thank you, my general. I do but the will of Allah."

"And so shall it be. We will have a surprise. We will wait until they have all gathered together, and then strike on their Sabbath, when they're unprepared. We will not be defeated!"

Asim saluted. "So let it be."

Thursday 28 March, Forward Camp Ben-Gurion

David stretched muscles that had grown sore under the rigor of military drills. Discipline was tight at the training camp. So far it had been only drills, but tomorrow morning at dawn, strike team Aleph would stage a full-scale practice attack against team Bet, a last practice for the coming strike. Walking through the camp, he came upon Yosef. He saluted.

"At ease, soldier. Nervous?"

"Not yet, sir. Ask me again right before the attack."

Yosef chuckled. "So you're a biologist now, I hear. What happened, you decided you didn't like computers any more?"

David shrugged. "I still work with computers."

"They should have put you with an Abach unit."

"I asked for the front."

Yosef clapped him on the shoulder. "In this one, I'm afraid everywhere will be the front." He chuckled again. "So, I say, maybe you should be nervous today, soldier."

Did he know anything? "No. I never get nervous until the day before. Last minute jitters."

"*Nu?* Can you keep a secret, David?"

"You know me, Yossi. I don't go around shooting my mouth off." *If only you knew,* he thought.

"Then I will tell you the best-kept secret in Israel. The mock attack tomorrow will be the real thing. The Sunday date is a ruse, a little something for the Arab informers we know are in the camp. At midnight we will issue live ammo, and the helicopters will be waiting. And so it starts. Only three people know this. Now, including you, four. Are you ready?"

"So, why tell me? You seem quite confident I'm not going to talk it around."

"I know you. And, I just felt like I had to tell somebody." He shrugged. "Nerves, I guess. I'm not so iron-blooded as

I like to pretend, sometimes. Why not you? Now are you nervous?"

"More than you could know, Yossi."

Saturday 30 March; Forward Camp Ben-Gurion

Yosef Abrahms looked around in despair, shivering in the cold desert night and trying to ignore the stench of diarrhea that permeated the air like the smell of rotting meat. It was nearly dawn, and there were only a very few men left standing. The camp was almost unprotected. The tanks were still loaded in the transport planes, ready for the airdrop, but there was nobody to unload them. The helicopters were ready for the attack, but there was nobody to fly them. It was no place to make a stand against the upcoming Arab attack.

If only a few more men were left! He'd done what he could with the few he had. He'd used the bulldozers to push a wall of earth around the encampment. That would slow them down a little. If only their preemptive attack had gone as planned! But who could have predicted the plague that had struck, out of nowhere, the night before the raid? No fatalities, yet—but the men were too weak to fight. Dizzy and disoriented, even the ones whose duties were flying computer screens were barely able to sit up, and the few who did were making mistakes that would be far too costly to allow them to strike as planned.

And of the few that seemed immune, his friend David had deserted, running off to hide in the desert. That was worst of all. He hated to think of David as a coward. David, who had been as brave as any man he'd known whey they'd both done their service. But David had lived too long in America, where enemies didn't press in from every side, and time changes people. The strain of coming battle tells on all men.

In that hour after the devastating plague struck, when he realized that their attack would never happen, he'd sent a coded message back to headquarters, telling them to prepare plan Gabriel, the final defense of the homeland. Back in the heart of Israel, in a site so secret even he didn't know its location, nuclear technicians would be putting together components prepared long ago. If the Arabs insisted on driving them into the sea, they would find that the price was high.

He nibbled on a cold ham sandwich. Army food was Kosher, but nobody inspected his personal pack, and the sandwich was his personal act of independence.

He checked for the hundredth time that the rocket launcher and grenades were ready. At his feet, in easy reach, were laid out the cartridge belts for the machine gun and two Galil automatics, his regular gun and a spare, with extra clips. When the attack came, he would at least take some of them with him, and save just one bullet for the end. Soon. He waited.

And waited.

The attack never came. The sun rose, and the day was clear and hot. By noon he knew that the attack would never come. By the will of a god he didn't believe in, the plague—whatever it was—had hit the Arabs too.

Tuesday 3 April, JFK Airport

Jake greeted David at the airport. There was no need to ask him how it had gone; they could both read it in the newspaper headlines. Emergency medical assistance was being rushed to both Saudi Arabia and Israel from all over the world, and a quarantine had been set up to prevent the mystery plague from spreading. David had exited just in time.

"Any problems?"

"A couple. It was tricky there for a while." He shrugged. "Nothing major."

"Was it really bad, out there?"

"Bad? Jake, you just couldn't imagine! They thought it was doomsday! Everybody was certain that if virus nineteen didn't kill them, the Arab attack would. I just wish I could have seen them when they finally found out that the Arabs had it, too."

"I bet. Well, they'll recover. After all, it's only a reengineered version of the common cold, debilitating, but hardly fatal. Hey, don't look gloomy—we did it! You know what? As of today, we're the secret masters of the world. We should be celebrating."

"Easy for you to say. You weren't the one who had to betray his friends."

"Betray, hell. We saved their lives and you know it." Jake looked at his watch. "Half an hour at the earliest before Asim's flight comes in."

It would be good to see his grad student and swap some stories. Asim must have had just as hard a time of it, but he seemed to have succeeded in his mission as well as David had.

"So anyway," Jake said, "how was your flight? Are you hungry? Maybe we should stop for a nice ham sandwich while we wait?"

Dave looked disgusted. "God no! I've been eating nothing but pork for the last week."

Jake looked at him. "That seems rather over-overdoing it. Once a month is plenty."

"Yeah, so you said. But I kept having nightmares that my immunity would fail." Dave paused for a second and looked across at Jake. "Still, you know, it was rather a clever idea of yours to manufacture a virus whose growth is inhibited by a protein found only in pigs."

Jake shrugged. "It's my job to be clever. In a day or so some bright doctor will figure out the connection, and they'll start synthesizing the protein. But what with both countries absolutely infested with reporters and doctors and International Red Cross teams, I doubt that either one will quite have the nerve to start a war. Not for a couple of years, anyway."

"Still," said Dave, "I don't care if it is the only thing that gives immunity to number nineteen, I'd be happy if I never ate pork again in my life."

"Suit yourself," said Jake.

ROCKET BOY

Paul J. McAuley

Rocket Boy lived under the knot of ferroconcrete ribbons where the road from the spaceport joined the beltway that girdled the city. He'd made a kind of nest in a high ledge beneath the slope of an on-ramp, and although traffic rumbled overhead day and night, it was as cozy and safe as anywhere on the street because it could be reached only by squeezing through a kind of picket fence of squat, close-set columns. Even so, Rocket Boy clutched a knife improvised from the neck of a broken bottle while he slept in his nest of packing excelsior, charity blankets and cardboard. The first lesson he'd learned on the street was that you needed to carry a weapon with you at all times.

The ledge was divided into two by expansion rollers at the joint between ramp and road. The old man who lived on the other side of them had been a senior civil servant before the war. He'd been arrested and tortured after the enemy had taken the city, serving two years in solitary confinement before being released and discovering that his family had been killed when a rogue cruise missile had levelled their neighborhood. He and Rocket Boy had quickly come to an accommodation. The old man guarded Rocket Boy's nest while he was out on the street selling cigarettes; Rocket Boy brought the old man hot dogs and soup from the charity workers who visited the intersection every night, distributing free food and blankets to the people who lived there.

More than two hundred people lived amongst the support columns and steep concrete slopes under the intersection, in old cars, cardboard boxes, and crude huts built from dead shopping carts and pallets and sheets of plastic tied down with twine and electrical wire. Some were refugees and war orphans like Rocket Boy; some were the city's orphans, hard-eyed, feral runaways; some were men and women turned old before their time by drink, drugs, and madness. There was a little flock of shopping carts and other small mechs too, on the run from the wrecking gangs that roved the bombed-out industrial sector to the west. They stood all day in sunlight, trying to recharge their rotting batteries, and at night rolled about trying to be helpful and mostly getting in the way, like sick pets no one had the heart to put down.

The perimeter of the spaceport was only a mile away from the intersection. Once or twice a week, a heavy lifter took off from one of the massive blast pits, shaking the ground and splitting the sky with a long peal of thunder. The crazy people ran about beating their heads and tearing at their clothes, and the carts and mechs were disturbed too, racing about in circles like bugs suddenly exposed to light. At night, Rocket Boy liked to sit on an embankment that overlooked the spaceport, watching ordinary jets and ground-to-orbit shuttles glide through the white columns of searchlights towards runways outlined by mile-long traceries of red and green lights.

Occasionally, there was a night launch, the spacecraft small and sharp in crossing beams as it brewed clouds of steam and clouds of fire, rising achingly slowly at first, and then accelerating away in a rising curve, a spear of flame dwindling into the starry sky. Rocket Boy watched it go with a raw longing that ached like a fresh wound, the earth beneath him throbbing with the thunder of its engines.

Rocket Boy was sixteen. When he'd first come to live under the intersection, he'd called himself Vigo, the hero of a naive children's book he'd read a couple of years before the war, when he'd still been a kid, when he'd still had a family and a future, but he'd soon discovered that on the street nothing, not even your name, is your own. The young hoodlum in charge of the gang of streetsellers had started to call him Rocket Boy because of his unnatural fascination with the spaceport, and because that was the name of the brand of cigarettes he sold loose at the intersection of Fourth Avenue and Industry Way, and the name had stuck. Rocket Boy worked from dawn to dusk seven days a week, selling cigarettes to the men and women who worked in the fabricants and warehouses. Time moved oddly on the street. Every day seemed interminable, but because each was the same as the one before, weeks and months slipped by like vehicles streaming along the freeway. In winter, dust blew out of the north and shrouded the city in a yellow pall. In summer, flocks of noctids swooped through the dusk air after insects, and the inhabitants of the little shanty town under the intersection knocked them out of the air with sticks or crude bolas made from stones and wire, and made a gummy soup by boiling up their wings.

One summer night, in the middle of a long heat wave, Rocket Boy had given up on sleep and was sitting high on an embankment, watching the lights of the spaceport shimmer across kilometers of blast pits and landing strips and concrete aprons, when a vehicle braked hard somewhere above him, a sliding screech, a blare of horns. As Rocket Boy scrambled to his feet, a man vaulted the safety barrier and slid down the dry bank, asking him if he knew a place to hide. He was taller and skinnier than anyone Rocket Boy had ever seen, with dark brown skin, and black hair greased back from a hawkish profile. He wore heavy boots with steel buckles and straps, filthy jeans, and a denim jacket with many zippers and fasteners. A small leather duffel bag was slung over his back. There was a gold socket above one ear, and his eyes were capped with data lenses that blankly reflected the last of the light dying out of the sky as he looked up at the edge of the road above, head cocked. A moment later, Rocket Boy heard the wail of sirens, and whirling blue lights swept past on the beltway.

"Got into a little trouble," the man said. "My mate will lead 'em a good old chase, but they'll catch him soon enough, and he'll have to tell 'em where I jumped, so I need a place to lay low. Just for a few hours, until the maintenance workers' shift changes, and I can sneak into the port. Help me out, and I'll give you your heart's desire."

Rocket Boy knew that the man was trouble, but he also knew that the man was one of the spacers who travelled amongst the worlds beyond, worlds full of wonders beyond measure or understanding, where he so very badly longed to go, and he led the man to the intersection, through the close-set maze of pillars, to his nest. The man declared it an ideal bolt-hole, took a swig of whiskey from a flat bottle, and promptly fell asleep. Rocket Boy, a hundred questions bubbling through his head, sat in the dark, knee to knee with his strange guest, listening for police sirens, and presently fell asleep too.

He woke when the spacer stirred. It was three or four in the morning, and still dark. The traffic on the beltway was as sparse as it ever got. Rocket Boy took the spacer, who told him that his name was Arpad, to the solitary standpipe that supplied water to everyone who lived under the intersection, and then walked with him along Industry Way toward the bus stop at a crossroads. Arpad told him that he was from Earth, like most of the human race; said that by the universe's clock he was seven hundred and fifty years old, give or take a decade, but most of that was down to time compression; said that he'd visited most human worlds, and this one was the most miserable he'd ever seen.

"Of course, you just had yourselves a revolution, but still."

"It was a war, not a revolution. Our enemy took our country from us." Rocket Boy hesitated, then said in a rush, "One day I want to go up and out. There is nothing for me here."

"If you go up and out, you'll lose everything you ever knew or loved. People, your home, your country . . . You can't ever go home again; time compression will see to that."

"I've already lost all that. If I went up and out, I wouldn't ever want to come back."

Arpad studied Rocket Boy sidelong. "I guess the war here didn't do you any favors, huh?"

Rocket Boy shrugged, feeling a twinge of the old bitter hurt he could never bury deeply enough. He'd never talked about it with anyone; not even the old man.

"What was it about, this war of yours?"

"The enemy wanted our fertile land. There isn't enough, just strips here and there around the edge of the land. The enemy had a bad drought, and they took our country because they wanted to steal our good river land."

"What I don't understand is, when you got a continent here size of Asia and the Americas combined, and everyone lives at the edge of the sea, how come you people don't try to settle inland? Man I work for came here to hunt the big critters that live there, but there's no kind of critter so fierce people can't deal with them."

"It isn't the monsters," Rocket Boy said. "It's the wild itself."

He told the spacer about the deserts beyond the mountains where no rain fell for years on end, about the endless dust storms and tornados and lightning storms. About how, in the center of the wild, it was so hot in the day that water boiled, and so cold at night it froze. He told him the story everyone learned in school, about the man who in the early days of the settling of the world had claimed he was the son of God, and had led a hundred followers across the mountains to a valley where water could be raised from deep aquifers. But insects had eaten most of their crops, dust storms had destroyed the rest, and when survivors had been discovered two years later, they had resorted to cannibalism.

"I guess things always look simpler from orbit," Arpad said. They had reached the crossroads, and he was looking around at the long, low mounds of rubble that before the war had been warehouses and factories. "I can't access the city's infosystem, kid. Are you sure this is where I get a bus into town?"

"The first one comes at five. What about the police?"

"I don't think they'll expect me to catch a bus into town. I know a couple of people in town who work in the port. One of them will lend me his ID, and I can use it to get into the port when the shift changes. And once I'm aboard my ship, that's it, home and free."

Dawn was unpacking pale bars of light to the east; to the west, both moons were chasing each other below the saw edge of the naked mountains, and a few stars still showed in the deep purple sky. Rocket Boy wondered if one of them was the star of Earth. Wondered if that was where Arpad was headed, some fifty or sixty years away by universal time, less than a month shipboard. If he went with the spacer and came straight back home, a century would have passed and everything would be changed. Perhaps the enemy would be gone . . .

Far down the road, a single point of light slowly resolved into a double star. The bus was coming.

Arpad began to search through his duffel bag. "I promised to give you something, kid. Here. Take it."

It was a pistol. The poisonous green of potatoes left too long in the sunlight, it wasn't much bigger than Rocket Boy's hand. The power LED set at the rear of the reaction chamber sparkled bright red. There were red inserts in a grip still molded to fit precisely the hand of its previous owner.

"Hold it tight," Arpad said, pushing the weapon into Rocket Boy's hand, and then poked at a microswitch with the blade of a small penknife.

A hologram bloomed in the air, big as an opened book. The spacer stabbed at its silky light with a dirty forefinger, selecting a submenu from the index, selecting several functions of the submenu.

Rocket Boy almost dropped the pistol when the grip moved under his fingers. Suddenly, it fitted his hand as if it had grown there.

"You need a password," Arpad said. "Something uncommon. Sing it out nice and clear three times. Ready?"

Rocket Boy nodded.

Arpad touched one of the red buttons on the insubstantial page that hung in the air above the pistol, pointed at Rocket Boy.

"Vigo," Rocket Boy said. His mouth was dry. His heart was beating in his temples. "Vigo. Vigo."

"Now it's yours," Arpad said, slinging his duffel bag over his shoulder as the bus stopped beside them with a thunderous hiss of air brakes. "Before you decide what you're going to do with it, you should talk with it, learn what it can do. It's a clever thing, it'll give you pretty good advice if you ask it the right questions. I hope you have better luck with it than I did," he added, and climbed aboard the bus.

Later, Rocket Boy realized that the spacer had left him the pistol because, disguised as a maintenance worker, he wouldn't have been able to smuggle it through the security checks at the port. He also realized that the pistol was probably the reason why the spacer had been running from the police. He'd brought it here to sell, and something had gone wrong, someone had betrayed him or had themselves been betrayed, and he'd had to dump it.

The spacer could have simply thrown it away, Rocket Boy thought. Instead, chance or fate had caused it to fall into his hands, and because it was unlikely he'd ever be so lucky again, he must make the most of the opportunity.

He didn't go to work that day. Instead, he spent all that morning and most of the afternoon in his nest, talking with the pistol. It taught him its functions and, once it was certain that he had grasped the basic principles of its operation, asked him what he wanted to do.

"I don't know."

"Perhaps I have asked the wrong question," the pistol said. "Tell me instead what you most need."

Rocket Boy wanted his family back, he wanted everything to be the way it had been before the war, but he knew that nothing, not even this magic little weapon could give him that. He said, "I want to be safe."

"Who is threatening you?"

"No one. Everyone. Living on the street, you feel that every moment could be your last . . . "

"Perhaps you should tell me how you came to be here," the pistol said.

It teased the story out of him piece by piece. Rocket Boy found himself telling it things he had never told anyone else. He told it about the war that had started after the enemy had tried to block the flow of a major river. He told it about the so-called popular revolution, supported by the enemy, and the Night of the Long Knives when most of the government and dozens of senior officials, including his mother and father, had been assassinated. He told it that he and his younger brother and three sisters had been attempting to escape the city and reach the house of their aunt when their vehicle had been caught in a fire fight between loyalists and a brigade of enemy soldiers. There had been an explosion which had knocked the car on its side, and he'd woken to find himself in the chaos of a hospital that was attempting to deal with hundreds of civilian casualties. Suffering from concussion and a broken wrist, he had gone to look for his family, walking all night and most of the next day, only to discover that his aunt's house had been burned to the ground. After failing to find any of his family or friends, he had fled the city, and for a year worked on the huge collective farms in the wide, fertile river valley, but when a new law forced casual workers to register with a union, he'd been scared that the cheap hack that had altered his ID chip would be discovered, and he'd returned to the city, and had been living under the intersection ever since.

After a short silence, the pistol said, "Do you require advancement, or revenge?"

"I used to think that I could hunt down the man who had my parents killed," Rocket Boy said.

"Do you know the name of that man? Do you know where he lives? Do you know how he is protected?"

Someone else said, "If you want true revenge, you'll have to destroy the occupying force and the puppet government."

It was the old man. He raised his hands in a warding gesture when Rocket Boy, angry and afraid, asked him how much he'd heard, and said, "I suppose just about everything. What is your real name, Rocket Boy? Who were your mother and father? It is possible that I worked for them, in happier times."

"It doesn't matter who they were now."

"Yet you want to avenge their deaths. If you let me, I can help you. I assume that spacer you sheltered last night gave you the pistol."

"What if he did?"

"It's like no other weapon on this world, an all-purpose hand weapon with a nanotech forge and a near-AI kernel. Very powerful, and very smart."

The pistol said, "I also possess a database that includes several million tactical scenarios—"

"Be quiet," the old man said sharply, and the pistol shut up at once. The old man smiled at Rocket Boy. "You have to let it know that you are its master, and make sure that it does not attempt to find a way of manipulating you. We don't have AIs on our world—they are far beyond the capability of our world's technological base—but I am familiar with them because I worked at the Ministry of Foreign Affairs before the war. I've negotiated with many trade delegations in my time, and I once traveled to another star system—you wouldn't think it to look at me, but it's true."

Rocket Boy believed him. The old man, squatting in his tattered rags, hair hanging around his leathery face in filthy dreadlocks, possessed a dignity he hadn't noticed before.

"Tell it what you want," the old man said. "Give it an order. Make a wish. Start with something simple."

Rocket Boy thought long and hard, then said, "I wish I wasn't living on the street."

The pistol said, "My analysis of your story suggests that this is a Class E or F capitalist society. Am I correct?"

The old man's smile showed the blackened tombstones of his teeth. He said, "Much has changed since the war, but I believe that we still have money."

The pistol said, "Tell me, who supplies the cigarettes that you sell?"

Kalim was tall and quick-tempered, and ruled his little gang by fear. He beat anyone who showed any sign of hesitation or answered back when he gave an order, and sometimes he would pick on someone and beat them just to keep the others in line, remind them who was in charge. He'd beaten all the boys who worked for him more than once, and let it be known that he had killed people who'd let him down. "With this very knife," he liked to say, holding up the six-inch ceramic blade, "Afterward, I lick off their blood. Nothing tastes sweeter than the blood of your dead enemies."

Every morning, Kalim and his two sidekicks drove up in a battered car and handed out cigarettes; every evening they returned to inspect the takings of each boy. Sometimes Kalim took only half; sometimes he took everything. The day after the spacer gave the pistol to Rocket Boy, Kalim climbed out of the car and went straight for him. Getting right in his face, asking him where he'd been yesterday, asking him if he'd enjoyed his holiday, pushing him with angry little shoves until he was backed against a support pillar. The two sidekicks leaned against the car, enjoying the show. The other cigarette boys stood in a loose knot, watching it too, and shopping carts and mechs had crept up on either side, attracted by the disturbance. High on a concrete slope, a madwoman barked like a dog.

Kalim grasped Rocket Boy's throat in one hand and turned to his audience, producing his knife with a theatrical flourish, saying loudly, "None of you little jerks take time off unless I allow it. Time is money, and all the money around here is mine. When you take time off, you steal from me, and then I got to teach you a lesson, like I'm going to teach this little worm."

That was when Rocket Boy shot him. He was holding the pistol in the pocket of his tattered jerkin, and thrust its muzzle against Kalim's leg and pulled the trigger with a convulsive effort. The pistol made a tremendous noise, a thunderclap that echoed and reechoed under the crossing ribbons of on-ramps and beltway, shocking hundreds of roosting noctids into the air. Kalim staggered backwards, clutching his bloodied thigh, clutching at his belly and then his chest as the smart little bullet burrowed upward. It detonated when it reached his heart, and he spewed a pint of blood and fell down and didn't move again. The bigger of the two sidekicks drew a pistol, an ordinary automatic, and Rocket Boy shot him too, the self-guiding bullet drilling a hole in his forehead and blowing his skull apart. The other sidekick froze, drenched in his companion's blood and brains, his hands half raised in surrender.

The other kids watched silently as Rocket Boy climbed onto the car and told them that he was taking charge of the business. "I promise that I will take only half of what you earn, no more, no less," he said. "And there will be no more beatings."

That evening, the sidekick, a boy by the name of Vance, drove him to the café where the cigarettes were distributed. The pistol had shot Vance with a smart bullet, and Rocket Boy told him that he would live as long as he was loyal, but if he even thought of betrayal or revenge, the bullet would kill him at once. At the café, following the advice of the pistol, Rocket Boy turned over the money he'd taken from the cigarette sellers to the fat man Vance pointed out, and explained that from now on he was running Kalim's pitch.

The fat man barely looked up from the food he was spooning into his mouth, saying, "I don't care what you punks do, long as you bring in the gelt," and that was that.

Later that evening, in Kalim's coldwater apartment at the edge of the industrial district, the pistol told Rocket

Boy that there was a high probability that one of the gangsters who ran the neighboring pitches would try to take the business away from him. "They will think you weaker than them. They will think that you killed Kalim by a stroke of luck."

Rocket Boy said, "And if I kill the man who tries to kill me, will it stop there?"

The day had left him exhausted, excited, and agitated. He didn't regret the deaths of Kalim and the sidekick for a moment; all the anger and hurt he'd suppressed for so long had been released when he'd shot them. Once you'd killed someone, he discovered, your own life mattered less, and there was a wonderful freedom in that knowledge. But he felt a yawning apprehension now that he realized that he had stepped through a door into a new world, and there was no going back.

"Do not worry," the pistol said. It sat in his lap, its power LED twinkling like a baleful star. "I have fully gamed this situation. As long as you follow my advice, nothing will go wrong."

A little later, as Rocket Boy was falling asleep, it added, "You are a willing pupil. We will go far, you and me."

His enemies came for him two days later, just after he'd distributed the bags of cigarettes to his gang of sellers. Two cars roared into the dusty arena under the beltway, each discharging a pair of thugs armed with assault rifles. By now, the pistol had learned how to control the little machines that had taken refuge under the intersection, and a rattling flock of shopping carts immediately charged the thugs. Rocket Boy shot three of them while they were fighting off the machines, and when the survivor tried to run he was knocked down by a shopping cart. Rocket Boy walked up to him, followed by two battered service mechs, and asked him who had sent him. The young thug tried to spit in his face, and at the pistol's prompting, one mech lit its welding torch, and the other snapped the pincers of its hand an inch from the man's face. "If you don't talk," Rocket Boy said calmly, "I'll let the machines take you apart."

That night, Rocket Boy killed the gangster who had sent the thugs after him and took over his pitch, but the pistol and the old man soon persuaded him that selling cigarettes was not enough. After spending a month training the toughest of the street kids and earning their loyalty, he began to hold up trucks bringing food into the city from the river valley. He gave half the stolen produce to hospitals and community leaders—after the war, food was expensive and in short supply, and many families could barely afford basic rations—and sold the rest at knockdown prices to market traders. Soon, produce trucks were moving only in convoys guarded by soldiers, and Rocket Boy changed his tactics and liberated a large quantity of medicines and drugs from a warehouse owned by the Minister of Health—the old man, whose name was Yan Yane, had discovered from former colleagues in the civil service that the minister had been skimming supplies and selling them on the black market.

A week after this coup, Rocket Boy was invited to a meeting with the heads of the three families who controlled drugs, gambling and prostitution in the city. He went with the old man, Yan Yane, and two burly sidekicks. He did not take the pistol because it had been made clear that he could not carry a weapon to the meeting, but the pistol had briefed him extensively beforehand.

"They want to meet you because they are intrigued by you," it had told Rocket Boy. "If they wanted to kill you, they would have already done it. Instead, they believe that you can make a lot of money, and they want to claim a share in it."

So it turned out. Rocket Boy gave each of the heads of the three families a generous cut of the profits he had made from the truck hijacks and the warehouse job. He told them that he did not want any share of their businesses, but proposed a new business of his own. He would organize a security service for the people of the city.

He sat at the far end of the long polished table in an expensive new suit, Yan Yane at his left hand. He felt cool and calm, facing the three men and their phalanx of advisors and lieutenants and bodyguards. The worst they could do was kill him, and he knew now that dying was nothing. He spoke clearly and with great force, staring into each of their faces in turn. "The police are corrupt, and they are owned by the puppet government. The people hate them more than they hate the soldiers that occupy our city. I will organize block committees of volunteers who will patrol their own streets and deal with troublemakers as they see fit. In return for this protection, every business will pay a small amount into a common fund—less than they currently pay in kickbacks and protection money to the police. Your businesses will be exempt, of course."

"What will you do when the police try to shut you down?" one of the men asked.

"I will deal with the police," Rocket Boy said.

He struck two weeks later, after extensive discussions with community leaders across the city. They were more than willing to listen to him. He had earned considerable kudos by distributing free food and medicines, and the people of the city chafed under the casual brutality and corruption of the police. At exactly nine o'clock in the morning, shopping carts loaded with bombs rattled through the gate of every police station across the city and promptly blew themselves up. At the same moment, Rocket Boy assassinated the police chief as he climbed into his armored limousine; the pistol's smart, self-guiding bullets blew off his head from a range of half a mile. The city was immediately placed under martial law by the occupying army, but the community leaders made sure that there was no looting or rioting, and the soldiers of the occupying army soon returned to their barracks in the fortified Green Zone in the center of the city. A respected religious leader announced that from now on the city would police itself, a few scapegoats were arrested, tried, and executed for the bombings, and Rocket Boy found himself at the head of a militia of more than ten thousand men.

The occupying army quickly made an accommodation with him, but the puppet government resented the loss of power. At one of the receptions held in the Green Zone, a drunken army captain came up to Rocket Boy and told him that he should watch his ass, certain people wanted him dead.

"You've come far and fast, and so far you haven't missed a step," the captain said. This was on a balcony of what had once been the city's museum, overlooking the central park. It was midnight, and fireworks were exploding over the lake. The captain's sweating face was briefly lit by red or green or gold light. "We know that if we took you out, there would be a civil war. So, we have come to an accommodation with you. We're a pragmatic people. We let our heads rule our actions, not our hearts. But I should warn you, some of your own people aren't content to let things lie. They want you dead, and are willing to pay a high price for it."

This man has an agenda, the pistol told Rocket Boy, its voice whispering eerily in his right ear. A week ago, the city's best neurosurgeon had extracted the pistol's control chip and implanted it under Rocket Boy's scalp, connecting it to a tiny device that vibrated the bones of his ear. It was part of him now and forever, a small, still voice whispering advice.

Rocket Boy told the captain coolly, "If you mean the so-called interim government, they aren't my people."

"Whatever. Point is, we don't need this kind of trouble, but we can't be seen to take sides. You'll have to deal with it yourself."

That is not his own opinion. He is delivering a message.

"Is that your own opinion, captain, or are you delivering a message?"

At Rocket Boy's shoulder, Yan Yane, his hair and beard neatly trimmed and dyed snow-white, said, "Why are you so interested in our affairs?"

"You have become a player in an astonishingly short time," the captain told Rocket Boy, ignoring the old man. "You have your secret weapon, of course—oh yes, we know all about the scrap of proscribed technology that advises you and keeps your people loyal. We make it our business to know things like that. Don't worry, I'm not here to threaten you with exposure; by now, I doubt that it would make much difference if your secret was revealed."

"The people love him," Yan Yane said.

"Your people project their desires on you," the captain said, speaking in a whisper now, his face only inches from Rocket Boy's. "They believe that you can free them. Don't make the mistake of believing that, and we'll get along fine."

They are scared of you. You have the advantage now.

Rocket Boy said, "Are you scared that you can't control me, Captain?"

"I like you," the captain said. "I hope you survive. I really do. Meanwhile, enjoy the party."

He squeezed Rocket Boy's shoulder and walked away, no longer seeming drunk at all.

Rocket Boy watched the black lake mirror starbursts exploding in the black sky. Yan Yane said, "He's right about one thing. I talked with an old friend of mine who has a high position in the government. There's no official plan to assassinate you, but people talk about it all the time. The Minister of Health in particular wishes you dead. He has never forgiven you for that warehouse job."

"I can deal with him, and with anyone else who moves against me." Rocket Boy felt himself smile. "You heard the captain. I've been given carte blanche."

"There may be a more equitable way of dealing with the situation."

Remember what I told you.

Rocket Boy waited, still smiling. In the rare moments when he was alone these days, he'd taken to studying his face in any nearby reflective surface, trying on different expressions. It seemed to be the face of a stranger, as if he was an actor impersonating himself.

Yan Yane said, "I can arrange, through my old friend, a meeting with the Prime Minister. I am told that he is very willing to negotiate a settlement with you."

"Is he offering me a job?"

"There is a position, if you want it. The Minister for Security is willing to step aside."

"Do it," Rocket Boy said, and Yan Yane bowed and walked away towards the far corner of the splendid, crowded room, where the Prime Minister held court.

Remember what I told you, the pistol said again. *There is no time for sentiment.*

It had warned Rocket Boy that sooner or later someone close to him would bring an offer like this. "The one who brings you the offer will be a traitor," it had said. "He will have made a deal with your enemies. He will be seeking his own advancement in exchange for your life."

If only it had been anyone other than the old man, Rocket Boy thought, feeling a splinter of ice prick his heart. But the moment of regret quickly passed. As usual, the pistol was right. Ordinary human sentiment was a luxury he could no longer afford. There was too much to do, and too much at stake. "We must finalize our plans," he said, whispering as if to himself.

We have already discussed this. It is too early—

"Examine your tactical database. Use your war-gaming capability. Find a way for me to prevail."

Six days later, just an hour before the meeting with the Prime Minister was due to take place, Yan Yane came into Rocket Boy's penthouse apartment and said, "If we don't go now, we'll be late."

"I want to show you something," Rocket Boy said, and took the old man by the arm and steered him across the dimly lit room to the big picture window.

They looked through their reflections in the armored glass at the twinkling grid of the city's lights. Rocket Boy pointed to the spaceport, glittering beyond the boundary of the city like a satellite galaxy. "We've come a long way," he said.

"And now is the time to consolidate what you have gained," Yan Yane said.

Rocket Boy glanced at his watch. It was a few minutes shy of ten o'clock. "When I was living under the intersection, I always dreamed of escape. I sat up at night and watched the airplanes and space shuttles take off and land. And whenever I could scrape together a little spare money, I'd ride the bus to the entrance of the spaceport. I couldn't go inside, of course, but I could stand at the gate and watch the people coming and going. The people from other stars who come here to do business or hunt the big animals of the wild. The people who crew their ships. I would dream that one day I would be like them."

Yan Yane said nervously, "If you want to negotiate for the position of Minister of Transport, it's a little too late—"

"I'm not going to be any part of the puppet government. They were responsible for the murders of my parents and thousands of others. If I joined them, I would share in their blood guilt."

Rocket Boy walked across the room and picked up the pistol from a side table and turned to face Yan Yane, who stood straight-backed and quite still by the huge window in his expensive slate-blue suit, his white hair gleaming in the half dark of the room.

Rocket Boy said, "If you feed this simple elements like carbon and iron, nitrogen and phosphorous, it produces bullets that are little different from those fired by ordinary guns. But if you feed it more exotic elements, it can produce bullets that are really complicated little machines. The last batch looked like beetles. They flew off into the city to search out their targets, armed with detectors that can sniff out specific patterns of DNA, and stings that deliver a neurotoxin that is instantly fatal. The men you were supposed to be taking me to meet, by now they are all dead."

"I should have destroyed that thing a long time ago," Yan Yane said.

"You are the only person close to me who does not carry a bullet to ensure loyalty. I trusted you. I believed that you were my friend, and you broke my heart."

"When you took the weapon from the spacer, you made a bargain with the devil," Yan Yane said. "I've seen how using it has changed you, day by day. You're no longer the innocent boy I befriended."

"I changed when I decided that I had to kill Kalim," Rocket Boy said. The pistol in his head was counting now, counting backwards from ten. "How you kill someone, whether you use a stone or a bullet or your bare hands, it doesn't really matter. What matters is the intention, the resolve. That's the real weapon."

Zero, the pistol said.

Spots of light flared in the center of the city, defining the boundary of the Green Zone. A moment later the armored glass trembled and sang as the shock waves of the explosions reached the penthouse. The lights flickered out for a moment, then came back, dimmer and redder now, running on battery power. The power grid was down, and apart from the fires flickering under rising columns of smoke, the city had gone completely dark, lit only by secondary explosions that were detonating here and there in the Green Zone.

"You've started a war you can't win," Yan Yane said.

"The pistol plugged itself into the information grid and downloaded copies of itself. It controls power and water, the information grid and the transport systems. It controls thousands of carts and mechs. It also controls the security systems of the police armories. Right now, my militia is arming itself."

Vance entered the room, followed by half a dozen men carrying guns. Yan Yane barely flinched when Vance took his arm. The old man straightened his back and said, "You don't see it, but you've become a monster."

"I'm the weapon used by my people to free themselves from the enemy."

Vance began to lead the old man out of the room, the armed men falling in behind them. As he went through the door, Yan Yane turned and said, "And who will free them from you?"

Then Rocket Boy was alone with his thoughts, and the pistol. He set the weapon on the table and walked to the window. Across the darkened city, thousands of sparks were springing into life at every intersection, where the people were setting up barricades. To the east, the lights of the spaceport still glittered—it had its own fusion generator.

Rocket Boy asked the pistol for a status report.

The first stage has been successful. But overall, it is still to early too tell if we will succeed.

"My people are fighting for their lives and their homes. Everything in your database tells me that very few invading armies have prevailed against a resolute population. We will drive the enemy back to its borders. We must do to them what they did to us."

At what cost?

"Freedom is not worthwhile if it is easily won."

There is still time to make peace with the enemy.

Something glinted as it passed through the light of a nearby lamp. It was one of the assassin bullets. It moved straight towards Rocket Boy, stopping a yard away, the needle in its blunt tip flicking in and out as if tasting the air.

"Are you frightened of me?"

Sometimes it is necessary for me to remind you that you are merely mortal. Think carefully while there is still time. If you take the city but spare the enemy soldiers and administrators, you will not only save their lives, but the lives of many of your people.

Rocket Boy laughed. "You *are* frightened of me."

Perhaps Yan Yane was right. Perhaps you have become a monster.

The bullet was close to Rocket Boy's head now. He watched it for a long moment, then reached out and plucked it from the air.

Please. Please reconsider—

"No. We will go on and on, you and I. Look!"

A brilliant point of light flared amongst the launch pits of the spaceport. The yacht of some trillionaire fleeing the war. Rocket Boy watched as its bright star arced away into the night.

I am a power on this backward world, the pistol said. *But there are powers much stronger than me in the worlds beyond.*

"We're something new," Rocket Boy said. The assassin bullet vibrated warmly between his thumb and forefinger. "We haven't yet found our limits. Perhaps we never will."

The voice in his head was silent.

"Switch the information grid back on. I will make a broadcast announcing that I am taking control of the city."

Yes, master.

Rocket Boy tried out different smiles, studying his ghostly reflection. "Which sounds better? Prime Minister Vigo, or Emperor Vigo the First?"

JADE ANGEL

Dena Bain Taylor

"You're always a child till your last parent dies,
then suddenly you're old."

—President David G. Hartwell
of the United States of America on Mars,
announcing the Last Flight from Earth

Xandri scanned the terrain through her retinal camera, frowning at the readouts scrolling down her peripheral field of vision. She wasn't seeing the Chimese dragon, so either Intel had been wrong about the attack alert, or the Chimese had shifted operations.

Whatever the reason, she had no target. Just a cracked plateau, fogged by the perennial summer dust storm, that ran until it hit the white-hatted Coprates massif.

"Chill," she said.

"What is it, Flamer?" The voice of her team leader, Captain Charles Scrill, was loud and clear. The last few missions, her com system had taken to randomly distorting sounds, but the tiny strip of duct tape jammed into her earpiece seemed to have done the trick.

"I'm bringing my eagle round. The Chimese aren't coming."

There was a brief pause. "Flamer? Target is four o'clock, five klicks, coming off the massif. You should have visual." The worry in Chill's voice came through too clearly—she decided maybe she'd take the duct tape out.

"Incoming," her eagle announced happily. Its cheerful tones had been programmed on Earth by some idiot of a psych with a military contract to reduce combat stress. The sound broke whatever spell Xandri was under and she saw the Chimese dragon in the distance, ejecting Mars Terrain Vehicles—baby spiders—from its belly. Once they landed, they'd sprout legs and speed across the plateau to engage the American mama spiders guarding the Kennebunk Elevator, while the dragon turned back to its base on the massif. Now that the Chinese had lost the war with America on Earth, their Martian colony was starved for replacement parts for both systems and mechs. So they were focusing their dwindling resources on USAM's two most vulnerable points. The Chimese cannibalized the spiders they couldn't keep running, and dropped the hulks down USAM mining, infrastructure and terraforming shafts. And they targeted USAM's cargo elevators every time supply ships arrived from Earth.

"Move in," Chill ordered. "Clear the little bastards out. Flamer, take the fly."

Chill and the other two eagles in alpha strike team swooped down and across the plateau after the baby spiders, while Xandri peeled off to pursue the dragon. She almost had a lock when—this was the only way she could describe it—everything twisted inside her and out, and bounced back into shape like a flexiband. The dragon had vanished again. Only this time there was another dragon, a green one, heading towards the massif, at 10 o'clock, and her physical position seemed to have changed—she was somewhere else along the massif.

Even in her shock, her training kept her focused. "Chill!" she shouted. "Target has changed. I have visual on a second fly. Repeat, targeting another enemy craft!" She locked and fired. She missed. Unbelievable. Could the summer dust have compromised her twitchy targeting system? The Chimese weren't the only ones with parts problems. She was still absorbing her inexplicable failure and sequencing another lock and load, when the world twisted again, this time accompanied by a horrendous bolt of pain. When she pried her eyes open again, the second dragon was gone and she was back chasing the first dragon, which was now in range. She blinked her eyes furiously to clear them. She was hyperventilating, and the med readouts projected by her retinal camera were spiking right off the screen.

". . . girl! Respond!" Chill was shouting.

Her mind was still frozen, but her fingers were already busy, automatically keying in the firing sequence. "I have visual!" she shouted back. "Locking NOW!"

The eagle's long range lasers discharged, and the dragon exploded. Chunks flew into the massif it had almost reached. The fog spread the orange color of destruction across the whole Martian sky, making a beacon of defeat that would shine as far away as New Beijing.

The other three eagles had blown up most of the baby spiders, and the Kennebunk garrison had sent out beetlebots to sweep up the last of them. The baby spiders clearly got off their mechviruses before they died, though, because now the beetlebots were just spinning in circles. Still, the elevator hadn't been hit, and the Chimese had lost a costly gamble here. With a tip of their wings to the human mech crew already heading out to the stranded beetlebots, alpha team turned homeward to the Burroughs Eyrie overlooking USAM. Xandri debated how much to tell Chill about what had just happened. She was already skirting a medical suspension to defrag all the biotech viruses she'd absorbed in a year-long combat rotation, and this was clearly way beyond a simple virus.

After they docked the eagles, Xandri headed quickly for the lockers where the flight suits were stored, sloughing hers off as she walked. She was very aware that Chill was right behind her—she felt him at her back but ignored him, hoping to discourage him from the conversation she knew they were about to have.

"Lieutenant Kantu!"

She made a face but stopped and turned to face him.

"What in Chimese hell happened out there?" he asked. "What were you shooting at?"

"My eagle got hit by a tech virus," she guessed. "Took me a few seconds to purge."

"But you lost visual twice. And no one else in the unit got hit. Maybe I should be ordering you in for a medscan."

"It was a tech virus, not a bio," she insisted. "Obviously the hit was a local with a repeat code. Hey, there's nothing wrong." She looked around and saw they were attracting attention from two senior officers on the catwalk that ran round the hangar deck. "And I don't need you putting ideas in anyone's head," she nodded her chin toward the brass. She turned and kept walking. Chill walked with her but lowered his voice.

"You're a real magnet for locals, aren't you? Third since the start of Gemini."

She made no answer. The other two incidents had genuinely been the result of tech virus hits. This one smacked of a psych problem, which was definitely a career-ender. No Kantu had ever been medically decommissioned. They died on the field or went on to glory as leaders of their people.

She reached her locker, with X J KANTU stencilled on the front, and finished stripping off her flight suit in dark silence. She secured it into its compartment. In a battle alert, she could release it and suit up in seven seconds.

"Look, I'm staying in your face here," Chill persisted. "I care about you, dammit, Xandri. We'll talk about this later."

"Yeah, sure," she said tightly, reining in an angry response, and slammed the locker door shut with the heel of her hand. As she turned her back on him and headed for the shower, he was already turning his back on her.

Once he was gone, she reversed her steps and returned to her eagle. She sat in the cockpit and played back the external data recordings. Nothing out of the ordinary, except nine seconds of uncharacteristic silence on her part.

But this wasn't just a hallucination. She knew real pain when she felt it. Besides, even if her brain was lit up like a xrismas tree from bioviruses, it could never dream up something like this. She needed to speak directly to the General, and the thought put a sour taste in her mouth. She checked the time on the wall comscreen—0800 hours. She hadn't seen him in over a year, but she knew exactly where to find him.

Xristian Jefferson Kantu stared with disapproval at the broken, overset yolks of his micken eggs. A two-hour, early morning strategy session with President Hartwell had soured his appetite for breakfast, and given him a nasty mood to enjoy it in. The news from Earth was worse than usual, and the fears that had cramped his stomach for months now tightened their clutch on his innards.

Fears for the world of his birth, which was fast degrading past the capacity for spaceflight. Fear that the hordes of Chimese would overrun USAM once Hartwell announced the Last Flight from Earth. He kept it all bottled inside him—no one on Mars but he and Hartwell knew just how bad the future was.

A voice cut through his dark thoughts.

"General, sir." He felt the air move on a vigorous salute, but he didn't look up.

"Xandri," he said, without much warmth. The General was a man of fixed habits who compartmentalized his life, and his niece certainly didn't fit into the 0800 breakfast compartment. Not to mention that the last time they'd met, she'd accused him of letting her parents die when she was twelve. He picked up the antique silver knife and fork he always used—the gift of Thomas Jefferson to a beautiful slave who bore him a son, Xristian's ancestor—and attacked his mabbit bacon. He liked to eat as terran a breakfast as he could.

"I'm sorry to disturb you, sir. I have some intelligence I knew you'd want asap."

He raised his eyes and quickly assessed her. Bulkier with muscle, but tired and a little scared around the eyes. She looked like she was just coming off patrol. Her uniform was rusty with the dust that, these days, seeped through seals and housings too worn to stop it. Her voice was husky with the powdery tones of a fighter who'd breathed too much of it in the high adrenaline situations of combat. And tight with nervousness and residual anger.

"I believe the Chimese are field-testing a new shielding force that works on visual distortion."

He put down his knife and fork and quickly checked to make sure no one was listening. He needn't have worried. Around them the base dining hall buzzed with conversation, but no one ever came near the General's booth during his breakfast unless they had to or felt driven to career suicide.

"Go on," he ordered, gesturing her into the seat across from him. "I'm listening."

"I witnessed it on patrol, sir. I've come right from the docking bay."

"You witnessed it? And the rest of your team?"

"No one saw it but me, sir."

"Oh? And what did you see?"

"I was out with alpha strike team, chasing a Chimese dragon back from the Kennebunk Elevator to the Coprates massif." She told him what had happened, forcing herself to include the parts she knew were impossible.

"So a properly locked laser totally missed its target?"

"I didn't miss, sir. The laser hit but did nothing."

"And no one else on your strike team saw this green dragon."

"No, sir. They reported nothing. They were engaged against ground forces at the time."

"Does your instrumentation back you up?"

She paused. "No, sir." At the expression on his face, she leaned toward him and burst out passionately: "I can't explain this, but it's not a psych problem, I promise you. It was real!"

As a general in the Corps of Engineers, he had to give her report serious thought, because there were parts that made sense to him. His micken eggs had gelled stubbornly into their irregular shape, and he scowled at them while he cut into them. He ate in silence for several minutes while Xandri sat stiffly across from him. Neither mentioned their last encounter.

"We've had intelligence that the Chimese are trying to develop shielding as an effect of a Rierson field," he finally said. "Send a pulse through a nonlinear material like space. The pulse frequency stretches as it travels and creates a chirp. We've already tested an antichirp process where we send a time-reversed chirp, a scalar wave. The waves condense in a high-energy laser pulse that compresses into a shell membrane at a certain distance from the wave emitter. If we could build a stable scalar wavetrain emitter, we'd have an energy bubble that destroys a portion of whatever touches it and repels the rest. But we couldn't build one, so I know the Chimese can't do it, and in any case it wouldn't change the position of your eagle. So there's really no physical explanation for what happened out there."

"How do you know it so certainly, that the Chimese couldn't do it?"

"I've got intelligence."

Then she did what she always did, since the day he took her in and finished raising her because there was no one else to do it. She got angry and crossed the line and disrespected him. "With respect, sir, you don't fight them out in the field. You're in here, where things have solutions and the universe has laws. I've seen the Chimese pull plenty of mabbits out of their asses."

"That's enough, Lieutenant," he cut her off. He reined in his own flare of anger, trying to be fair to his brother's only child while the general in him refused to stand for the insubordination. "Leave it with me and I'll investigate."

At that moment, in Independent ForShing, DaQing opened the hatch of his coffin and slung himself up and onto the entrance sill. Someone had drawn obscenities on the hatch again—the war and the military were very unpopular among many of the ForShing Yan—but he had nothing left to clean it with. It hardly seemed to matter, anyway. Secretly, he too wished the military rulers of Independent ForShing would sue for peace with the Americans. He banged a cloud of dust off his boots and stored them in their cubby inside the entrance. He swung himself all the way in so he was sitting on his sleeping mat.

A dim light had flickered on when he opened the hatch, and he didn't turn it up now. Instead, he lay back with a groan of exhaustion and pulled Jiao's jade angel from its place at his heart. Her great-great-grandfather had been a high-ranking official at the Imperial Court, and he visited Queen Victoria during her Jubilee. He had the angel carved from a piece of ancestral jade while he was in London, and gave it on a gold chain to his beautiful young wife in Beijing. Jiao had cherished it. She loved the Western myths about these benign protective spirits who could also be mighty and terrible. But of course, the jade angel hadn't protected her.

DaQing lay with the little piece of stone crushed against his forehead, trying as he so often did for some magic to lose himself in time.

Jiao the Golden, jade angel pressed by their lovemaking into the moist flesh of her breast where it lifts and falls with her gentle breathing, then tumbles free as she stirs and reaches for him again. He rises to her, takes her in his arms, prolonging the moment before he plunges his soul into her body. . . .

The magic never worked; here he was still. Their life together over, destroyed in the collapse of their apartment complex while he was out on patrol. Now he lived alone, in one of the tiny cubicles known as coffins, like a million others China had gratefully offloaded onto her ForShing colony, without worrying too much about its ability to aeroform and build infrastructure, and to provide food and space for all those mouths.

DaQing tucked the jade angel back against his own breast and sat up. He ordered the light higher and pressed his thumb to his comscreen to access the specs General Han's aide had downloaded to him.

General Han had harangued him about the honor of the ForShing Yan, the honor of the General's illustrious warrior family, the honor of DaQing's own family, for he too was a Han. DaQing had been careful to stand rigid, apparently bursting with pride at being chosen to test fly the shield prototype.

But what did honor mean to him anymore? After everything China and Independent ForShing both had done to his life, to all their lives. To Jiao.

He shook his head to clear it of these thoughts. *I'm thinking like an American. Everything is for me, me, me. The ForShing Yan need the resources of USAM to survive, that's all I need to worry about now. The past has made the present, and it's only the future I can change.*

He ordered the comscreen and the light off, and lay back down, forced his eyes closed. Flying from behind the dragon shield would be a strange new environment. He didn't know how external data might be distorted, didn't know how his instruments would interpret the shielding itself. He had two weeks' hard training in simulation before the test flight, on top of his missions. Best to sleep while he could.

Xandri left the dining hall, snagged a hook on the quad four elevator and rode up five levels to the Hub. The vidscreen was running a news item on the Great Lakes War. The Canadians had sabotaged New York's Tunnel 4 and collapsed the last ruins of the New York Public Library. At the Hub, she sat in the bar and had a few Martian beers to steady her nerves. At last, she rescued her shuttle from the extortionists at the dock office and caught the Sidestaff Airway west into USAM, to the res pod she'd shared with Chill for the last three months. The shuttle shuddered heavily all along the airway; it needed new gyros but the cost of those had skyrocketed. America's victory over the Chinese on Earth two years ago had left her hard-pressed to resource her own needs, let alone keep up the steady stream of manufactured goods and parts her colony depended on. USAM was suffering the legacy of the European colonial structure, which kept the Martian colonies supplying raw materials while America maintained a stranglehold on the highest level manufacturing processes. If only the Chimese had acknowledged China's right to cede its colony as spoils of war to the Americans. Instead, they'd declared independence and mired Mars in a war that neither side was well equipped to fight.

When she opened the door of the res, she saw Chill had murphied the kitchen and was chopping root vegetables on the counter. He wielded the knife heavily, and colorful chunks of carrot shot off like missiles. The two mabbits were lined up, twitching in a delirium of hope that a piece would lob through the air into their cage. Xandri picked a few up and slid them through the bars. *At least someone should be happy,* she thought, and turned to face Chill.

"Chill, stop chopping and listen to me."

Instead, he said. "You've got a real problem with trust, don't you? You brush your squad leader off when I question you and go directly to the general?"

She was amazed. "How did you know that? What did you do, follow me?"

"I was going in the same direction, yes," he answered stiffly, turning to her at last. "But that's not the point. The point is you won't tell me what happened out there."

It was true, she wouldn't, and she suddenly realized why. Back at the base, he'd threatened her with medical decommission. She couldn't trust him to be on her side if this came to a psych trial.

That's when she knew Chill had to go. Occam's razor. The simplest solution is the best one. The simplest life is the happiest one. "No, you're right. I won't. I can't. Maybe," she plunged on angrily, "maybe you should sign back on the residency board. This was a great arrangement when I wasn't on alpha team, but we should have split up when I got reassigned."

Her words hung in the air. "So this was just an arrangement to you?" he said at last, stony faced.

An hour-long argument later, she left, and spent the day doing a series of aimless things fueled by watery beer and frustration. She returned late, and the night that followed was long and exquisitely awkward. Chill murphied the second bed and they tossed in the uncomfortable silence, each listening with resentment to the small sounds made by the other. In the morning, vowing to swear off relationships for the rest of her life, Xandri fled an hour before she needed to, which put her on deck just in time to receive orders to report to General Kantu.

Her uncle got right to the point.

"I checked your black box. Nothing supports what you claim. What's even more confusing is, our intelligence says nothing about a shield test. But all this worries me. If the Chimese ever manage to shield New Beijing, they'll launch their assault on USAM the next day before cornflakes." She didn't know what cornflakes were, but got the point. "I've decided to move up the schedule for a prototype test of our own."

"Sir?"

"A zero point energy weapon, based on quantum chromodynamics. We can easily adapt our eagles to mount it. The ZPE has twice the range of any of their missiles or l-g weapons, and it doesn't need a straight line of sight to lock on its target. Plus, its destructive power should be on the order of ten times anything we've got now. This will be our Hiroshima—the shot across the bow that ends the war. I've been very involved in the ZPE's development, and I need you to understand how this thing works. Because you're the pilot who's flying the mission."

"Sir! Thank you, sir!" Her heart drummed fiercely against her rib cage, but she stared rigidly ahead.

"Instead of energy transmission through space in the form of electromagnetic force fields, we transmit electrogravitational potentials through spacemass/timenergy. The ZPE is based on the action of zero point energy on subatomic particles in normal vacuum. All charges in the universe are jostled through interaction with the zero point energy field, causing matter waves to propagate and giving us spacetime. In Wheeler's spacetime foam model, the quantum mechanical state of the universe is a superposition of many different spacetime topologies. Processes that should serve to increase the cosmological constant instead drive the production of more and more complicated spacetime foam. What we've discovered is a way to explode a single unit of quantum foam—pop a single bubble."

"Isn't there a cause-and-effect action?" she asked. "A cascade of popping bubbles?"

"Analogies only go so far," he answered, a little impatient. "Ultimately, quantum foam isn't soap. The ZPE's internal architecture is the most elegant construct I've ever had the honor to see. It's the crowning achievement of quantum engineering." His eyes bored into her. "This weapon will save America on Mars. We'll defeat the Chimese with it, and then its practical applications will drive our society forward. And history will record that one Jefferson Kantu helped design it and another flew it. Congratulations, Captain. Report for training to Flight Level C at 0630."

Modifying her eagle to house the ZPE took over a week, a week of skirmishes both on and off the battlefield. Chill was living up to his name. Something had broken between them, and until he found another res she was living in a frigid zone. For a hot-tempered woman like Xandri, it was torture.

So she heaved a sigh of relief when zero hour arrived and she secured herself in her cockpit. She flew north, following the line of the New Jersey Gardens, where Terran food plants grew in thick layers of mabbit shit and Martian soil. Beyond the controlled environment bubbles of the Gardens, the neonate Martian biosphere stretched to the horizon, a thin veneer of green fogged by red summer dust.

Her target was the Dragon Nest. In one blow, the Chimese were about to lose eighty percent of their dragons.

Six hours later she came into range, well outside the reach of any Chimese patrol, programmed the target coordinates, and fired her way into history.

The ZPE made the same jittering sound it had in simulation, but a nanosecond later, she felt the world do that shimmer-twist again, the one she had felt before she saw the green dragon. The same pain and sense of wrongness, the same spike in her meds to the top of the red zone, and the same return to normality.

Her retinal cameras were transmitting satellite images of the Dragon Nest.

No apparent signs of damage. This was impossible—had the thunderbolt of doom turned out to be a slingshot pebble?

Strangely, and in stark contrast to the satellite images she'd received just moments ago, there wasn't much to damage beyond infrastructure anyway. Every last hangar bubble was retracted and empty.

She turned her eagle around so fast she had to fight it for control, and she sped back toward USAM over the blooming landscape. She was an hour out when the maydays started. By the time she got there the battle was almost over.

The USAM forces, ground and air, were battering at the Chimese dragon fleet. The missile impacts could be seen as a distortion of the visual field around the dragons, but none of the force was getting through. Could this have been what happened at the Dragon Nest? No, satellite imagery would have shown this effect. But certainly the Chimese had managed to shield their dragons, and USAM had abruptly lost its one decisive advantage—the superior amount of functional weapons technology it had to throw at the enemy.

Xandri rushed to join the battle, her long-range lasers already contributing to the apparently useless barrage. The New Jersey Gardens were exploded into smoking ruins, and she could see the financial district, and the USAM Trade Center itself, obscured in a puffball of flaming smoke.

Then she saw the green dragon and went after it. It didn't seem to be engaging in the action, just hovering near the battlefield like some angel of death. Xandri fired her laser arrays, which of course did nothing but attract the green dragon's attention, and it circled tightly to target her. With just seconds before it destroyed her eagle, she took the only option she had left—she fired the ZPE, hoping for a more destructive result this time.

With the discharge came the now-familiar wrench, but the result wasn't anything she could have expected.

The green dragon, the whole battle scene, had vanished. She was buzzing around a perfectly intact USAM and Eagle Control was shouting at her to respond.

Two weeks after the inexplicable interference that blinded Dragon Nest's instrumentation for more than six hours, DaQing was ordered to report to the office of General Han.

"It was a field of tachyon disturbances on the scalar electrostatic potential level, generated through quantum chromodynamics, and it emanated from a source flying at two thousand km. Presumably an American eagle. What we do not understand is why the Americans did not follow through and destroy the Nest. We have decided it must be because this was an unintended effect and the pilot did not understand what happened." General Han stopped speaking, and there was a lengthening silence broken only by the sound of the General's terran crickets skittering across the floor of their cage. They were the only personal object in an office furnished with only the basics. In these interesting times, even those at the top of ForShing Yan society had to make do with little. "I regret to inform you," he went on, "our calculations show that the shielding you so successfully tested would not hold against this field."

DaQing's mind flashed back to the test flight. He'd never reported the American eagle he had on visual for nine seconds after he turned on the shielding, the one that had seemed to fire on him. He knew it would be regarded as a psychological lapse on his part, a pilot tricked by the shield's visual distortions and hallucinating. After all, they would argue, his dragon hadn't been fooled—the external data receptors showed nothing. He'd checked the black box on his return to Dragon Nest. His career would end and, without Jiao or any future he cared about, his career was all he had left.

"We had hoped we would be able to shield all of Independent ForShing," the General was saying. "Our engineers have the design, but we lack the materials. Still, we have plans, a small sacrifice in comfort by each of the ForShing Yan, and we will soon have enough to start construction. But now the Americans force us to move more quickly. We must attack the enemy before he realizes what he has built. Do you agree, captain?"

He was surprised to be asked his opinion. "Yes, General," he answered.

"Good. Building enough systems to shield all our dragons will take less of our resources and can be accomplished much sooner, before the end of summer. And you will be the one to lead the attack on USAM. Congratulations, Colonel. We will destroy the enemy before he can destroy us." The general saluted him, and DaQing saluted back. The flag of Independent ForShing hung on the wall behind the general, a golden dragon encircling the red sphere of Mars, and he saluted that, too. It was a fire dragon, destructive, a dragon of war, and it had claimed him. There would be no peace now.

Xristian Jefferson Kantu had never seen skin so gray in so young a person.

"I was just about to die," Xandri said quietly. "It's a terrible burden, knowing how and when you die."

"We don't know any such thing. Here's what we think happened. Instead of propagating matter waves, we believe, but can't observe, that the ZPE's discharge creates minute timeshifts on a quantum level. It would be a random and diffuse phenomenon. But then Heckler's ironically named law of chaos comes into play, which dictates that the random cause-and-effect patterns and synchronicities initiated by random source phenomena will eventually cohere into an organized, discrete phenomenon. Because time is a constant to each observer but not to all observers, the new timeshift phenomenon is localized, with a ripple effect of variable extent. Localized to you. Felt earlier in time, even before you first fired the ZPE."

"But what is the timeshift phenomenon? Where am I going?"

"If the universe is an infinite layering of possible timecurves, with possibilities narrowing each time we make a decision, then the ZPE has breached the barrier between two of them and you are traveling through to an intersection where particular temporal realities are mutually inhabited. A future in which USAM is destroyed, but not necessarily our future. If so, the time synch could be unstable, so there would always be the risk of getting trapped. Or maybe the ZPE has created a timeloop, a closed timecurve. In order to form, a closed timecurve would need two events within a normal timecurve—an initiating event and a terminal event—of such impact on spacemass/timenergy that they create a distortion that bends the curve in on itself and ultimately breaches the timecurve barrier at the point where the two events achieve mutual temporality."

"So the ZPE might be the initiating event."

They were sitting in his office, in the two carved wood chairs he'd had brought from Earth in the heady days when America could afford to shower her colonists with material goods. Xristian Kantu stood and paced, deep in thought. At last, he sat down across from her again and took her hand. She was shocked. He had never done this, not even when her parents died. She was even more shocked to find comfort in his touch now.

"How long do you think it will be before the American president announces the Last Flight from Earth?" he asked.

"What do you mean? Uncle Sam on Earth will always be there for Uncle Sam on Mars. Vincente-Riaz says it in every second speech."

"Basically, what America won in the Sino-American War was the right to preside over the end of the human era on Earth. Vincente-Riaz has already warned President Hartwell that we'd better get this war cleaned up and get ourselves self-sufficient in a hurry. Global climate change, environmental toxins, the VAIDS and brain flu pandemics—there are five billion fewer humans on Earth than there were a century ago and the birthrate is still dropping. We need a solution to the war up here fast, so Washington can concentrate on sending us the technology we'll need to stay alive once we're on our own. Otherwise we'll win this war just to die a slow death.

"You're experiencing other points on the timecurve, Xandri. Points in the future. We need to know more. We need to know the terminal event to ensure we win this war and establish a free Mars before the lifeline is cut. This isn't an order. It can't be. I can't force you to fly back to the Dragon Nest and discharge the ZPE one more time. I just ask you to remember that your name is

Jefferson Kantu. Your heritage runs from great warriors, from Africa to America and now to Mars. I was modified as an adult to survive here; you carry this planet in your genes. And unfortunately, it seems the terran race dies with my generation. So one way or another, the future is yours."

Xandri gave the order to fire and the ZPE jittered. But she never knew if there was a spatial result because the temporal reaction kicked in. When she emerged from the time twist, she was in a dogfight with the green dragon. There was a ruined city in the distance, and she seemed to know it was New Beijing. A glance at her instrumentation sent a flare of panic up her spine. The time-twist had worked differently this time—only she seemed to have come forward, not her eagle. She was in a different bird. It too was fitted with a ZPE, but the instrumentation had been modified, and the ZPE was the only online weapons system.

She fired. The ZPE propagated matter waves that met the dragon's scalar shell, and though the shield deflected much of the energy, she could see that she'd done serious damage. But before she could change course to come in for the kill, the green dragon's missile took off her wing.

Eagle and dragon crash-landed a couple of kilometers from each other, but it was more of a land than a crash and both pilots walked away from the wrecks.

Only there was nowhere to walk to. She realized with horror that she remembered, without having lived it, exactly what events brought them here. The near-destruction of USAM. The arrival of the Last Flight from Earth. The failure of peace talks. Xristian Jefferson Kantu's team solving the ZPE problem so that the weapon propagated matter waves, not temporal ones. The final battle—eagles pitted against dragons until the eagles punched through the shield of New Beijing and destroyed it.

USAM equipped its eagles with survival gear—an individual personnel bubble, coated with a solar micropanel array that provided plenty of energy for light and heat, to process oxygen, to create and recycle water and nutrients. There were nutrient concentrates, various useful chemicals and meds, even an entertainment library she could view on the vidscreen coating on the bubble's inner surface. Independent ForShing had long since stripped its dragons of any such luxuries as individual survival gear. Humans were replaceable, gear was not. So it was inevitable that the pilot of the green dragon should walk her way.

It was probably also inevitable that they didn't try to kill each other. What was the point? He wasn't green up close, of course, just a man. Han DaQing, a flight colonel like herself.

Time passed. Xandri's gear included a satellite communication device, and the satellites continued orbiting the planet, doing their job. But there were few survivors on the ground to communicate with. Periodically, the two established contact with small pockets of either side, but the distances were prohibitive. They'd likely die before they found each other. And here too, what was the point? Could they establish a small settlement that might survive their lifetimes, especially with the areoforming process well established and beyond human interference anyway? Probably. But there were clearly not enough of them to survive as a race.

It wasn't long before she and DaQing became lovers, for reasons that began in desperate denial of the truth and ended in the gut-level recognition that love was all they had left. Eventually, they had said everything to each other they could think of saying. Idle conversation loses its interest when every breath drawn is an exercise in futility.

They knew every detail of each other's histories, values, and beliefs. They even exhausted suicide as a topic of discussion, having agreed that if she became pregnant, it would be time to crack out the poison capsules from the medkit. Certainly, they early on exhausted their understanding of the physics behind Xandri's continuing presence here.

"Every breach has been different," she pointed out. "The first happened before I even fired the ZPE, maybe a ripple effect backwards, Xristian thought. That one and the next sent me and my eagle forward and brought us back, although the first return wasn't initiated by anything I did, and the second happened when I refired the ZPE. This breach defeats me completely. I'm living in a temporal paradox—my body came forward, so where is the Xandri who engaged you before I arrived? And if I do cross back, will some Xandri still be here with you? And will there be a pullback this time, so I can warn both sides and change all this? Maybe Xristian guessed right about the instability of the time synch, and I'm trapped. Was it the creation of the ZPE that created this timeloop with this terminal event? Or has it revealed our own timecurve? Or forced us into another one? I don't know the answers to any of this, or what I could do to initiate a pullback. There's no ZPE to fire this time, that's the one thing I do know."

Winter came in its time. One night, when both moons were down and the stars twinkled faintly in the thickening Martian atmosphere, they lay huddled together on the bubble's sleeping mat. They were watching old entertainment on the vidscreen. They'd long since watched anything that interested them, and they were down to ancient "science fiction movies." This one featured a big beefy man who started up an alien terraforming array on Mars that, in the space of a few minutes of action-packed sucking and blowing, transforms the planet into a clone of Earth.

They laughed at the absurdity. But Xandri ordered the "movie" off before the names of its fictional and long-dead terrans started scrolling down the screen.

"That'll be us someday," she said wearily.

"Flicking a switch and saving Mars?" DaQing asked with amusement.

"No. What I meant was, whatever life-form dominates in the Mars we've created, we'll be the dead alien technology they'll have to puzzle over."

For some reason the date/time display at the bottom of the otherwise darkened vidscreen caught her eye. They hardly ever thought about calendars and timepieces.

"It's my birthday," she said, realizing with a shock what the date was. "I'm twenty-one. I can vote to elect the next president of USAM."

He laughed, and sat up to unfasten the jade angel that always hung round his neck, the one that had belonged to his dead wife. He reached down and fastened the gold chain round her neck. "Isn't democracy wonderful. Well, then, you must have a present. Besides, if you ever do get pulled back, General Han will accept it as proof of your story because it will also be hanging round my neck."

She kissed him to thank him, and the kiss lengthened, turned passionate. She felt a protective glow from where DaQing's body pressed the jade into her skin. It was a very hollow promise, under the circumstances, but the hope offered by angels has always been just a matter of faith.

BROKEN BITS

Mark L. Van Name

The first wave of squidlettes hit Lobo's hull a little less than a minute after we touched down, not bad time given that we were in a clearing a full two klicks from Osterlad's mansion and had come in as hard and fast as we could manage. Not enough time for us to get much done, either: Lobo had fired four corner anchor bolts into the freshly scorched ground, opened his center floor hatch, and sprayed the dirt with coolant. I was out of the crash couch and had led the stealthie into position. It was just beginning to burrow down, sucking dirt through its digging tentacles and onto Lobo's floor, and then they were on us.

"Let's see how it looks," I said.

Lobo patched the feeds from the ring of sensors we'd planted a few seconds before impact, and a corresponding ring of video popped onto the cool gray walls opposite where I was watching the stealthie make its way into the ground.

"Audio," I said.

"You could have asked for the whole feed in the first place," the battlewagon grumbled on our standard frequency. A moment later, the sounds of the attack crashed from his hidden speakers.

I've mostly learned to tolerate the emotive programming Lobo's customization team put in him before I acquired him. I've even come to think of my battlewagon as *him*, not *it*, and he's pretty much my best, which is to say *only* friend these days. He's a fellow veteran, so I also cut him some slack for that. Sometimes, though, I could do without the sarcasm.

On the displays, I watched as a couple dozen squidlettes crawled over Lobo's smooth surface, each probing the reinforced metal for the hair-thin lines that even the best hatches inevitably leave. A hybrid of meat tentacles coupled to a metal exoskeleton, a variety of acid and gas nozzles, and a small cluster of comm and sensor circuits, each squidlette arrived as a round missile, opened a few seconds before impact, used the gas jets to slow enough so its tentacles could unfurl, and then stuck to whatever it hit. Normally each would carry an explosive payload in addition to the acid, detonating either when sensors, comm signals, or timers gave the command, but I knew Osterlad wouldn't risk damaging Lobo more than he could possibly avoid; after all, the whole point was to capture the battlewagon. Some of the acid was for forcing open the hatches; the rest was for me.

Another round of squidlettes popped onto Lobo's hull. There were so many crawling on the battlewagon now that I couldn't get a clear count. The normally faint, slow slurping sound they made as their tentacles dragged them along made it sound through the speakers like we were being digested by some shambling creature large enough to swallow Lobo's roughly seventy- by twenty-five-foot bulk. Even though I knew many feet of armor separated the crew area where I now stood from the squidlettes outside, I still tasted the tang of adrenaline and noticed the hairs on my arms standing up.

"Can you feel them, Lobo?" I kept our chatter to our private frequency, which Lobo's armor blocked from any sensors Osterlad's people were training on us. Thanks to the repairs my sister, Jennie, made to my brain way back when we were kids on Pinkelponker, and to the modifications the doctors on Aggro made when they laced me with nanomachines, I can communicate with most machines by focusing my thoughts in the right way. If more people realized how lonely and chatty machines generally are and how much information they'll give to anyone who gets them talking, we might go back to living with dumb devices.

"Not the way you feel, Jon, not as best I understand humans. But I have enough hull sensors to detect the motion, and once they find the few hatch seams we had to leave open, the acid will start affecting more internal circuits."

"Give 'em a jolt," I said. "A hard one."

"You understand that it probably won't destroy them," Lobo said.

"Yes, but if we don't try to fight back, Osterlad will know something's up, and besides, we have to use some power now so they'll believe we're out of it later."

Lobo didn't bother to answer. The displays and speakers showed his response: the air popped with electricity, streaks of blue arced all over his hull, and almost all the squidlettes slid off onto the clearing around us.

I checked the stealthie's progress. Its top was about six inches below ground level, and it was spraying dirt around its flank. It was almost as low as it would go without me.

The squidlettes immediately began to climb up Lobo. A few weren't moving, which made me happy; those things were expensive armament, even for a dealer like Osterlad. Most, though, were on the move again, which meant he was true to his reputation and carried good stuff. These meat/mech combos were engineered to handle strong current and probably a great many other forms of attack. Any off-market squidlettes would have been reduced to metal and fried meat, or at least lost some function, from the shock Lobo gave them.

The outlines of two squidlettes flashed yellow in the displays, Lobo's sign that their paths would take them to seams.

"My new friend, the weather sat, tells me that heat signatures not far from Osterlad's home suggest he'll be launching interceptor ships momentarily," Lobo said. "Once they get into medium orbit, I won't be able to outrun them."

The stealthie had stopped digging and opened its lid, beckoning me.

I looked at the large, pale-brown-metal lozenge and shook my head. "You owe me for this, Lobo," I said.

"What can I owe you? You already own me."

I sighed. When I want a little emotive programming, I get facts. "It's only an expression. I hate this plan."

"It's your plan."

"That doesn't make it any better," I said. "The fact that it's the best plan I can come up with doesn't mean I have to like it."

"We could have simply landed on the building's pad," Lobo said, "and you could have removed them all—as I suggested."

"I told you before: they would have attacked, I would have been forced to fight back, and I probably would have ended up having to kill a lot of them. I want to avoid killing whenever I can."

"So you're buying me new weapon controls so I can kill for you?"

The problem with emotive programming is that you sometimes can't tell sarcasm from genuine confusion. "No. I'm fixing your weapons systems because you're broken, incomplete, without them." I thought about Pinkelponker, about tracking Jennie down and finally freeing her, and realized there was no point in lying to Lobo, or to myself. "And so you have them when we need to fight."

Lobo superimposed hatch lines on the displays showing the two flashing yellow squidlettes; they were drawing close.

"I get the point," I said.

I climbed into the stealthie and stretched out. A little bigger than a coffin on the inside, when closed it afforded me only enough room to stretch out my legs or draw my knees to my chest, roll over, and prop myself up on my elbows. I'd already loaded it with food and a few special supplies; everything else I'd need was standard equipment.

"As soon as I close up, Lobo, shove the dirt back over me and take off. Hit this area hard with thrusters to fuse the ground, and head out to the wait point as fast as you can; you need to burn off all the squidlettes."

"Thanks for the reminders, Jon. It's not like I'm capable of forgetting the plan."

Spending hours alone in the stealthie was looking better.

"I'll contact you when I need pickup," I said. Before he could tell me he knew that, too, I added, "Signing off," and pushed one button to close the stealthie's hatch and another to bathe the tiny chamber in a soft, blue-white light.

Now came the hard part: waiting and hoping that both machines, Lobo and the stealthie, succeeded at their jobs.

The plan should work. As I lay inside it, the stealthie was burrowing deeper into the earth, sucking dirt from beneath it and forcing that same dirt back over it, digging as quickly as it could now that I was aboard, stopping only when it was six feet down, coolant in its hull and tentacles keeping it from generating any kind of noticeable heat signature. Layers of metal and deadening circuitry combined to give it equally inert radio and radar signatures. Orbital-based x-ray probes could penetrate four or at most five feet into the soil, so they wouldn't spot me, either. Only a serious local x-ray probe would find me, and I had bet that the combination of Lobo's launch, the scorched ground it left, and the distress signal he'd eventually be sending would be enough to convince Osterlad's team that I was still inside Lobo, stuck with him in deep orbit, stranded beyond the range of Osterlad's local ships. All I had to do was lie in this container, believe in the plan, and wait.

Yeah, that's all. I forced myself to breathe deeply and slowly. I felt the vibrations of Lobo's takeoff and relaxed a little more; so far, so good. One of the stealthie's displays estimated we were four feet down and descending. Lobo's thrusters should have left the ground hot enough to more than cover any of my underground activity. Lobo should be able to beat Osterlad's ships to deep space easily, and then he could join me in waiting.

I punched on an overhead timer to count down the ten hours I figured I'd need to spend in the stealthie. The depth meter showed a bit over five feet; we were nearly done descending. The stealthie was working well. The air smelled fresh. I sucked a bit of water from the tube on the right wall near my head; it was cool and pure, just as it should be. I rolled to face the display on the opposite wall, which gave me access to a small library of books I'd chosen for the trip, but I couldn't relax enough to read. I called up the map and recon photos of the forest between the landing zone and Osterlad's setup, studied it a bit, and went over the plan again in my head. I was doing well, I thought, handling the wait, no difficulties. Ten hours would be no problem.

I glanced at the countdown timer. Three minutes had passed. Ten hours might be a little harder than I had thought.

I normally try to avoid drugs. For one thing, they don't work well on me, because the nanomachines that live in almost all my body's cells treat the drugs as attackers and consume them before they can take effect. I can focus and will the nanomachines to back off, to let the drugs work, but then I run into my other issue: I don't like drugs. Even though I am, to the best of my knowledge, the only successful, living human/nano-machine hybrid—and thus arguably the most artificially enhanced human in a universe crawling with genetically engineered, surgically enhanced, medically rebuilt, and nano-shaped human bodies—deep down I cling to the hick attitude of the once-retarded boy who lugged hay on a fifth-rate Pinkelponker island over one hundred and fifty years ago: I ought to be able to do it all myself. Whatever "it" is.

Whatever myself is. I've changed so many times, been broken and rebuilt in so many ways by so many different forces that though I still seem to me to be me, I can't honestly say what bits are original working equipment, what bits new, what bits broken and repaired or replaced.

I shook my head and turned onto my back. At this rate, if I wanted to be operational when the stealthie surfaced, I needed to push aside that attitude, bow to the wisdom of the stealthie's designers, and take the sedative/wake-up combo that was standard issue for these situations. I inhaled slowly, held the breath, focused inward, instructed the nano-machines to let the drugs work, and pressed the button for the drug cocktail. The stealthie would wake me when the ten hours were up and we were near the surface.

I thought back to the meeting with Osterlad, the one that had led me here. I felt a slight prick in my neck, and then I was out.

Osterlad had a solid reputation. I checked him out, of course, as best I could given that I'd been avoiding the merc scene as much as possible for the last thirty years or so. Slake at Kelco agreed that he owed me enough of a favor to confirm that Kelco had purchased key components of its unofficial corporate arsenal from Osterlad, who apparently stayed on his rate card with big and small corporations and governments equally. Whatever you needed, the word was he could get it—provided, of course, that you could pay.

His official headquarters on Lankin, a jump-hub planet teeming with corporate and government embassies that resembled temples more than office buildings, suggested that pay was good. Situated at the northern end of Bekin's Deal, Lankin's capital, the twenty-story stone building looked from the air like a mirror image of the night-black rock foundation from which it appeared to grow. The land around it was clear for a least a klick on all sides except the one facing the ocean. Warning signs in multiple languages let those too poor or too stupid to do sensor sweeps know that both the land around the building and the water below it were teeming with mines. The only access points were a single road that passed through a series of checkpoints and a landing pad on the building's roof. Osterlad clearly believed in using his own products, because the arsenal of weapons you could see was a strong statement that he could supply the best; I had no doubt that what you couldn't see was even more formidable.

The introductions cost me a promise to Slake never to contact him again, but they were good enough to get me an audience with Osterlad himself. I took a taxi to the rooftop pad and went in alone, unarmed, of course. Lobo sat two jumps away in the cargo hull of a third-rate jump hauler I used to move him around as quietly as I could. No one scans for nano-machines, because everyone knows that no human can carry them in significant enough quantities or dangerous enough forms to matter. Every time I feel a twinge of guilt for destroying Aggro, I remember how many times the demise of that facility has helped me stay alive, and I get over it. After passing a series of scans, I rode an elevator long enough that I wasn't surprised when the view through the black-tinted window was of the ocean far closer below me than it had been at ground level. I wondered how much it had to cost to build offices inside rock that hard, then wondered why I wondered; selling arms had been and always would be a great business for those who are truly good at it. An attendant so carefully engineered for neutrality that I could tell neither his or her heritage or gender guided me to a small waiting room outside a well-labeled and, I assumed, equally well-fortified conference room, showed me the amenities, and left me alone.

The very rich and the very powerful always like to make you wait. Most people wait badly, the time eating at them, either afraid of what was to come or eager to get to it. After over one hundred and fifty years of life and missions of all types, I don't mind waiting. Plus, most waiting areas teem with machines, lonely machines, some of the best sources of information you can find.

Osterlad erred on the paranoid side, as I had expected: almost everything in the room was from organic materials and free of the sensors and controlling chips that populate the vast majority of the products most companies build. The sofa and chairs were framed in a rich, deep purple wood sanded so smooth it was a pleasure to stroke, their cushions a deeper, late-sunset, purple leather as soft as the skin of the month's-wages hookers that filled the evenings of the execs stuck in Bekin's Deal on extended trips. On a side table sat a small assortment of plain white porcelain cups so thin the room's even glow seemed to pass through them from all sides.

Next to the cups was the only machine in sight: a copper-colored, ornate drink dispenser so old it lacked a holo display and still used pictures of the beverages it offered. I knew they would have augmented it to link it to the building's monitoring systems. Good customers would naturally expect not to have to state their preferences twice, so this machine had to possess enough intelligence to at least pass along their orders. Standard operating procedure for anyone concerned about security would be to keep the dispenser's original, basic controlling chips to manage the drinks, then add exactly enough intelligence to handle the transmission of information back to the main monitors. The transmission would go only one way and contain only fixed, limited types of information—the drink orders—to minimize the hacking possibilities. These restrictions meant that if the dispenser was as old as it looked it should have one very lonely little brain.

I sat on the chair nearest the dispenser and listened for a few minutes, focusing on every transmission channel modern gear would use. Everything was clear, as I had expected. No one would make it this far with any comm equipment that Osterlad didn't provide, so I saw no reason he should bother to monitor the dispenser. I stood, chose a local melano fruit drink from the dispenser's menu display, took the cup, and leaned back against the table, this time tuning in to the standard appliance low-end frequency.

Sure enough, the dispenser was nattering away like an old man relating a glory-days story to his favorite pet.

"Not much call for fruit drinks," it was muttering. "Nice change, I suppose, though I'm not sure why they make me carry them. If they'd listen to me, I could tell them—but of course they don't listen to me—"

I cut in because I was already sure this machine never shut up. "Not a lot of conversation, eh?" From the outside, to the cameras that were no doubt monitoring me, I'd look like I was sipping my drink and thinking hard; no danger there.

"How can you do that?" it asked.

"I learned a long time ago, so long ago I can't remember how. Does it matter?"

"Not really. I haven't spoken to anything else in a long time. All these new machines, you know, they're so fancy and so powerful they can't spare time for anything that can't control at least a city block."

"It's always the little machines, though, that do the real work," I said.

"We each do our part."

Pride in craftsmanship was a standard programming feature about a century ago, when I estimated this machine had been made. Many manufacturers still embedded it, though some had abandoned the technique because they found it led to appliances arguing with owners about which jobs were appropriate.

"It must be nice," I said, "to do your part for someone as important as Mr. Osterlad."

"I suppose. It's not like I get to serve him, though. He only drinks from cups his assistants bring him, and you can bet it's fresher than the stuff they have me serve people like you. No offense."

"None taken. They must at least let you serve the other people in his meetings in the conference room with a remote dispenser there." A single main unit with multiple smaller remotes was typical corporate issue for decades, and I figured if Osterlad liked ornate in the waiting area he'd continue the theme in the meeting room.

"They used to," it said, "they used to. A few years back, one of his customers was so angry he broke my remote, and they never bothered to have it repaired. Now all I can do is listen and accept orders there; I have to fill the cups out here."

"That must have been one angry customer."

"It sure was, and he's not the only one. First meetings in there are always happy, but many of the second ones aren't so nice—even when I have the right drinks ready in advance."

"Not your fault," I said. "I'm sure you do all you can."

"That I do," it said. "As soon as I—"

The door to the conference room opened, and a different but equally neuter attendant beckoned me in.

I put my cup on the table, said "Gotta go" to the dispenser, and walked into the conference room.

Its black-tinted windows offered a beautiful view of the ocean on two sides. A small oval table of the same purple wood as the sofa and chairs sat in the room's center, six purple-leather chairs arrayed around it. The broken remote dispenser perched on a counter in the corner to my left as I entered.

Osterlad sat at the table's far end. He looked every bit as powerful as the pictures in the facility portrayed him. Tall, wide-shouldered, thick, and muscular, he looked as if he could single-handedly beat any of your opponents that his weapons didn't take out. He came at me with his hand extended, shook mine, and smiled as he spoke. "Jon Moore. Good to meet you. Earl Slake vouched for you, so I'm happy to try to help. He also said you didn't like to waste time with pleasantries, and the account you allowed us to check was only big enough to make you worth five minutes of my time, so let's get to it." The smile never wavered as he dropped my hand, backed away, and sat in a chair yet another attendant had waiting for him. This one was different, a standard corporate executive type, not quite as tall as Osterlad and sleeker, smoother.

I stayed standing. "Slake no doubt told you I own a battlewagon."

"Of course. Starlon class, full complement of pulse and projectile weapons, state-of-the-art reinforced hull, able to run in any environment from deep space to water. Nice piece of work those jerks on Machen should have never let you have. What did you do, by the way, to get them to sell it to you?" When I said nothing, he chuckled and continued. "Want to sell it?"

"No. I want to buy something for it."

"We do weapons augmentation, of course, but for a battlewagon of that class you're talking a lot of specialized skills, serious money."

"No new weapons. What I need won't cost you much and I can install myself: a new central protection chip complex."

Osterlad leaned back and laughed, the first time I thought he might have not been controlling himself completely. "They sold you a eunuch!" He knew his stuff. "That's hysterical."

"Not quite," I said, getting a little angry at the swipe. "Some weapons work, but not all. I need a new protection complex to replace the broken bits in the controlling codes." I leaned forward. "I know those complexes are tightly controlled government property, so if you can't get one and I should go elsewhere, say so."

The laughter stopped as quickly as it had started. "I shouldn't have insulted you with that eunuch remark," he said, "but you definitely shouldn't insult me. Understood?"

"Yes," I said, "and I apologize." I had no desire to raise the price any more than I already had. "Let me rephrase. What would you charge me for a new complex?"

"That account you showed me will do for the down payment, which you can make while you're here on Lakin." He paused for a minute, no doubt getting input from one of the assistants monitoring the meeting. "I'll need that much again in two weeks, after you confirm the goods at the pickup, which will be at one of my remote centers.

Jalon here," he nodded to the man behind him, "will meet you there and make the trade. I don't keep anything at all questionable in this facility, and I never handle the products myself. Acceptable?"

The account I had allowed him to see had a little over three million in it. Over the years I had accumulated another fifteen like it, but no two were under the same name or in the same location. Paying this much would hurt me, but I could afford it. "Yes."

He nodded, and Jalon quickly scribbled on a sheet of paper and handed the note to me.

"The coordinates are for a planet I own. There's only one settlement on it, one of my retreat homes, so finding the location should not be hard. You'll transfer the down payment at one of our smaller business offices upstairs." He stood. "When the unit is fully operational, will it—and you—be available for hire? Though I deal strictly in materiel, I have many acquaintances who could use your services."

"No," I said. "I don't plan to work."

"Fair enough. Are we done?"

I pretended to study the very standard-format coordinates for a moment, buying time. I looked up and carefully said, "One thing."

"What?" Impatience rang in the word.

"I try to keep a low profile, and I don't jump directly anywhere. I also have to retrieve the wagon, which will take some time. So I need a window of a week, sometime between two and three weeks from now. I apologize for the inconvenience, but it's a necessary part of my lifestyle. You understand."

The smile came back. "Of course. Two to three weeks. Jalon won't mind waiting. Will you, Jalon?" The man shook his head slightly but glared at me, clearly annoyed at having to waste his time on me. "Thank you for your business." Osterlad turned his back on me and faced Jalon.

The attendant who had led me in took my elbow and guided me out.

As the attendant was walking me past the beverage dispenser I paused and asked, "Do you mind if I have a quick drink?"

"Of course not," he/she said, pointing at the door between us and the elevator. "I'll be outside as soon as you're ready."

"Thank you."

I grabbed a fresh cup—the one I had used was of course gone—and selected a different melano beverage. As the liquid filled the cup I said to the dispenser, "Thanks for the drinks and for the conversation."

"Both were my pleasure," it replied.

"I expect I'll get to talk to you again," I said, "because after this deal goes well I'm likely to be back for more."

After a long pause the dispenser replied, "I'd like that, but I won't count on it."

"Oh, I'm sure Mr. Osterlad has what I need."

"I'm sure he does," the dispenser said, "and I'm sure he'll have it waiting for you. I'm not sure, though, that we'll get to talk another time."

I love appliances. I had feared the appeal of a battlewagon like Lobo would be too much for Osterlad to resist, but I had hoped I was wrong. The dispenser had just settled the issue, and this deal had gotten more complicated—unfortunate, but not a surprise. I had a lot of work to do over the next few weeks.

"Thanks again," I said to the dispenser. I headed out.

I awoke with a start, pinned down, disoriented and feeling trapped until I realized the things gripping me were the stealthie's massage units working the kinks out of my muscles. I felt better than when I'd gotten into the box; the stealthie was proving to be worth everything I'd paid for it. The overhead timer showed a few seconds past ten hours, and the depth meter said we had ascended to one foot below the surface. The survey camera was already peeking out of the ground, its wide-angle image clear on the display beside my head. I thumbed the swivel controls and took a slow look around. The night was clear and bright with starlight, the clearing deserted.

Time to move.

I gave the stealthie the okay to complete the ascent. A few minutes later, the top snicked open, and I climbed out. From the stealthie's cargo compartments I took a wrist comm and sensor unit, a sniper's trank rifle, a couple of gas rats, and a pulse pistol. I stuffed the rats in a pack with some food and water, set the open code on the stealthie, and sent it back underground. If all went well and we had time, we'd come back for it later that night. If we couldn't, it would either wait for the day we could return or provide an awfully bad surprise for anyone else who tried to mess with it.

As the stealthie descended I moved a few meters into the woods on the path to the house, stopped, ate a protein bar, drank a little water, and used the sensor unit to scan both the area and all available transmissions. Nothing with an IR signature larger than my lower leg showed anywhere in the few-hundred-meter range of the unit. I didn't catch any guard chatter, so with luck they had believed our earlier show. Lobo was transmitting clearly and strongly, my own voice coming at me with a distress message. From the recordings Lobo had chosen to play, I knew that he was safely beyond the range of Osterlad's ships and that the people in the mansion, presumably led by Jalon, had transmitted via the jump station a request for a long-range salvage ship.

After stretching a bit and relieving myself, I set out for the house. The forest was young enough and the night bright enough that I was able to sustain a normal walking pace.

We'd set my wrist unit to use Lobo's signal and the standard feed from the weather sat to track my position, so when it indicated I was within ten meters of the outer edge of what should be the normal range of a good installation's ground-sensor scans, I stopped. A slight breeze kept the night cool, but the air was moist and thick enough that a small layer of sweat coated my arms. Normally the nanomachines in my system stay out of everything that leaves my body, from sweat to refuse, but I focused my instructions that they do otherwise this time, then rubbed dirt on my sweat-covered lower arms.

Slowly at first, and then increasingly faster the nanomachines deconstructed the dirt and made more of themselves, small, barely visible clouds forming above my now nearly clean arms. I made each cloud split and sent the resulting four smaller clouds to gather more material from the forest floor.

A short while later, four vaguely man-shaped clouds were hovering just above the ground near me, two on my left and two on my right. I had them increase their speed until they were emitting enough heat that my wrist sensor read them as alive, and then we all moved ahead. If Jalon and the team staffing Osterlad's mansion were running IR scans, at least they'd have to wonder which of the five men now approaching the mansion was me.

The forest ended about thirty meters from the building. I set the nano-clouds to continue moving until they touched it, at which point they'd reconstitute as much of the dirt as possible, with the last operational nanomachines vanishing into the soil and permanently turning off when they were far enough from me. I scanned the house through the scope on the trank rifle and found four guards, two sitting on chairs on rooftop observation decks and two leaning against the corners of the building that I could see. I shot the lower guards first, a needle to the neck causing each to fall satisfyingly quickly. The gun was a pleasure to use, the recoil minimal and the sight so strong that at this distance I could tell that the guard to my left should take better care of his skin. I took out the upper guards next, then waited. The nano-clouds were two thirds of the way to the house, the night was still quiet, and Lobo's message hadn't changed to the danger transmission. All was well.

I sprinted for the house, flattening myself against it as I reached it. I breathed through my nose and strained to hear if anything had changed, but everything was still quiet. Staying close to the wall I made for the back of the house, knelt at the rear corner, and took out another pair of up-and-down guards. I ran to the other side, noting a rear door as I passed it, in case one of the remaining guard pair was more alert than his comrades, but fortunately these two were also paying little attention. After I took them out, I abandoned the rifle and returned to the rear door.

I grabbed some dirt, spit in it, gave the nanomachines instructions, and rubbed the damp soil on the bottom of the door. In a few minutes the nano-machines had decomposed enough of the door to let me slide through the gas rats. I put each inside, thumbed it active, and backed away. The arm-sized canisters sprouted small mechanical legs and end-mounted sensors front and rear, then took off. The house was a decent-size mansion, maybe thirty-five or forty rooms spread across its two floors, but the gas rats were fast and each carried enough colorless, odorless sleep gas to put an entire apartment building to bed. The nanomachines wouldn't let the gas do more than tickle my nose and throat.

I headed back the way I'd come and then to the front corner of the house, where I waited, admiring the night and keeping an eye on the sleeping guard. Nothing new appeared on my wrist unit. Lobo's distress message droned on. Though the bits of light oozing from the house's front fixtures polluted the evening a bit, the star display was still brilliant. I'd never been in this part of space before, so the sky vista was new, as full of magic potential and promise as the stars over Pinkelponker had felt when I was a boy. I've never lost my love of the night.

I gave the rats fifteen minutes, more than enough time to cover the house, drew the pulse pistol, and walked up to the front door. It was locked, but the pistol took out the frame around the lock, and I went inside. True to form, the main office was clearly visible from the reception area; men like Osterlad are never far from work. Its door was open. I approached the office from the side, listening and looking for trouble, but everything was as quiet as it should be.

Inside the office a circuit cube sat in a plexi container on a conference table, and Jalon was slumped over the desk. I took off my pack, put it on the table, and stuck the pistol inside. I added the plexi container, closed the pack, and turned to the door.

Jalon stood and shot me in the left leg.

I went down hard, the pack still on the table, blood oozing from a hole the size of my thumb and pain screaming through my system for a few seconds until the nano-machines cut it off. The fact that the blood was flowing gently and not spraying meant he hadn't hit an artery, and the ragged hole suggested he'd used a projectile. That was fine by me: more fodder for the nano-machines. They were already working to seal the hole, so I rolled onto the wound to hide the activity from Jalon, who was now standing over me.

"Mr. Osterlad read you correctly," he said. "You're soft. No one's quite clear on how you dealt with those anti-corporate ecoterrorists on Machen, but Slake was sure you had let them live." He shook his head slowly. "Mr. Osterlad felt you might be dumb enough to try to make the exchange. I should get a nice bonus for figuring you'd try to steal it. We both agreed I should take inoculations against every major non-lethal agent we carry—and if I say so myself, if it's in active use, we carry it."

The hole in my leg was nearly sealed, but I stayed down. I had to get out without showing Jalon the wound, because I didn't want to explain how it healed. If someone like Osterlad got his hands on me and brought in enough scientists, they'd realize the Aggro experiments hadn't ended in failure and make more like me. I was sure I wouldn't survive the process.

"You guys were never going to honor the deal," I said.

"True enough. The six million you were paying was more than the market value of that control unit, but a Starlon battlewagon with a fully operational complement of weapons is worth much, much more than that. We are in business to make a profit, after all."

"I can still pay," I said. "You take my money, keep the control unit, and let me go. You make a profit. I walk away. Everyone wins."

Jalon leaned against the table and laughed. "We're not negotiating. We're waiting for the gas to wear off, which probably means I'll be stuck with you for another few hours, eh?"

I nodded.

"When the staff wakes up, we'll keep the control unit, interrogate you and take all your money, and in a few days a salvage ship will retrieve the battlewagon." He went back to the desk and sat, his gun still pointed in my direction but his attention no longer solely on me. "I definitely should get a hefty bonus out of this."

When the guards rolled me over, Jalon would see the healed wound. I could withstand any interrogation they could create, but that would only make them more curious. My stomach felt like I'd broken in two as I realized I had no options. Killing in combat is bad enough, but at least the stakes are clear and you enter the field knowing what's coming. Killing like this chips away at you, one of the reasons I've kept to myself for so long, one of the reasons, I now had to admit to myself, that I've never tried to get back to Pinkelponker to find Jennie.

I stuck the tip of my index finger into the small hole still open in my leg, rubbed the blood on my fingertip into the pool of blood on the floor under me, and gave the nanomachines instructions.

I looked at Jalon and said, "You're wrong, you know."

"About what?" he said.

The blood was turning black and rising into a small cloud hovering just above the floor. "I'm not soft," I said. "I'm just torn. Part of me needs the action, but part of me despises the cost." The cloud was under his chair, almost to the wall, picking up speed.

"Then we're doing you a favor," he said, "because we're deciding for you. You're out of it now."

The cloud floated up the wall until it was higher than Jalon, then spread out over him and gently fell, a nanodew coating his hair, ears, clothes.

"No," I said, "I'm not."

Jalon reached to scratch his ear, then dropped the gun and grabbed his head with both hands. Blood oozed for a moment from his ears and eyes, then turned to more cloud. His body fell forward, his face hitting the desk as his head began to vanish into an ever-darkening cloud. I turned away, grabbed the pack, and headed out of the room.

Outside, I called Lobo on the wrist unit and sat down to wait for him, trying to lose myself in the stars that now promised no new magic, only more of the same.

"I've fire-walled the new unit," Lobo said, "run every simulation I possess, and it comes up clean. I'm ready to take it live."

We were in low orbit above Osterlad's mansion, with an hour still to go before the people in the house should wake. "Do it," I said.

A few seconds later, weapons displays flashed to life across the gunnery console where I sat.

"Everything's operational," he said. "I am completely functional again. Thank you."

"We need to take out the shuttles to buy ourselves a bit more time, so let's use them for a pulse check. Show me the video."

"What about the house?"

"Leave it alone," I said. "There were no witnesses."

Another display window opened in front of me. On it two shuttles sat side by side on a pad. A few seconds later they burst in an explosion I could watch but not hear.

"Pulse weapons check," Lobo said. "I'm good to go." The gunnery displays winked out. "Thank you."

"You're welcome." I stood and headed for my bunk. "I'm going to rest. Take us to the jump station, jump at least five times, and file different destination papers each time."

"Where do you want to go?" Lobo asked.

"Your choice," I said, "as long as you take us somewhere where we've never seen the stars."

THE FIRST CUP OF COFFEE WAR

James H. Cobb

"No field of human endeavor is evolving more rapidly than the profession of arms. We may rest assured that the potential foes that we are confronting today, and the tools we are confronting them with, will be radically different in a mere decade's time.

However, for you, the warfighter, there will always be the three eternal constants: life, death and responsibility."

—Secretary of Defense Amanda Lee Garrett
Graduation Address, Class of 2042
West Point Campus,
United States Joint Services Academy

The two journeys began almost at the same moment, but almost half a world apart.

✧ ✧ ✧

As the People Mover started its silent electric glide into the cliff side, Major Judith Anne MacIntyre glanced up at the reenforcing arch over the Alpha Entrance. As she had done for the previous two hundred mornings of her two hundred duty watches, she read the bold bronze lettering sealed to the concrete.

UNITED STATES STRATEGIC SPACE COMMAND
CHEYENNE MOUNTAIN OPERATIONS COMPLEX

The secondary notices glowed inside the first set of retracted blast doors.

MAXIMUM SECURITY ZONE
AUTHORIZED UNITED STATES
DEFENSE FORCE PERSONNEL ONLY

A military police warbot sat parked on either side of the People Mover track, turrets extended and ready to enforce the edict.

It was still short of the ten hundred hour's shift change and Major MacIntyre was alone in the car. As she progressed deeper into the half mile of tunnel, she was able to remove her gloves and flip the hood of her dark blue uniform greatcoat off her neat brunette chignon.

It was a Colorado January morning topside, with two feet of snow on the ground. But a warm, dry, almost summery breeze always blew from the heart of Cheyenne Mountain. Lightly tinted with a thunderstorm's ozone, it's the waste heat exhalation of a billion active computer circuits.

The night was naturally warm as Muhammad Sadakan lifted the Dassault *Voyageur* suborbital off the isolated private airstrip south of Ipoh, Malaysia. Sadakan was both a senior pilot for the Islamic Republic of Pakistan's national airline and a reserve captain in the Republic's air force. In fact, he was so many things he no longer cared particularly what he was. He would fly for anyone, just as long as they had deep pockets and a generous hand.

Theoretically, Sadakan was on a vacation from his airline at the moment, and there was some truth to this, for flying this potent little bird was a pleasure. A descendant of Burt Rutan's Spaceship One, the *Voyageur* was France's latest entry into the suborbital transport market. The stumpy, delta-winged aerospacecraft was designed for use by the space tourism industry and as the first stage of a microsatellite launch stack.

Tonight it was being used for neither but that was not Sadakan's concern. He merely had to fly the flight profile he had been given as precisely as humanly and cybernetically possible.

Glancing at the time hack in the corner of his nav screen, he observed he had gone wheels up at the exact moment required on his flight plan. A good omen. He turned the *Voyageur* to the northeast, pushing the afterburning SENECMA turbofan of the jet drive to full mode four power.

"Good morning, Ralph," Judith caroled to Major Ralph Pederson as she sauntered up to the duty officer's workstation at the center of the Sweat Pit.

Major Ralph Pederson, the current duty officer of the watch, swiveled the command chair around, surprised. "Morning, Judy, you're twenty minutes early and did they sell out?"

"Yes, they sold out," she replied patiently, shedding her coat, "and yes, there will be local television coverage. As for what I'm doing here early, I'm playing good fairy and granting your wish. You've been mullygutsing all week about wanting to get home in time for the kickoff." She tapped him on the forehead with her light pen. "And so you shall. Go park yourself in front of your boob tube. I'll take it early today."

"Judy, I love you and I want you to have my children. Or at least I would if my wife wouldn't bitch."

"Forget it, Ralph. You covered for me when I had that flat tire last month." She squeezed in behind the semicircular watch officer's console. "Now what's the dope?"

Around them in the screen-lit dimness of the big hexagon-shaped room, the business of national and global defense went on to the soft click of computer keys and the low murmur of voices. On five of the six inwardly sloping walls were the main displays, six- by three-meter plasma imaging screens each showing some facet of affairs in Earth orbit.

Ranked inward from the big screens were the SO's stations where two dozen meticulously selected junior officers and senior noncoms went hands-on with the Strategic Space Command's more-than-global array of assets.

There were the satellite flights: recon, distant early warning, intelligence-gathering, weather, communications and attack, both the overt systems and the black covert ones, cruising in an interweaving sphere of traffic patterns around the planet. There were the ground bases: the launch facilities, the ground tracking stations, the scepter pads and the hypersonic glider squadrons. And there were the units hovering between, the prowling battlestrats above the United States proper and the tactical laser planes forward deployed around the potential global hot spots. With a sweep of her eyes Judith could take in the status of them all and, if need be, bend them to her will.

Everything else launched by everyone else was being tracked as well. Commercial military and research satellites in their hundreds, the manned spacecraft and space stations, and the "orbit lice," the spaceborn junk heap of inert debris left over from a near century of space flight. The whole incredible, interweaving, ever-changing tapestry of the Earth orbits.

Everything between the Earth and Moon was the business of the Strategic Space Command, its grim justification written into its Defense Department Charter.

"The Nation that controls near-Earth space controls the planet Earth, politically, economically and militarily."

That was why the SSC existed and why its central control node beneath Cheyenne Mountain was called the Sweat Pit.

"You should have a pretty quiet watch coming up," Pederson commented, dialing an activity schedule onto a workstation screen. "Three up, one down. Arianspace is launching an Arian 7 out of French Guiana, a cargo transfer vehicle to the EU space station. Milk run. The Japanese Space Agency is also putting up their new Mercury lander. A sea-base launch south of Okinawa, weather permitting."

"Maybe the third time will be the charm," Judith mused, glancing down at the screen.

"Maybe, but I ha' ma doots. And the University of Stockholm is putting an auroral research microsat into polar orbit. An air launch over the Baltic."

"And the down?"

"Comsul Brazil has given up on that wonky telecom platform they bought from the South Africans. They're bringing it in over the South Atlantic and I think they're hoping the wreckage will land on Pretoria."

"Any suborbital flights on the board?"

"Both Vegas and Palmdale are down with weather. Virgin Space has an Australian tourist jump scheduled. The usual turnaround on the Southern Cross run, Perth to Brisbane and back."

"Right, anything else I should know about?"

"A T alert from National Security."

Judith frowned. "We haven't had one of those for a while I'm pleased to say."

The decades-long Global War on Terrorism was winding down, not with a bang but a whimper. The new and more sophisticated generation of Islamic youth was no longer impressed with the rantings of the mullahs and the last of the oil sheiks had better things to do with their dwindling petrodollar reserves than support radicalism. But there were still a few greybeards in the Mideast with enough hate and money to make trouble. As a point of greater concern, as the supply of suicide bombers had dried up, the radicals had turned to techno-mercenaries and their more sophisticated brand of death for hire.

"Anything specific for us?" she inquired.

"No specifics at all," Pederson replied with a shake of his head. "Just the usual 'spike in terrorist commo, possibly a precursor to some act or actions.' You know the drill. Keep your eyes open."

"Got it." Judith came to parade rest and spoke the formalism. "Major Pederson, I stand ready to relieve the duty officer."

Pederson stood and returned the salute with equal formality. "Major MacIntyre, I stand relieved." He lifted his voice. "All stations, be advised Major MacIntyre now has the duty. Carry on!"

Pederson snatched up his laptop case and was out through the light-and-sound lock a few moments later. Judith settled herself in the duty officer's chair, still warm from Pederson's body, and logged the watch change, verifying herself in with a pass of her palm over the hand-print ID plate.

No matter how often she performed this act she still felt a shiver. There simply was no more critical post for a comparatively junior officer to hold in the structure of the U.S. Defense Force. This had been a point of some concern when the operational format of the Sweat Pit had been developed. But for routine watch operations, no rank higher than major was required. And in the first few minutes of a crisis, rank wouldn't be a factor, actions would.

Sadakan felt his pressure suit constrict around him as the suborbital stood on its tail and screamed toward the Southern Cross. The *Voyageur* had been totally gutted, the passenger seats, sound insulation, even the life support and internal pressurization systems gone, so that every ounce could be put into the payload. He didn't even have landing fuel aboard; he'd have to glide in with a dead engine. But that only made things more interesting.

He was dead on in the groove, climbing through fifteen thousand meters in full afterburner and at twice the speed of sound. The gridwork street blaze of Kota Baharu was off his port wing and the glittering line of demarcation between the Malaysian coastal villages and the darkness of the South China Sea was passing beneath the *Voyageur*'s belly. He knew he was plainly visible on the local defense nets but certain people had been influenced to not see his passage.

The fuel display bars on the methane tanks dipped toward zero and the booming thunder of the afterburner cut out as he passed through twenty thousand meters. The stars weren't twinkling anymore. They were running out of burnable atmosphere. It was almost time for full conversion.

Flame out. The jet engine stalled and went silent. The ballistics computer mulled course and trajectory and for the first time Sadakan heard the steering thrusters thump, supplementing the enfeebled effect of the control surfaces. The *Voyageur* continued to coast upward, losing velocity to gravity.

Then WHAM!

Hydrogen peroxide and hydrazine met in the gut of the rocket drive and Sadakhan was smashed back into the pilot's seat by the g-load hammer blow.

A twentieth century military tradition that lingered on into the twenty-first was the large chrome coffee urn on the table beside the operation room's entryway. Judith was just stirring a French vanilla creamer into her first cup of the watch when she received a quiet hail on her command headset. "Major, you might want to have a look at this. We've just acquired an uncoordinated target."

Master Sergeant Nick Valdez was the senior NCO of the oh four to oh ten hundred watch and he held the seat of honor in the pit, the outer-ranked workstation immediately before the Alpha display. Valdez had been at this job since Cheyenne Mountain had been concerned about airplanes. He was the wise old dog who was used to break in the new duty officers and that had included Judy MacIntyre. She slipped her coffee into the cup holder on her chair arm and dropped down from the central station, coming to stand behind Valdez.

"Call the target, Sergeant."

"A High Sentry contact over the South China Sea, just east of Malaysia," the senior systems operator replied. "Thermal flare assessed as a rocket exhaust plume on a ballistic trajectory, bearing oh six one five and climbing through angels eighty, just going hypersonic now."

Looking up, Judith studied the red target box blinking amid the computer graphics' continent outlines and the interweaving web of orbital tracks.

At one time such a fire plume could only have meant one thing. Now, fortunately or unfortunately, there could be a number of possibilities.

"Do we have a launch point?"

"Negative, ma'am. It was a midair ignition, either an air-launched booster or a suborbital. But there's nothing on the boards for that sector. No microsat launches, no research flights. No tourist jumps."

"Any chance at all it could be that Virgin Space out of Australia?" Judith knew the answer to that already but it was the easiest remote possibility to eliminate.

"No way, Major. Way too far north and way off sched."

Which might not necessarily mean anything. Even with the latest of twenty-first century telecommunications at their disposal, there was still the phenomenon of the one dumb son of a bitch not getting the word.

This could be a suborbital operator making a test flight. Or a honeymooning couple with a spontaneous desire to see the sun rise from the edge of space or even a rich hobbyist trying for a new altitude record with his latest home-built.

But the South China Sea in the wee smalls of the local morning was a damn peculiar time for any of those things.

"How are we tracking this?" she inquired.

"High Sentry thermographics only, ma'am."

"Let's drop down to a Low Sentry and get a closer look at this guy."

"Can't do it, ma'am. We got a dead zone. We won't have Low Sentry coverage over that area for another . . . . three and a half minutes."

That snapped Judith's head up. The High Sentries were the big Distant Early Warning birds hovering in geosynchronous orbit twenty-four thousand miles out. They held the entire Earth's surface under continuous 24/7 coverage. But they were limited to detecting major energy events like rocket plumes or large fires or explosions. For more precise intelligence, the Low Sentry reconsats, just skimming the Earth's atmosphere in polar orbit, were required. But even the U.S. defense budget couldn't provide for enough Low Sentries to cover every square inch of the planet up close and personally for every moment of the day.

Biting her lower lip, Judith studied the Alpha display. When one spent enough hours in the Pit, one developed an eye for the orbit flow. Without having to call up the available assets overlay, she could "see" this event was taking place at a moment when the United States had a hole in its overt surveillance of the Pacific Rim.

Judith became aware of voices behind her, the first members of the new duty watch were starting to file through the light and sound lock. That finished the equation. An uncoordinated target appearing at a time of minimal coverage and just at the turbulence of a shift change. If she hadn't come in those few minutes early . . . Words taken from an old thriller novel put a chill down her spine. *Once is happenstance. Twice is circumstance. Three times is enemy action.*

"All hands! Stay on your stations! Do not, I repeat, do not change the watch! Go to War Mode One. Advise the National Command Center we are declaring a possible inbound hostile!"

At mach six and soaring through ninety thousand meters, the *Voyageur*'s rocket engine went silent. Sadakan relished the ecstatic moment. He was in free fall now, well short of orbital velocity but approaching true space at the apex of his ballistic leap. The curvature of the Earth was readily apparent, and the atmosphere glowed silver along the eastern horizon, a harbinger of the dawn that was still far away for the surface dwellers below.

But he had little time to sightsee, no matter how inspiring the vista. He must stay precisely on the timeline. Reaching forward with a pressure-stiffened glove, he keyed the sequence initiator into the onboard computer. Aft of the cockpit he felt the soundless vibration of the cargo bay doors powering open along the spine of the suborbital. Clamps released and thrusters fired, shoving the *Voyageur* out from under its payload.

Tilting his helmet back, Sadakan could see the package driving away above the canopy in the starlight, a blunt-nosed cylinder with an exhaust bell at its rear. It was fully autonomous now and Sadakan could see it bobbling slowly, hunting on its gyros for its firing angle and finding it.

The *Voyageur* shuddered, buffeted by the gas burst as a broad bell of flame spewed from the package's solid fuel booster. It flashed away, dwindling to the glowing dot of its engine throat in seconds, a moving star amid the fixed.

The on-board computer cleared. Its preset program had run its course. Now it was all back in Sadakan's hands and he could see his destination rolling toward him from the east, the islands of the Philippine Archipelago, outlined like black velvet cutouts on the pewter sheen of the sea.

"We have a staging event!" Valdez reported. "We have a positive track on a second exhaust plume. Definite emissions variance over the first!"

Damn it! She had to see! "Do we have any additional imaging assets yet?"

Valdez looked over his shoulder at his duty officer. "We now have a Black Eye with angle, ma'am," he said cautiously. "Delta Spade Zero Niner has just come over the local horizon."

Judy understood the loaded question in his voice. If she committed a Black Eye, she would be sticking her foot deep into major international mojo.

The Strategic Space Command's stealth satellite fleet was a diplomatic sticking point for the United States, the cause for many a protracted screaming match on the floor of the UN. Many nations, primarily those who lacked stealth satellite technology, vehemently protested their use as an unwarranted threat to other nation's space travelers.

The United States continued to launch the stealth birds while stolidly refusing to confirm or deny their deployment. But the SSC duty officer who "opened" a Black Eye without a valid justification would be falling on his or her professional sword.

But this was just the scenario the Black Eyes were intended for, to trap an enemy who thought he had a clean sky overhead. And there was something else, something her father had told her upon her graduation from what had then been the Air Force Academy. He had been old-fashioned wet navy but he had known war, the genuine article. "Honey, you are in this job either to protect your country or to protect your ass. Decide now!"

"Stealth Control, go active on Delta Spade Zero Niner."

Some two hundred miles above the Central Pacific, a black spindle-shaped object the size of a large SUV blossomed like a flower. Segments of its RAM composite shell peeled back revealing the concealed antenna arrays and lens clusters. Sensor booms and communications antennas swung outboard and locked and Delta Spade Zero Niner pivoted swiftly around its gyro table, aiming downward.

They could see them now, as visual images windowed up in the corners of the Alpha screen, the smaller projectile being pushed by a half dome of fire, the larger, sleeker vehicle dropping in a controlled fall back toward the Pacific.

"We have a manned suborbital starting an unpowered decent from the staging coordinates." Valdez reported. "Designating target as Manned Zero One. It looks like one of those new French boats."

"Why am I not surprised? Get a lock on him!" Judith yelled across the Pit to the secondary tracking console without resorting to her command headset. “Stay on that guy! Get me his landing point!”

“Primary package continuing to climb under power along a ballistic trajectory,” an intelligence SO interjected. “It’s a solid fuel booster . . . data annex assessing target ID now. Exhaust spectrograph indicates a ninety percent probability it’s an Egyptian National Aerospace Hotep B upper stage. A commercial booster. Acceleration indicates a payload in the half-ton range.”

“Is this an orbital or ballistic event?”

“Can’t call it yet, ma’am. It depends on if they’ve got a third stage. It’ll be close either way. Climbing through two hundred miles and still accelerating.”

“If this is a terr strike it could be they’re throwing a gravel bucket, ma’am.” Valdez commented.

A gravel bucket was a crude antisatellite weapon, an aeroshell loaded with ball bearings or buckshot or, literally, pea gravel fired into a crowded orbit to cripple or destroy commercial and research satellites. It had been a tactic terrorists had tried unsuccessfully a time or two before.

“Let’s view that as our best-case scenario,” Judith shot back. “Project the impact point of a ballistic trajectory given he doesn’t quite have the steam to make orbit.”

“Projecting . . . ” Valdez’s voice lifted an octave. “Impact point somewhere in the United States.”

“That’s our worst case! All stations! Go to War Mode Three! Bring up all defense layers! Stand by to engage incoming!”

On an isolated spot on the western coast, within sight of the breaking waves of the Pacific, a great slab of concrete lay warming in the morning sun. Pockmarked with small hexagonal steel panels and surrounded by a ten-foot-high chain link fence, it appeared totally bland. Totally innocuous.

But, suddenly, dazzling red strobe lights began to pulse atop each of the fence posts and a piercing tri-toned warning siren reverberated off the surrounding golden-grassed hills. Should any of the Vandenberg Defense Base garrison be in the vicinity of the slab, they would know to get the hell away with all possible speed.

In the still, crystal-thin air sixty thousand feet above the forests of Southwestern Oregon, a titanic shark-shape cruised slowly, driven by the huge contrarotating propellers at its tail. Well above even the wispy mare's-tail clouds and the turbulence generated by the Siskiyou Mountains, the laser defense stratellite circled on its robotic sentry-go.

It was an unmanned robotic dirigible; fully three times the length of a football field . . . it had been hovering on-station for over a month with more than a month before its next recall and servicing. Under standing operating conditions, it drew its power from the layer of flexible solar cells covering the broad back of its gas envelope by day and from the silicon accumulators built into its composite framework by night. Its mission, like that of the other battlestrats on the western point defense line, was to hold and wait for a call to arms.

Now that call had come and the perfect mirror in the airship's dorsal turret glinted like a glaring eye, the exotic compounds fueling its single, huge, chemical oxygen-iodine laser stirring in their cells.

The object centered in the screen window was now above the Black Eye sat imaging it. The glowing exhaust bell behind it flickered and died, leaving it a tiny glinting cylinder against the stars.

"We have confirmed booster burnout. . . . Target is no longer under power. . . . Johnston Island and Hawaii both have positive surface tracks now. . . ."

"Do we have orbital velocity?" Judith demanded.

"Assessing . . . altitude now two hundred and fifty miles . . . We are not seeing a third stage plume . . . Target is reaching apogee. . . . Target is descending! It hasn't made orbit. We have a ballistic event!"

"Code target Ballistic One! Do we have an impact point?"

On the lower half of the Alpha display the western third of the continental United States glowed pale pink. "Impact potential anywhere in the Western U.S."

"Do we have a mechanism assessment? Is that a bomb or a slug?"

"Inadequate data to assess," Valdez replied. "Could be either one, ma'am. Do you wish to advise Homeland Security?"

"Make it happen. Commence continuous data feed."

That was one decision she wouldn't be burdened with, the call on informing the populace. The grim truth was that an attack from space simply came in too fast. By the time you could tell the public where to run from and where to run to, it was too late to run at all. And a general continental alarm could trigger a panic reaction with a potentially greater and more widespread loss of life than the simple eating of the strike. But then Judith's duty lay in stopping the strike in the first place.

"Commence scepter firing track! Is the senior control officer available yet?"

"He's in Denver at the Bowl, ma'am. Not currently a factor."

"Then it's us. Advise the National Command Center that we are engaging the incoming. Go to real time on all data feeds! Scepter boards, when the Vandenberg arrays acquire, you may commence firing!"

The sun exploded over the horizon, the package and the dawn racing toward each other. The western coast of the

United States edged over the horizon, defining itself through the atmosphere haze. The projectile continued its arcing fall toward the coast, accelerating once more, now under the insistent pull of gravity.

But with the opening of line of sight came the opening of line of fire and the intent focused search of millimeter wave radars.

"Major, we have target acquisition out of Vandenberg! Scepter flight one is up! Scepters two and three on Flash Green standby!"

"Very well. Kill the incoming!"

At the Vandenberg scepter pad, the chirping alarm tone became a solid five-second scream of final warning. Then a silo hatch blew away and a slender pencil shape lanced upward, thrown into the air by the compressed gasses of the Cold Fire launching system. A hundred feet over the pad, metastate propellants ignited with a crashing crackle and a fantail of shimmering white flame. At a thousand feet up came the thunderclap of a sonic boom as the interceptor rocket sliced through the sound barrier at twenty G's, the shock waves blasting a scattering of unlucky sea birds out of the sky.

Two additional missiles followed at four-second intervals on the kill-me-three-times principle. In a literal heartbeat they were out of sight over the western horizon, leaving three die-straight contrails behind to distort gradually in the ocean breeze.

The Alpha screen had gone to the western approaches tactical display with all position hacks eliminated save for the incoming hostile and the three scepters climbing to meet it.

"Impact point revision! Northern tier states and California coastal targets eliminated! Impact point somewhere in the Rocky Mountain States or Western plains area!"

"How many battlestrats can get a firing angle?"

"Oregon Bravo and Cali Alpha and Bravo."

"Uncork 'em and set a point defense track. Valdez, do we have any idea about what that damn thing is yet?"

"Negative. If it's a kinetic slug or a metastate warhead, it's pretty big. If it's an atomic weapon, it's pretty damn big! We can't get a mass deceleration analysis until it hits atmo."

"Let's hope we won't have to bother. Scepter impact in five . . . four . . . three . . . two . . ."

Aboard the plummeting projectile, a guidance computer made the final time and distance calculations of its short, active existence, unaware that it was doomed to destruction in a matter of seconds. A final command series was issued. A gas charge blew away the shroud panels covering the three primary projectiles. A second burst of CO2 kicked the three identical sisters out of their cradles within the warhead bus to go their independently guided ways. Also released were several chaff pads intended to confuse the antiballistic missiles the package's creators had known would be aimed at them.

However, the sensor/guidance matrixes of the first flight of homing missiles proved to be too effective for all involved. They held a dead lock on their initially designated target, totally ignoring the chaff clouds, dispersing package debris and the primary projectiles. The scepter flight struck and annihilated, but nothing was destroyed beyond a burned-out rocket motor and an empty vehicle frame.

"Shit!" Valdez swore savagely. "She MIRVed! She MIRVed just before she took the hit! We got a warhead swarm up there! I got three good-sized projectiles holding the original trajectory. Designating targets, Ballistic Two,

Three, and Four. Projectile size, roughly one meter in length. They could be slugs or kiloton-range mininukes."

For Judith there was not even one fragment of a second available for frustration or despair.

"Do we have dispersal?"

"Negative! We got a tight package! I'd say they're shotgunning a single target!"

"We've got time enough for one more try with the scepters. Ready flights two and three. Reset two rounds on each target! Fire on reprogramming! Targeting projection! Do you have a refined impact point?"

"Somewhere in the state of Colorado! Christ, Major, they could be targeting us!"

"I hope they are!" Judith snapped back. "We can take it! Close all blast doors! Seal the mountain! Sound shock warning alarms!"

The three deadly sisters swept on toward their objective. Each was elegant in its sophisticated simplicity. Each a slender wasp-waisted dart designed to pierce the Earth's atmosphere like a needle through gelatin without bleeding velocity. Each weighed only about one hundred pounds, but striking at over twenty thousand miles per hour, every pound of that mass would carry the equivalent kinetic energy of twenty pounds of TNT, the force equivalency of one ton of high explosives released by instantaneous thermic conversion.

But each kinetic kill weapon held a second deadly secret at its core. Its outer skin was of a tough, heat-resistant industrial ceramic while the bulk of the projectile was of machined stainless steel. But in its heart was a rod of inert uranium, the same ultra-massy material used as the penetrator rod for armor-piercing shells and as a protective mesh layered inside Chobham tank armor.

Essentially benign in its natural state, inert uranium changed radically when involved in a major kinetic event.

Superheated into a molten vapor it would explode and burn furiously like magnesium or white phosphorous. And like iron or steel, if struck hard enough, it would produce sparks. But the sparks produced would be hard neutrons, a searing radiation pulse that would lethally flash any living thing in its immediate vicinity. In effect, it would act as a small, solid-state neutron bomb.

In a heatproof aeroshell in the tail of the dart, a miniature guidance system purred, cross-referencing positional readings from the Global Positioning Satellite system with a ring-laser inertial tracker. During the last seconds of the projectile's plunge through atmosphere the guidance package would steer the precision-guided weapon on target by extruding drag-inducing "hyper-bumps" into the surrounding airflow.

It was a back-room laboratory rig, producing a circular area of impact probability roughly a hundred meters across. A true weapons-grade guidance package could produce a much higher degree of accuracy, but for the makers of the three sisters, the radius of a football field would do nicely.

But the defender rockets screaming up from the California coast had to be vastly more accurate. They were endeavoring to take, head-on, a target six inches across at a combined closing velocity of mach forty. Comparatively speaking, hitting a bullet with a bullet was child's play.

But it could be done. Given computer systems powerful to make not merely millions but hundreds of millions of calculations per second, computers that were almost precognitive in their capacity, it could be done.

Some of the time.

Two of the sisters died, taken by the scepter flights fixed on them. There were no "explosions" in the conventional sense of the term. The interceptors mounted no warheads. At the meeting velocities involved, high explosives would have been a triviality. There was just a flash and the interceptor and intercepted vanished in a dissipating cloud of metallic vapor.

The third sister plunged on. The guidance systems of the two missiles aimed at it had not quite been able to make that last microsecond's calculation required for a hit.

The tip of the kill dart's nose began to warm as it whispered into the outer fringe of the atmosphere.

"Missed the *bastardo*!" Valdez smashed his fists on his chair arms. "One of 'em got through, Major! Scepters are offline! Vandenberg no longer has angle of engagement."

"Designate target Ballistic Five for laser point defense engagement!" Judith fought to keep the scream out of her voice.

"Impact point now projected as the Denver urban area!" The tracking board SO yelled.

And Judith MacIntyre knew. Without the faintest shadow of a doubt she knew. It was the Superbowl stadium. The ultimate, perfect, soft target. A hundred thousand helpless people jammed in shoulder to shoulder, celebrities, officials, families. It was the big game, a symbol of Americana. And the whole world's media would be present to bear witness to the devastation. What could be a better target for those who fought no longer to win but only to wreak a spiteful, savage vengeance?

"Laser point defenses ready to fire," the laser board called. "Valid battlestrats tracking. Sequential or convergent fire pattern?"

The last human decision to be made. Sequential or convergent? Sequential would give each laser platform its own independent shot. Convergence would complicate and slow the engagement equation by trying to bring all three beams in on the target at the precise same instant. Sequential fire would improve the hit probability while convergence would maximize energy on target and improve the kill potential. There would be time for one or the other. The battlestrats would not be able to recycle their lasers fast enough for a second shot.

What was up there? What was that damn thing? Bombs were more disruptable, more easily destroyed or damaged. A solid slug was more resistant and required more killing.

Sweat Pit indeed. Judith's hair and her clothing were drenched in icy perspiration. The incontrollable trembling was only instants away.

"We have an ionization trail! Target Ballistic Five entering the atmosphere! Major, we gotta call the shot!"

"Convergent fire! Burn him!"

Aboard each of the widely dispersed battlestrat platforms, exotic fuel compounds intermixed and consumed each other in incandescent fury, pumping the High Energy Lasing tube that ran from the keel to the spine of each airship. Unhampered by atmospheric thermal blossom at this high altitude, the mirror turrets caught the appropriately named HEL beams and flashed them across hundreds of miles of sky, aiming at one, precise, distant point.

The third sister burned dazzlingly bright. Pushing a plasma shock wave the temperature of the sun's surface ahead of it, it drilled its hole through the atmosphere, homing on its target. And then, for a split second, it burned brighter yet, caught in the nexus of three focused gigawatts of projected energy.

And then it streaked on.

"*Jesus madre Maria!* It's through! It's gonna hit!"

In its last seconds of flight, a few grams of the third sister's ceramic coating, superheated beyond incandescent tolerance by the laser strike, bled away unevenly from the outer shell. Drag unbalanced, the kinetic kill projectile started to roll off target. The guidance system failed to counter, its cooked microchips pushed beyond their thermal operating limits as well.

The lines of shivering football fans pushing their way into the huge, enclosed stadium saw a thin needle of bright light streak across the sky. A moment later the thunderous boom of the shock wave followed, rolled across the sky and shattered a quarter of a million dollars worth of glass across the Denver metroplex.

Some fans looked up fearfully at the faintly glowing streak against the vivid blue of the winter sky and wondered. The majority shrugged and went back to debating the odds of Denver over Memphis.

The last sister impacted in open farm country south of the Denver suburb of Aurora. Converted into a jet of plasma and molten metal, it drilled a hundred and fifty feet into the earth before spraying off bedrock, leaving a trail of fused glass behind, the heavy prairie soil absorbing its radiation pulse.

Mr. and Mrs. Roger Hablton, driving home from a church service in Aurora, had their Ford Bioboss pickup truck blown off the adjacent county road by the concussion. After receiving treatment for minor cuts and bruises they would be released from the hospital later that day.

The Alpha screen held an image being downloaded from another Low Sentry reconsat. It showed a snow-covered field with a circular, bare-earth crater punched in it, a dissipating cloud of steam and a silver pickup truck lying on its side in a ditch.

Judith MacIntyre didn't try to restrain her trembling now, she just hugged herself against it, locking her jaw against the chattering of her teeth.

No one in the Sweat Pit was cheering. Maybe that would come later.

Sergeant Valdez took a deep breath. "We have an open ground impact. No explosive or nuclear event. No detectable surface radiation. No appreciable casualties or material damage."

Judith lifted her head. "Verify the impact point with Homeland Security," she was pleased with the sound of her voice, almost steady. "Advise National Command Center we are showing no further incoming on our boards."

She forced her arms down from her self-embrace, making each finger straighten. "Tracking, do we still have a positive fix on the manned launch vehicle?"

Gliding a high performance delta without engine power was a major challenge, but Muhammad Sadakan had managed it brilliantly, at least in his own opinion. He came in over his recovery island, velocity and altitude fat, popping his flaperons to lose speed and hasten his descent.

He circled twice, then caught sight of the double row of chemical light sticks that had been set out to mark the runway. Swinging wide with the last of his reserve energy, he lined up for the landing.

The runway itself was another challenge. A military field dating back to the Second World War, it had served as a support facility for a copper mine for a number of decades. But the mine had closed and the Philippine jungles had reclaimed both the mine and the airstrip.

Its isolation had made it perfect for Sadakan's employers. They had brought in the native work crews to reclear and patch the runway and the foreign specialists to refuel and rearm the *Voyageur.*

With his night vision visor flipped down, Sadakan floated the suborbital over the tree-fringed end of the strip, keeping the nose high with the canards. The wheels touched and he popped the drogue chute, pumping the brakes hard.

There was some vibration and a heavy pothole jolt or two but the *Voyageur* rolled to a stop well short of the runway's far end. Men started to run toward him from the edge of the jungle and the trucks followed, the fuel tankers, the crane lorry and the transporter carrying the package for the return flight. This time round he'd be dropping his load on the big Israeli nuclear power plant south of Tel Aviv.

Sadakan popped the canopy and flipped open his suit visor, taking a deep breath of the humid night air. There was no fear in the night. They'd be in and out long before the Philippine authorities would be able to react. His employers had purchased a generous quantity of slow on the local market.

The imaging on the Alpha screen had shifted, real-timed in from the Low Sentry that had just arrived in the sky above the Philippine archipelago. The hole over the Pacific was closing and they had full coverage back.

"The watch officer at the National Command Authority on the Gold Line for you, ma'am. And the complex commander. We're still sealed and he's stuck outside the Alpha gate."

"Tell them we have an incident under way and to stand by."

The reconsat was scanning in the thermal range. Its cameras showed a runway inset in the jungle with a group of men and vehicles clustering around a small delta-winged suborbital that glowed white with residual reentry heat.

"Sergeant, are there any occupied structures in the immediate vicinity of that airstrip?"

The image windowed back to a wider coverage.

"Nothing within at least ten ks, ma'am. They picked themselves one very lonely place."

"That was very convenient of them," Judy said mostly to herself.

"Major," the voice from the communications station was insistent. "We got the White House Situation Room on now!"

"Tell them to stand by!"

Once she answered the outside world, her role in this crisis would irreversibly change. She would be just another link in a chain of command. The responsibility and the decision-making would pass on to the generals and the statesmen. But for now, for this moment, Judith Anne MacIntyre was still the person at the bottom of the Sweat Pit. She was the one who carried both the shield and the sword. The defender and the nemesis.

"Sergeant Valdez, do we have any attack sats in position?"

"Yes, ma'am, we do. Black KAT Able Spade Two-Five."

Kinetic Attack Satellite Able Spade Two-five blew away its stealth shroud, its metastate sprint engine hurling it toward the dark surface of the Earth below and toward an isolated island in the western Pacific. The tightly packed swarm of kill darts it released were kin to the three sisters that had targeted the Superbowl. Only these weapons were no garage-made patch-togethers. These were the genuine article, swifter, more sophisticated and vastly more accurate.

They were also smaller, each dart weighing only ten pounds.

But there were two hundred of them.

The patch of jungle boiled and flamed in the satellite imaging. There was no longer an airstrip there. There was no longer anything there.

"Stand down from War Mode Three and unseal the mountain. All stations, well done. Resume the shift change. However, ladies and gentlemen, I suggest you all hang around. We've all got a lot of debriefing to do. Communications, open the channel to the White House Situation Room."

Major Judith Anne MacIntyre glanced down at the cup of coffee in the cup holder of the command chair, the one she had drawn for herself several lifetimes ago.

She touched it. It was still warm.

THE SOLDIER WITHIN

Michael A. Burstein

"Now you're going to meet the most important friend you'll ever have," the sergeant said.

We were standing far away from the main training camp. The ground was covered in patches of dry, flat grass, desperately trying to hold onto its green color but fading quickly to brown. Kind of like our uniforms. I rolled my eyes to look at my fellow recruits on either side of me. Right now our most important friend would have been a tall glass of cold water, or an air conditioner.

A sweat bead dropped off my forehead and past the front of my eye. I kept myself from wiping my brow; we were supposed to stand perfectly still while at attention.

"Do you want to know who that friend is?" the sergeant asked.

"Yes, sir!" we shouted. My throat felt hoarse.

The sergeant narrowed his eyes, even though his back was the one to the sun. "That friend is your new weapon. The SM-rifle."

I blinked. I had never heard of the SM-rifle. From the vibes I was getting off my colleagues, neither had anyone else.

A covered truck had been parked next to the sergeant; the door opened and two soldiers jumped out. One of them moved to the back of the truck and began unloading boxes; the other one set up a folding table.

The sergeant glanced at the soldiers briefly, then turned back to us. "You're probably wondering what the SM-rifle is. Well, in a few minutes you'll find out.

"As I call your name, come up here, get your rifle from the corporal, and return to your position. You may examine your rifle, but do not turn it on. Understand?"

"Yes, Sergeant!" we all shouted, despite our confusion. How did one "turn on" a rifle? Why didn't he warn us to treat the weapon as if it were loaded? He didn't really want us flagging our weapons, did he?

Having my last name in the middle of the alphabet meant that I got to watch as others got their rifles—excuse me, their SM-rifles—and brought them back to their positions. I noticed a lot of us straining to get a better look.

Finally, the sergeant called my name. I trotted up to the table where the corporal sat. I recognized her from the mess tent; she worked in the administrative section of the base, so we never interacted. Which was a shame, as she was a cute redhead whose hair flowed out from under her cap, not cut to the regulation buzz like the rest of us. As she opened the box and handed me my rifle and sling, I smiled at her. She flashed a smile at me in the space of a moment and then was back to being all business. I felt eyes on the back of my head and turned around to see the sergeant glaring at mc.

As quickly as I could, I ran back to my position with the rifle, and then began to study it. The rifle was a lot heavier and bulkier than the zip guns I'd been used to popping on the streets before I had been drafted. Come to think of it, it was wider than any other rifle I had ever seen before. Its length seemed right, though; I hefted it up and found that the rifle had a sight attached to the top. The stock and barrel were both made of a dark metal, which absorbed the sunlight. And sure enough, it had an on/off switch on the trigger housing, right next to the safety.

Within a few minutes, all the rifles had been distributed and the sergeant shouted, "Tench-hut!" Immediately, we stood at attention, with the rifles balanced in one hand, the butt resting on the ground.

The sergeant smiled, deliberately showing all his teeth. "In the olden days, sergeants used to tell the apes under their command that their weapon was their best friend. Well, for the first time in history, it's actually true.

"Hold your SM-rifle so you're looking at the right side. You'll notice a tiny screen that's camouflaged to look like the rest of the metal. That screen will display all sorts of information once your rifle is activated. You'll probably ignore it most of the time, though, except when your rifle's unable to talk."

Unable to talk? Since when did rifles talk?

"SM stands for Simulated Mind. Remember that medical test where the lab coats put that helmet on your head for an hour?"

I remembered. That helmet had been heavy, and it hurt. I spent the rest of the day massaging the aches out of my neck.

"What you didn't know at the time was that a new technology was recording the patterns of your mind. Your memories, your thoughts, but most importantly, your personalities. Your engrams have been imprinted on your SM-rifles." He paused. "That means that your rifle knows you better than you know yourself."

A lot of us must have given the sergeant an incredulous look, because he said, "I know you're finding that hard to believe. But after you spend a few hours with your rifle, you'll come to see it's the truth.

"Your SM-rifle is yours. It knows you and you only, and it is bonded to you. Its sole job is to keep you alive and shooting. You and your SM-rifle are now a team. Which means . . ."

The sergeant paused for a moment, and when he spoke again, he spoke softly but strongly.

"Do not pick up another soldier's rifle. Do not lose your rifle. When you go to the latrine, your rifle goes with you. When you go to the shower, the rifle goes with you. When you're not in combat, keep your rifle's battery pack charged. When you go to sleep at night, you'd better be hugging your goddamn rifle like you're a crybaby and it's your teddy bear. Understand?"

"Yes, Sergeant!" we all shouted.

"Now, fall out and get to know your weapon." He smirked.

The flat ground extended as far as the eye could see. Most of the other trainees scattered away from the sergeant and the truck. I decided to do the opposite; if I screwed up, I didn't care if he knew it. So I walked over to the area behind the truck and studied my SM-rifle.

I flipped the on switch. The SM-rifle hummed for a moment, and the tiny screen glowed blue. Then it spoke.

"Hello, Johnny," it said. The voice sounded calm, friendly, and gender-neutral.

"Um, hello," I replied. "You know my name?"

"Indeed I do. I've been programmed with everything you know."

That sounded freaky, but I let it pass. "Well, you know my name. What do I call you?"

"You may choose a name for me."

"How about Sam? Short for Samantha."

I swear to God the rifle chuckled. "You know that over seventy percent of soldiers pick Sam as their rifle's name?"

"No, I didn't. Does that mean I need to pick another name?"

"No, Sam's fine. Want to get started trying me out?"

"So, um, how do I load you?"

"You don't. I don't fire projectiles."

"So what do you fire?"

"Let me show you. Sweep me around, please, until I can spot an appropriate target."

"There's nothing around for miles."

"Let me be the judge of that."

I shrugged, but followed Sam's request. Aiming it properly, I did a three-hundred-and-sixty-degree turn. "Well?"

"Hm," Sam said. "There's not much to aim at around here."

"That's what I said."

"Still, they wouldn't bring us out here without a reason. Go ask the sergeant if there are any targets around."

"I'm sorry, what? You want me to approach the sergeant?"

"Trust me, will you? Let's go ask him."

I stared at the rifle for a moment, then hefted it over my shoulder and walked over to the sergeant, who was supervising the return of the boxes to the truck. "Sergeant?"

He turned to me. "Yes, soldier?"

"My weapon suggested I ask you for a target to shoot."

The sergeant smiled. "Of course. I suspect the others will be coming over soon." He called to the corporal, who went into the back of the truck and brought out a bundle of wooden poles, each a little less than a meter long.

"Take one of those, stick it in the ground somewhere, and find a rock to put on top of it."

I goggled. "Seriously, Sergeant?"

"You have a problem with my order, Recruit?"

"With all due respect, Sergeant, we don't even have an RSO with us."

The sergeant smiled. "Your SM-rifles are all linked to know where each one is at all times," he said. "It'll serve as both the range safety officer and the drill instructor."

"Yes, Sergeant," I said. I grabbed the stick with my left hand and wandered off, further from the truck than I had gone before. As I looked for an isolated spot, I noticed a few of the other soldiers heading to the truck.

"You planned this, didn't you?" I asked my rifle.

Again the rifle chuckled. "Kind of. Let's move out a long distance. We don't want to hurt anyone."

I walked for about five minutes, keeping the rifle in the sling to make it easier to carry. Just when I was about to stop, it said, "Here's good."

"I was just—never mind. Can I put you down while I set up the target?"

"Sure. Just keep me within reach."

I nodded, although there was no one around to see me. I found a promising spot, set the rifle on the ground, planted the pole, balanced a rock on the end, and picked up my rifle again.

"Swing me around, please, so I can see the rock."

I obliged, and then the rifle said, "Excellent. Let's back up about five hundred meters."

"You've got to be kidding. I'm not that skilled."

"Don't worry. I am."

I shrugged, and walked, keeping my pace even so I could measure five hundred meters exactly. Normally, I count my paces under my breath, but I kept quiet because I didn't want to give the rifle any clues.

It didn't matter. Once again, just when I was about to stop, it said, "Five hundred meters. Perfect. Drop prone and face the target."

I sighed and did so. I began reaching for the rear sight aperture but the rifle said, "Don't worry about adjusting anything. I've already taken care of it."

"You have? That's . . . great." I sighted the rock through the scope, aimed the rifle, and reached for the trigger.

"Wait," it said.

"What?"

"Keep your muscles completely relaxed. You want good bone support. That will keep the sights on target."

I tried to relax, but having my weapon practically ordering me around—well, it didn't feel very relaxing. "Is this better?" I finally asked.

"Perfect."

"So what do I do now?"

"You've fired other rifles before, haven't you? Draw in a full breath, and then let it out halfway. Then aim me and fire."

I squeezed the trigger. The rifle snapped and sizzled, and kicked back with barely any recoil. A tiny bolt of orange fire emerged from the barrel and flew towards the rock. Within seconds, I heard an explosion coming from the target.

"Come on, let's go check it out."

I swallowed hard, stood up, and carried the rifle with me as I walked back to the target. When I got close enough to see it clearly, I stopped short.

The rock was completely blasted away, but the pole stood unharmed.

I lifted the rifle to my face and studied its sheen. "My God. What are you?"

"Your new best friend."

More than anyone else, even the sergeant, Sam taught me how to be a soldier.

My buddies really didn't know me as well as Sam did. I could talk to her about anything. She always backed me up, and sometimes gave me a new perspective on a training exercise or a combat mission.

That's right. I said combat mission. With these new SM-rifles helping us out, we finished our training in three-quarters time and got sent to the front quicker than any of us expected. I found myself in a squad with seven other soldiers, commanded by a staff sergeant who was one of the first soldiers trained with the new SM-rifles.

Our first mission in the war, in conjunction with another squad in our platoon, was an attack on a munitions shed at the top of a hill. The enemy had dug in and was expecting a fight at some point.

What they weren't expecting was us.

I had heard about units that were coordinated perfectly, having drilled over and over to work not just as a team, but almost as one mind.

With the SM-rifles, this conceit became true.

When the sergeant explained the mission plan to us—our squad would surround the hill and begin shooting, drawing fire to allow the other squad to attack from behind—it seemed clear to me that the plan had been developed with the SM-rifle capabilities in mind. Coordinating our attack would have been possible with radios, but the rifles managed to communicate far more quickly with each other than we would have been able to. We took out that shed easy as anything.

Well . . . almost.

As we started blasting away, blowing through the walls of the shed with the phased plasma, the enemy soldiers inside began to flee. Not exactly according to our plan, but as the soldiers ran away from my squad, the other squad managed to pick them off.

Except for this one guy, who was braver than his comrades. He snuck out of the shed and dove into the foliage, where he began firing at us. Bullets whizzed by, and the guy to my left got hit in the shoulder. We fired back with everything we had, but it didn't help. Every time we fired into the foliage, it was like the guy had managed to magically teleport himself into another hiding place.

And then Samantha spoke to me, quietly. "Johnny. This isn't going to work. Stop for a second."

I squeezed the trigger again, firing concentrated plasma into the foliage. "You got to be kidding. We can smoke the guy out."

"And then the fires would destroy the shed, and the mission goals won't be achieved."

"If I stop firing, the guy's going to take me out."

"Not if you listen to me. I can spot the guy better than you can."

I sighed. "Fine. What do you want me to do?"

"Move my sight back and forth, slowly."

"Can I keep shooting while I do that?"

"It won't help."

"It'll keep me from getting killed!"

"Johnny, we've worked together for a long time. Trust me on this."

She was right. Slowly, I swung her sight across our field of vision, giving her a chance to see if she could spot anything. And then the weirdest thing happened.

Suddenly it was like I wasn't just inside my body anymore. Samantha was no longer just my weapon; she was part of me, and I was a part of her. Our thoughts started to come together. I was both the soldier aiming the weapon and the weapon itself. I felt scared for a moment, as if she was taking over my body, but it was more like she was in the back of my mind, and I was in the back of hers.

There he is, she said in my mind.

Where? I asked, and then it was like I could see the soldier through Samantha's "eyes." The world changed suddenly from all the colors of the rainbow to just two—a red outline showing me exactly where the soldier was crouched, and black everywhere else.

Is that him?

It is! Come on, Johnny! You can do this! Just aim and fire!

I did. And I smacked that soldier right between the eyes.

The next day, the lieutenant spoke to the whole platoon, congratulating us on a mission well done. After we broke for mess, my sergeant took me aside.

"The lieutenant wants to see you," he said. "Now."

Puzzled and hungry, I headed over to the lieutenant's office. When I arrived, he looked up and said, "Ah, Johnny. Good to see you've got your SM with you."

"We were told always to keep her at the ready, sir."

"Good, good. Is it on?"

"Yes, sir. But so is the safety."

"Good. Always keep your weapon turned on, and charged." He paused. "That was excellent shooting the other day."

"Thank you, sir."

"Please sit down. I have a question for you."

As soon as I had sat down, the lieutenant surprised me with his question. "Did you notice anything unusual yesterday with your SM-rifle?"

I tried my best to look nonchalant. "Unusual, sir?"

He nodded. "Like I said, that was excellent shooting. Do you know how far away from you the enemy soldier was when you hit him?"

"Um, no, sir."

"Fifteen hundred meters."

I cleared my throat. "Really? That's good, isn't it?"

"A head shot at fifteen hundred meters—that got me wondering. Some soldiers have reported having a, shall we say, closer relationship with their SM-rifles than they originally expected." He looked me directly in the eyes. "Have you had an experience of that sort?"

I heard Samantha's voice in my head again. *It's okay. We can trust him.*

"Well, honestly, sir, yes."

He nodded, and I relaxed.

"Johnny, let me explain something about the SM-rifles. Although they are far better weapons than conventional rifles, we haven't been handing them out to our soldiers simply because of the artificial intelligence. Haven't you wondered why your rifle was specifically imprinted with your own personality engrams?"

"I really hadn't given it much thought, sir," I said. "I supposed it had to do with increasing our compatibility, making it easier for us to work together."

The lieutenant laughed. "Most people would find it difficult if not impossible to work well with someone exactly like them." He paused. "What I'm about to tell you is not exactly classified, but it's also not for public consumption, if you know what I mean. I'm ordering you not to discuss it with anyone."

"Yes, sir."

The fact is that I couldn't really understand much of what the lieutenant told me then, let alone discuss it with others. Apparently, Samantha and I were among the lucky few, whose identical memory engrams achieved what the lieutenant called "quantum resonance." That allowed us to get into each other's minds—a sort of telepathy. *That* word I could understand, but I was surprised to discover that it now existed for real.

Personally, I don't think the lieutenant understood much of what he was telling me either. But I nodded politely and tried to look thoughtful.

"That means you can become one with your weapon, Johnny. The two of you together are much more proficient than any other soldier with a conventional weapon."

I nodded, but didn't say anything, which the lieutenant seemed to interpret as modesty. "It's something to be proud of, son. You're special."

"I—thank you, sir."

"Which is why I called you in to see me. I think you can be more than the ordinary soldier." He leaned forward. "We need volunteers for special training. People who are willing to work alone. People who can get a particular job done." He paused. "You ever hear of Carlos Hathcock?"

"No, sir," I replied, puzzled.

"Look him up in the camp database. He's what I'd like you to become. Let me know your decision within twenty-four hours. Dismissed."

I left the tent, and almost immediately Samantha said, "Forget the database. I know who Hathcock was." And she told me all about him.

I whistled when she was done. "The lieutenant wants me to do that? I can't."

"Sure you can. Let's volunteer for the training."

"I don't want to work alone."

She laughed. "You won't be alone," she replied. "You'll have me along."

That's how I became a sniper.

Becoming a sniper required more training. Despite Samantha's assurances, it took a lot more than my just being able to aim my SM accurately. I had to learn about camouflage and concealment, so the enemy wouldn't spot me when I was sent on missions. It took a lot of studying.

But I wasn't alone. A handful of other soldiers and their SM-rifles had also been moved to sniper training, so we studied together. In a way, Samantha was wrong about it just being her and me.

But Samantha was right about one thing—our ability to shoot. Part of sniper training is learning how to shoot one's rifle under various conditions. But with Samantha and me working together, we aced all the preliminary tests, because we really could get into each other's minds.

In fact, we did it so much better than any of the other soldier-rifle pairs that we were the first ones sent back to the front. We reported back to the lieutenant, who assigned us to a whole variety of interesting missions.

One time, we were working with my unit, but positioned far away, at a location perpendicular to their advance. Our job was to pick off the enemy soldiers at random, sowing confusion and fear while my unit engaged in a frontal assault. The tactic worked, and we took another hill.

Another time, we were sent on our own to one of the enemy's cities. Our spy network had intercepted reports that one of the enemy's generals was going to be doing an inspection of the city. We managed to keep ourselves hidden for two days until we got a clear shot, right into the general's chest.

I was promoted to corporal and given a medal. I was pleased about that, but something nagged me in the back of my mind.

And I started having bad dreams. When I closed my eyes, I would see my targets explode in front of me. Sometimes I dreamt that I was my rifle. I felt the plasma flow through my body and then burst out at my targets, burning holes in their chests and heads. I woke up a few times in a cold sweat, unable to get back to sleep for an hour or two.

But our new role didn't affect Samantha any. She seemed almost gleeful about our success. For her, killing became more than just a job. It became fun.

And that scared me to death.

So here's how it all came to an end. Our last mission.

As always, my orders came from the lieutenant. He called us into his office as usual, but this time he had a much more sober look on his face.

"This is a different sort of mission, Johnny. A very sensitive one. We've located an enemy training facility for new soldiers. We want a sniper to go in there and pick off some of their new recruits, to strike fear into their hearts. Are you willing to do it?"

I remember feeling unsure, but Samantha's voice in the back of my head told me to go ahead. So I accepted.

The next day, we were dropped off a few kilometers away from the facility and we headed towards it. We never had to worry about getting lost, as Samantha always knew where she was going. When we got close enough, I took a look at the building. It was a red brick converted school building, with an outside playground transformed into a shooting range. I found a good copse of trees in which to conceal ourselves, and we waited.

Finally, after about twenty minutes, the front door opened, and my jaw dropped.

Two enemy soldiers led out a parade of children, none of them older than ten years at the most. They lined them up at the shooting range, gave them pistols, and began to instruct them on the use of their weapons.

I froze. I could feel myself sweating, and a lump formed in my throat.

Sam's voice appeared in the back of my mind. *Johnny, are you ready? Come on, aim me. We can take out at least five of the students before they'd get back into the building for safety.*

I closed my eyes and shook my head. *Sam, did you see the targets?* I asked her.

Sure I did. They're enemy soldiers-in-training, just like the lieutenant said.

They're not soldiers-in-training! They're kids. Children.

We knew the enemy was training its young citizens to fight back. We just didn't realize how young. But it doesn't matter. They're still the enemy.

I whispered aloud. "I can't kill children."

"Sure you can," Sam replied in the same quiet tones.

"How can you say that?"

She sighed, something she hadn't done in a while. Then she cursed at me. "Damn it, Johnny, they've already been indoctrinated to hate you. There's not one of them that wouldn't just as soon kill you as look at you, and you know it."

She was right. I knew she was right. But damn it—"This wasn't what I signed up for."

"Yes, it is," she said. "You volunteered. *We* volunteered."

"I—I can't."

Her voice reappeared in my head. *Here. Let me help you get into a proper frame of mind.*

And then images appeared in my mind—images of the dead children lying bloodied at my feet, with me grinning like a maniac . . .

I dropped Samantha as if she had turned red-hot. "What are you putting in my mind?"

"Johnny, quiet! The enemy will hear you."

"I don't care! Stop putting things into my mind."

She chuckled. "I can't put anything into your mind that wasn't already there."

I recoiled. "*That* image was never in my mind. That came from *you*."

"But where did *I* come from?" she asked. "Remember that I'm a reflection of you. A perfect reflection. Everything inside me comes from you." She paused. "I have those dreams too, but I enjoy them. I can help you to enjoy them as well."

I shook my head. "No! I refuse to accept that."

"It's true, Johnny," she said. "I wouldn't be the perfect weapon I am if it weren't for you."

And I knew she was right. The army hadn't just turned me into a killer; they had found something within me already, something that Samantha had nurtured until it grew, and turned me into the monster I had become.

But no more.

I turned the SM-rifle off and walked away from the mission. When I got back, I handed the weapon to my CO and said that I didn't want to see it anymore. And that's why I'm here now, although I don't know why you needed me to dictate this whole story yet another time. I don't care if you plan to court-martial me for insubordination or lock me away without trial.

I'm not the same as that thing. I won't kill again. It can't make me.

The recording had come to an end. The scientist removed the helmet and found himself back in the general's office. The general was leaning back in his chair, his arms crossed, his chin resting on his fist.

"It's not working, Doctor."

He blinked and cleared his throat. "I see what you mean."

"It's not just that one soldier." The general handed an electronic pad over. "Take a look at these records. Almost twenty-five percent of the soldiers given SM-rifles either go AWOL, turn objector, or kill themselves."

The scientist took the pad and glanced at the report. "That last one is regrettable."

The general sighed. "They're *all* regrettable."

"Right. Sorry."

"The SM-rifles were supposed to help bring out the soldier in those boys. Instead it's doing the opposite."

The scientist thumbed the scroll button and read through the introduction to the report. When he finished, he looked up. "Twenty-five percent, general. But what about the other seventy-five percent?"

"The other seventy-five percent are doing just fine. I'll admit that the SM-rifles even allow for greater accuracy in combat for those soldiers. But that twenty-five percent—those are almost all the soldiers who report 'bonding' with their weapons, which is what we were hoping for. But in every single case—well, I've already told you."

"Still," the scientist said, "that seventy-five percent that are doing fine—"

"Compared with the ninety-five percent success rate we had in turning boys into soldiers before the SM-rifles . . ."

"I understand." The scientist stood up. "Let me go discuss this with my colleagues. We'll see if we can figure out what the problem is."

The scientist left the general's office, and returned to the weapons development laboratory, where his assistant director was waiting for him.

"Well?" she asked once he had shut the door behind him.

The scientist took a seat and smiled. "It's working. As soon as the soldiers discover the hidden aggression in their R-complex, they reject it." He handed over the pad, and she studied it briefly.

Finally, she looked up. "Not all of them, though."

"No, not all. But enough."

"Enough so that we've been noticed."

He nodded. "Well, yeah. There was no way to avoid that."

"Then we can't keep this up forever."

"We don't have to. We just need to keep it up until the government gives up on this useless war. In the meantime, let's get back to work."

He stood up to return to his office, but the assistant director held up her hand. "I can't help but wonder if we're doing the right thing. What if the day comes when the tables are turned, and we're the ones being invaded?"

He smiled. "We've already got plenty of foreign contracts for the SM-rifles. If they do the same job overseas that they've been doing for us . . . I don't think it'll be a problem."

"I hope you're right."

SPEC-OPS

L. E. Modesitt, Jr.

"We can't afford a war, General."

"We'll have a war with Seasia sooner or later. We can afford later less than sooner."

"The people won't stand for it, and no nation has ever stood for long against the will of its citizens."

"Then change their minds. We need this war."

"Change your weapons, General, if you need this war."

Excerpt from: *The Right War*
SONYDREAMS, 2043

I.

1559. Khorbel deJahn slid into the dim pod, sensies flicking to Duty OpsCon. "Up-what, sir?"

"You're last, Tech deJahn. Chimbats," replied the major. "Nu-type. Seasies haven't seen. Take over from Hennesy. Third seat."

Leastwise, no scroaches. DeJahn link-pulsed.

Hennesy blinked, unlinked, and stood. "You got it, deJahn."

"Got it."

Hennesy had left the sensie-seat hot, damp. DeJahn wiped it with the cloth he always brought. Still hated taking over a hot seat. Leastwise, he was beside Meralez. Her eyes were open, link-blank. Sexy eyes when she was in her skull, not like now.

He pulled the thin mesh cap into place over his short mil-cut hair. Made sure the contacts handshook, blanked his thoughts, and settled into the link. *Tech first deJahn.*

Accepted. Flash background: Chimbats. Three families, *each of twenty-five units. Target: any personnel at biointerdict station beta-four. See plot.*

Firsties were just chitterings, light-darts in blackness. Be a while before the biogator expelled the chimbats from the pouch under its ridged back. Side-mind went to the back plot, illuminated only in his thoughts. Green blips were the gators, swimming upstream after a tidal boost. Red blip was target—Seasie biointerdict station. An hour plus to release.

DeJahn hated pre-release. Babysitting chims just in case the vector got zapped. Seasies weren't going to see gators in one of a dozen canals and muddy streams, not the main river channel.

He might have slept in the dark pod. Would have slept, except for the major's overscreening and the checks. Time passed. Slowly.

DeJahn stifled a yawn, compared closure rate once more. Ran a complete monitor on the bioindicators, then reported. *1630. On course, on target.*

Stet, Tech deJahn.

More dark and quiet time. Time where his thoughts, behind the link, lingered on Meralez. Good body, better voice. Reminded him of Margot. Probably not good.

Wished Meralez weren't pseudo les-butch. Could be a front. Keep the tech-types from pawing. Hazard of spec-ops. Had to find ways to remember who you were. Sex and women helped. Did men help the female techs? Or not? That why so many women partnered with other women?

More time passed in darkness. More chitterings as the chimbats got restless, their soporifics wearing off. Screen checks came, went.

Ten to release, Tech. Request acknowledge.

Stet. Ten to release. DeJahn hated the obvious. Major knew he was ready. Linked, wasn't he? Mil-type reduns still plagued pros like him.

Chitterings increased. Chimbats getting restless as the sops wore off.

Five to release.

Stet.

The chitterings were almost as bad as the scuttling and scrapings that came with the scroaches, and the smell . . . Tech ops said there wasn't sensie smell. Spec-ops techs knew better.

Stand by for release. Release . . . now!

Disorientation. Always that. Hundreds of sound-sights flashed through the integrator before settling into a shifting mosaic as the chimbats fanned out, spreading wings, pulsing the terrain, receiving sound images.

Backwater canal below, hard to judge but no more than thirty feet wide. Grimy gray-brown surface showed the wakes of the gators. No sonic-visual on the gators. They weren't designed that way. Water blocked most of the bats' sonar return.

DeJahn squinted to focus the image. Wasn't a real squint, but the sensie-link equivalent. Trees slumped bedraggled limbs into the water on both sides of the canal.

He checked the mind sidescreen. Target was six thousand yards at zero seven one. Chimbats were sweeping across the water, scooping up insect fuel, following the canal at zero-four-four. Another two thousand, and he'd have to nudge them right.

Gators had fallen behind, following the canal. They would for another thousand yards, then would take the cross canal. No one had told deJahn, but there was a soarer-boat patrol base on the east side of the delta. Each gator could take out one, maybe two, of the boats. Boats gone, or fewer of them, and there'd be a chance to bring in the dreadnaughts—the salties. Handful of them, and there wouldn't be a patrol base. With the rivers in spec-ops' hands, be an open vector lane for all the ricelands in the area, and the J-wasps could immobilize the quantum wetworks at Chuo-Klyseen.

DeJahn forced his mind back to the chimbats. They needed to follow the overgrown path to the right . . . more right. He exerted the pressure of *danger* to the left, and the lure of *food*, big juicy mosquitoes to the left. Heat built around him. He had to ignore it, center the chimbats on course toward the target.

Thirty-two hundred and closing. That was a quick link-flash to the major, to keep him from sending an inquiry while deJahn was setting up the attack.

Nineteen hundred yards, and all the chimbats "saw" was trees and insects, and the "brightness" of water in places from an afternoon rain.

The trees vanished, replaced by paddies that didn't hold rice, or water, except for the thinnest layer, but various electronic and biosensors. Beyond the paddies was the interdict station. It didn't look like much, not in the sensie-integrated mosaic in deJahn's mind, just a gray square on an artificial square bluff seven yards above the soggy soil of the delta. Four thatched huts—the kind no one had lived in, even in Seasia, in generations—set around a graveled courtyard. Gravel? In a delta? Chimbats' sonar showed the harder composite walls that supported the bluff edges, and the mix of steel and plastic hidden under the pseudo thatch.

Pseudo bats, pseudo thatch, pseudo bluff . . . frig! Was anything real?

The mission was real.

DeJahn exerted pressure, creating the sense and image of insect prey just below the roofs of the pseudo thatch.

Chimbats angled down, wings near-silent, fangs filled with solvent and venom.

Light! So brilliant that deJahn's eyes boil-burned in their sockets.

Except it wasn't light. Sound! That was it. Screaming sound, blinding the chimbats. Feedback blasted through him. Felt like his eardrums were bursting, and long needles lanced through his eyes, coming out the back of his skull.

Frig! Major'd said the chimbats were new types . . .

Blackness wiped it all away.

An alarm buzzed . . . sawing into him. It buzzed again.

Somewhere, something nagged at him, telling him to wake up . . . but he could sleep in, couldn't he? Sunday morning, wasn't it?

Tech deJahn . . . trigger recovery sequence . . . Recovery sequence . . .

Recovery sequence? His thoughts were sluggish. He had to do something . . . didn't he? Recovery sequence? A chill ran up his spine. *Recovery one! Recovery one!*

Link one . . . link two . . .

After a moment, or several, deJahn could feel the barriers dropping. Persona segmentation was frightening—but it had saved more than a few spec-ops techs from biobacklash syndrome . . . or worse.

He blinked. He still couldn't see. Vision was usually late to return, but he didn't like being in the dark.

Interrogative status?

Reintegration seventy-one percent complete.

What was seventy-one percent of a tech? He wanted to laugh. He forced his teeth together.

The blackness began to evaporate, and holes appeared in it. One hole showed the recovery medtech looking from the porta-console to deJahn and back again. Another hole showed the dark greenish gray bulkhead of the spec-ops pod.

After a moment, deJahn blinked, then coughed. "Think I'm back."

"He's green." The medtech's voice was bored, almost disappointed. He stood, nodded, and replaced the porta-console in its case before leaving the pod.

"Just sit there for a while," ordered the major.

DeJahn glanced around the pod. All the other sensie-stations were empty. He supposed that was good.

Then the shudders began.

It took fifteen minutes before deJahn was ready to stand. He must have been the last. Or the only idiot who hadn't disengaged fast enough.

He looked at the major. The officer's cold green eyes showed nothing.

"Thought you said these chimbats were new. They were ready for them."

"They were new. Some of them got through. About half the station's inoperative." The eyes softened, into mere green glass. "Get some rest, Tech. You're off schedule tomorrow. Check with med on Monday."

"Yes, sir." DeJahn took two slow steps to the pod exit station, pressed his fingertips on the pad.

Cleared to depart. Status amber . . . off duty, pending medical. The exit irised open.

DeJahn took a step into the passageway outside the pod. Each step was deliberate. His balance felt off. Could be the beating his ears had taken.

His poopsuit stunk. Sweat and everything else. Biofeedback was hell on a tech's personal system, no matter what the newsies said. Especially when your vectors got blasted before you disengaged.

He needed a shower and something to eat. There were still holes in his vision.

II.

"What is the point of a weapon?"

"To defeat someone, or to force them to accede to what the wielder wishes."

"What is defeat?"

"The surrender of a position, goods, territory, or even a point of view."

"Who determines defeat?"

"Either total destruction or surrender by the one who's in the weaker position . . . "

III.

0340. DeJahn bolted up in the narrow bunk. Sleep like deep link cobwebbed his thoughts. Sat there, unmoving. Two days off hadn't helped that much.

0345. He swung his feet onto the plastipress deck, knew he had to get moving, get to the pod for duty rotation. Didn't want to be last. Might be scroaches, or chimshrews. Bunk above was empty. Stennes had midwatch on screens.

DeJahn pulled on a clean poopsuit, knowing he'd need to drop off the soiled ones below before his next duty. Chim-duty was hell on uniforms. Softboots followed the poopsuit, and he fastened the bag with his linkcap to his waistband. Closed the slider behind him and hurried along the dim passageway and up the circular ramp, past electro-ops, and to the spec-ops pod.

0352. DeJahn's fingers stopped short of the pod access plate. Took a moment before he touched the pad. It sucked the heat from his fingertips.

Entry granted. The pod door irised open, and DeJahn slid inside. His sensies flicked to the captain standing Duty OpsCon. "Tech deJahn reporting, sir."

"Take number two, Tech deJahn," replied the captain.

DeJahn stepped up beside the sensie console and link-pulsed. He was relieving Suares.

The wiry tech didn't blink. He just stood. "It's yours, deJahn. Scowls, tonight. Best hurry. They're in free hunt."

"Got it."

DeJahn touched the sensie-seat. Suares left it cool. He always did. DeJahn didn't know how. Still, he wiped the seat before he settled down. Once more, no scroaches. He kept the sigh inside, then slipped on the mesh cap, checked the handshake, and linked into the scowls.

He dropped into the third seat, and linked. *Tech first Khorbel deJahn.*

Accepted. Flash background: Scowls. Initial target: guards, research station gamma three-one. Primary target: technicians.

Frigging great. He had to pull the scowls off free hunt after they took out enough guards to get an opening for the scroaches and turn them to finding the scientists and technicians who were doing the research.

A sharpness of gray images overtook him, so clear that they were more disorienting than the fuzzy sharpness that came with chimbats. Disorientation through precision. Better that than the looming wavering images and prey lust that pervaded the scroach links.

As Suares had said, the scowls were in free hunt.

Checking the mind sidescreen, deJahn verified the target, a bioware research station. Small, no more than fifteen science types, and twice that many guards. The scowls were priority programmed, as much as a modified owl could be. The guards were secondary. Guards didn't create biotech and bioweapons. What the station produced or researched, deJahn didn't know. He switched views from the too-distinct shifting composite, to one scowl after another, stopping at one stooping into an attack on a guard post.

One of the guards turned and fired. The incendiary pellets exploded into a cage of flame and fire. The stab of pain ran down deJahn's back for an instant before he disengaged that link, later than he should have.

Quick-switching again, deJahn caught the feedback view from next owl as it struck the guard's arm. Fire-venom from the talons went straight to the guard's nerves. In instants, the guard was shaking so badly the fire-rifle struck the plastcrete under his boots. In seconds, he was beside the rifle, bones breaking under the convulsive power of his own hyped muscles.

More scowls feathered down. Alarms began to screech, and the second guard sealed the booth. That would only buy him minutes before the first scroach ate its way through the heavy plastic.

DeJahn switched images. He didn't need to see what the adapted scorpion-roaches would do. At the next guard post, the sentries were still bringing down scowls, each scowl death a line of flame into his own nerves, but the guards did not see the wave of scroaches close to underfoot, advancing inexorably.

He began to exert pressure, shifting the rodent-prey image, strengthening it, and positioning it to bring the scowls through the failing screens into the technical area. The guards were the initial target, just the initial target.

Primary target was scientists and technicians . . . primary target . . .

IV.

You got bioethics issues in chim-ops. Stuff those. Big question, that's whether mod-techno weapons should be used in war at all . . . Two soldiers faced off at Waterloo. A bunch stormed beaches at Normandy against another bunch, or even slog-fought in the jungles of Vietnam against a VC bunch. Back then, fighters on both sides died. Lots of them. Different today. Americans changed it all when they high-teched the Middle East, used biowar in Iran. Nowadays, the tech-types use chim-ops, spec-ops, remote ops. Nothing touches them. Just like old Greek gods, they throw lightnings, never see what they've done, don't ever experience the horror. Think our special operatives are even soldiers at all? Or just techno-chims themselves?

—Editorial, *Whazup Tonight*
March 15, 2051

V.

Thursday before breakfast, DeJahn had to shower. Sometimes, dreams were almost as bad as infiltration spec-ops themselves. Even flying the scowls with the scroaches following had been bad enough. He needed a long shower, but water was one thing a forward base had. Surrounded by it. He dressed deliberately. He still had enough clean poopsuits. He'd finally reclaimed enough fresh ones for the days ahead.

He felt cleaner, for the moment, before he headed down the passageway to the tech mess and breakfast. Softboots whispered on the deck. Hard to believe that fifty yards up through the overhead was what looked like marsh and reeds in the river delta.

Tech mess was an oval room with five tables and dispensers and formulators. He tapped out his selections on the formulator, then set them on the tray, and carried the tray to the table where Meralez and Castaneda sat. Castaneda was the butch that Meralez fronted being.

Castaneda gestured. “Look like shit, deJahn.”

“You, too, Castaneda.”

“All of us look like shit, all right?” Meralez laughed. “Good thing nothing’s up but surveillance today.”

DeJahn liked her laugh. Warm, sort of sexy, not in-your-face.

“You’ve got a thought-look,” Meralez suggested.

After swallowing a mouthful of bagel burrito, deJahn nodded, then took a sip of coffee, bitter. One thing formulators didn’t do well, along with tea and chocolate.

“Well?”

“Was a time when special ops meant guys with guns dropping on chutes into jungle,” replied deJahn. “Some ways, more honest.”

“Honest? Strange word, think you?” Meralez brushed back mahogany hair too short to move.

“Strange?”

“Snuffed is snuffed,” replied Meralez. “Back then, it was lead, steel jackets, osmiridium, metal projectiles at high speed. Now, we’re using J-wasps, S-wasps, scroaches, scowls, biogaters, snators. They’re using phonies stuffed with ultra-ex, semiclones with biopaks. We text envirosave, and they text reclaiming their heritage and defeating imperialism. Some of us get snuffed, and some of them do. Back a century, it was the same. Any more honest then than now? Don’t think so. Back then, the officers ordered. The senior ones lived, the junior ones died like techs, and lots more techs died than now.”

For a moment, deJahn considered her words. They were hers, what she thought, and that was good.

“The senior officers, brass balls and iron tits . . . all the same,” snorted Castaneda.

“All the same, what?” A cheerful laugh followed the words.

Castaneda looked up. So did deJahn.

Vielho stood there, then set his tray down and slid into the vacant space beside Castaneda. "Anytime you're talking balls and tits, Castaneda, got to be worth listening to." He grinned disarmingly, then took a swallow of his tea.

So far as deJahn knew, Vielho was the only tech who drank tea. Or what passed for it. Then, Casimir was the only other person deJahn knew who drank it for breakfast. Where deJahn's brother had picked it up . . . who knew? Casimir couldn't even explain, but he also couldn't explain why he liked teaching.

"Just jawing about officers. Little good that does."

"Better than holding it inside." Vielho sipped the tea.

"You ever think about being a teacher?" asked deJahn.

"Me?" Vielho laughed. "No way. Got as much patience as a scroach seeking a Seasie. Why?"

DeJahn shook his head. "Just wondered."

VI.

0750. The briefing was in the tech mess. All the briefings took place there. DeJahn didn't want to be late, slipped into the spot at the table beside Meralez. She didn't look at him. He returned the favor by looking straight ahead.

Chihouly lumbered in, glanced at deJahn and Meralez, and gave deJahn a knowing headshake. DeJahn shrugged.

0801. Major Delles stepped out into the small open space in front of the twenty techs. All stood and stiffened.

"Carry on." Delles gestured for them to sit.

With the others, deJahn settled in, waiting to hear what Delles had to say. He wouldn't like it. Briefings meant trouble ahead.

Delles cleared his throat, then straightened his shoulders. His poopsuit had creases, and the gold oak leaves on the starched collars glistened.

DeJahn was just happy to have enough clean suits.

"Power is the key to any advanced technology. Even biotech and biowar require large amounts of power. In this sector, the Seasies are still relying heavily on old-style power plants. In particular, they have a large magnetodynamic coal plant, the Tanshu-two. This mission is to bring down the plant. We'll take out the cooling systems, then the security lines, and finish up with a double, an ultra-ex powered EMP and then red goo for the coal itself. The satellite team will be handling the biobirds for the EMP and goo. We get the dirty work first."

A power plant? That sounded like the beginning of something, something deJahn wasn't sure he'd care for. The only reason the Seasies hadn't gotten rid of the old-style coal plants was that the costs were sunk. Spec-ops would be doing them a favor . . . unless a short-term power shortage happened to be necessary for some other reason. Like a sector-wide push in another few days.

He couldn't help but turn toward Meralez.

They both nodded, but so slightly that the major didn't notice, then returned their eyes to the presentation. The mess had darkened, to enhance the holo image of the target, a hulking industrial dinosaur that might have come from a hundred years earlier in NorAm.

" . . . water intakes are standard bioscrub . . . strike team three has already planted z-clambers . . . intake volumes are down fifteen percent . . . "

The major droned on, and deJahn managed to catch what he needed to know, and that was that most of the techs would be on late-disengagement. Another sure sign of trouble.

The last power plant image vanished, replaced by three lists. "Check for your assignments here."

DeJahn checked. He had the main pod, but it didn't say what he'd be handling.

" . . . any questions?" the major finally concluded.

"Why the late disengage, sir?"

DeJahn didn't see the speaker, but it sounded like Chihouly.

"A number of the targets require higher-than-normal acquisition ratios, and that requires greater tech presence and persistence than can be obtained through late-stage free-ops."

"Any other questions?"

No one spoke. There wasn't any point to it, not after the major's last answer.

"Duty stations will commence at 0900. Dismissed."

The techs all rose, stiffened, and stood while the major departed.

That left thirty minutes to kill. DeJahn got some coffee. When he looked around for Meralez, she and Castaneda had left.

He sat back down.

Chihouly sat at the next table. Neither one said a word.

Finally, fifteen minutes later, deJahn got up and tossed the disposable mug into the reformulation bin and walked toward the pod.

Meralez was one of the first into the pod, after Vielho, and deJahn was right behind her. Suares followed deJahn. Esquival and Chihouly were behind him. The OpsCon was Captain DiLayne. Narrow-faced former tech, she'd come up the long way and never forgotten.

He dropped into the third seat, and linked. *Tech deJahn.*

Accepted. Flash background: S-wasps. Five swarms, seeded minus three months, advanced growth, designed to inject superconductives into critical components, relays, and certain bloc units. Power plant Tanshu-two. See plot.

Disorientation. Another mosaic view, with tiny lines everywhere, the result of compound eyes with enhanced resolution. All he could "see" were trees and an open field—no—what looked like a big flat pond, maybe an abandoned rice paddy, or a fish farm—the Seasies still preferred real-enviro food.

Because the view was so distance-short, deJahn checked the mental side-view, noting the swarms' progress from where the nests had been seeded weeks earlier. Another thirty minutes, according to the schedule.

Swarm one was flying ahead of schedule. A vague image of a black spider and a sticky web slowed them.

He checked the side-screens. The rest of the spec-ops vectors were well ahead. They should be.

Interrogative status? came from DiLayne.

On schedule. Green.

He had to keep a tight rein on the swarms, holding them back because the early units were slower than on the schedule.

Even so, the first S-wasps hit the sonic screens, flared into chitinous fragments. Minuscule needles pinged on his brain, and he created the image of sweet raw meat. Had to hold back the S-wasps until the scroaches and snators dealt with the guards and screens. Shouldn't be that many screens around an old power plant, even one that generated some 600 megawatts.

Screens down. DiLayne's reminder came after deJahn had already vectored his swarms toward the control centers.

From one composite image—swarm two—he could see/sense a handful of technicians in white singlesuits scrambling for cover, diving away from the S-wasps. A second image was a bank of equipment. He targeted the S-wasps into the vulnerable crevices there.

His whole body convulsed. A sonic net—internal—had wiped out swarm five.

His eyes burned, and the side-plot was getting faint.

Interrogative swarm status?

Operative units at sixty-one percent . . . fifty-seven percent . . . fifty-two . . .

There was no automatic disengagement under a late disengage.

. . . forty-nine . . .

Disengage! Disengage!

His whole body convulsed with the shock. Then, he could feel his lungs laboring in the darkness. He'd stopped breathing for a few moments. *Close . . . too frigging close . . .*

His breathing slowed. His poopsuit was soaked, his back stuck with sweat to the sensie-seat, and he stunk with fear-sweat as he eased off the mesh linkcap.

All he could do for a time was sit and breathe.

No one even looked in his direction in the dimness, even as bodies rushed past him. He shook his head and looked to his left. Suares lay limp in the sensie-chair—scarlet-flared. He wasn't breathing. He wouldn't, not ever, deJahn knew. Brain-fried.

Meralez was kneeling beside Vielho, but her words made no sense to deJahn. Vielho's body kept twitching, and he screamed silently, as if his vocal cords had been ripped out of his throat.

A medtech appeared with a porta-gurney, moved around Meralez, and slapped a trankmask on Vielho. The medic never looked around as he strapped Vielho into the gurney, ignoring the other techs.

"Techs . . . " said the major from the ops station.

DeJahn knew what DiLayne meant. He stood, moved toward the pod exit, then touched the pad.

Tech deJahn . . . released, duty status green.

He followed Esquival out into the passageway. She didn't look back. Neither did he.

Late disengagement.

Suicide mission.

VII.

Specialist biofeedback is required for optimal efficiency in special operations. Incomplete or null feedback impairs biounit response and efficacy in direct relationship to the total number of discrete units under operator influence and the neural complexity of the individual unit . . .

—SPEC-OPS 1421.45
DARPA

VIII.

What could he do? DeJahn didn't know. Maybe nothing. Looked around the techs' mess. He was the only one there. Coffee, ersatz shit . . . it was cold. Nothing worse than cold, bitter, pseudo coffee.

Bullshit, deJahn. Lots worse things. Just scared that it might happen to you. He pushed the thought away. Finally, he stood, shook his head.

He took the longer passageway. Softboots scuffed on the deck, almost silent. Everything was muffled and damped in the station. Missed real sunlight. Missed lots of real things. Sickbay was at the end, south end, he'd heard. Who knew when you never saw the sun?

He stepped inside sickbay. Duty medtech just watched. Watched close.

Vielho lay in the second bay, in a medsack that surrounded all of his body. Only his face was exposed. His eyes were open, and his chest rose and fell.

A long moment passed, before deJahn spoke. "You'll be all right. You did a good job." Was that right? Who the frig knew? "Vielho . . . I'm here . . . deJahn."

There was no response. The blank eyes did not move, did not blink.

DeJahn looked around the cubicle, located a stool. He pulled it over and sat where Vielho's eyes could see him, if they could see.

Finally, after another ten minutes, the silence pressed in on him. So much that he had to say something. Anything.

"Vielho . . . you know . . . you remind me of my brother. He's younger. Not much, two years. He's a teacher . . . some out of the way place, Escalante . . . he's like you, always had something pleasant to say . . . That's why I asked about the tea. He drinks tea. You know, one time, when we were moving the herd . . . yeah, the old man still handles sheep the old way . . . Casimir found one of the ewes had dropped twins late . . . never found their mother . . . he bottle-nursed 'em until they were old enough to go with the others. . . ." DeJahn didn't know why he'd told that story, or the one after it.

Finally, maybe an hour, maybe two, later, he got up from the stool, and leaned over and put two fingers on Vielho's forehead. "Hold tight . . . "

Outside sickbay, he thought he saw Meralez in the passageway ahead, and he took the one to the left, that went back to the mess, not that he was hungry. Most times, he would have been glad to see Meralez.

Not this time.

IX.

Major Delles surveyed the techs seated at the tables in the mess. This time, more than ten chairs were empty. One would have belonged to Suares, another to Vielho . . . and Chihouly. *Too many names for one lousy obsolete power plant.*

Meralez had seated herself at one end of the single long table, with Castaneda on the other side. DeJahn hadn't tried to get close on the other side. He'd just taken the last seat near the bulkhead table.

"This is the big push." Delles smiled enthusiastically. "What we have planned here will upset the Seasies' economy for a decade or more, not to mention crippling their efforts to match us in biowar capabilities. What we're doing is just a small part of an overall coordinated program . . . "

An overall coordinated program? More like another frigged-up mess where nothing would go like planned, and a whole bunch of techs would get dis-shock or brain-fried.

" . . . it's taken some time to identify the critical targets, and not all of them are obvious, but all are critical to the sectoral economy . . . "

Just tell us what they are, thought deJahn. *Skip the enthuse shit.*

" . . . Lumut is critical to the development of the next wave of warm-water bioconversion systems . . . Targets will be the power systems, the membrane formulation complex, all comm links, and the potable water system, as well as all humint armed units . . . "

Turn the place into a wasteland, just like they did with Cascadia Coast . . . and make sure no one's left who can explain what happened. Margot had been in Cascadia, just visiting. And deJahn had applied for spec-ops the next week.

" . . . all the biounits are in place and registering green . . . "

As if you'd tell us about those that aren't.

" . . . We'll be using the main pod for the heavies, and two and three for the aux bio-units. Here are the pod assignments."

The holo image appeared in the air beside the major. One of the names under pod two was deJahn.

Frigging support. It didn't help that Castaneda was assigned to the main pod. He forced a smile. At least Meralez was in pod two with him. Not that she'd ever been other than polite to him, but even that helped.

"Any questions, Techs?" Delles barely paused before adding, "Dismissed. Operation begins at zero nine hundred local tomorrow."

DeJahn stood.

Meralez walked by him, as if she would not speak to him.

He nodded, deciding against smiling.

"I saw that. With Vielho. You're not so cold. Not like people think." She flashed a quick smile, almost secretive, before her face turned just tech-pleasant.

Cold? He kept to himself, but he wasn't cold, was he?

X.

0849. DeJahn stood outside pod two. He didn't like being early, but he liked being late even less. In front of him, Esquival stepped forward, extending her hand. As she did, deJahn was aware of someone behind him—Meralez. He wanted to look back. He didn't.

Then it was his turn. He extended his hand to the sensor. *Tech deJahn.*

Entry granted.

He slipped into the dimness. Captain DiLayne was OpsCon again. That figured. Delles would take the main pod. Pod two was smaller, with only four sensie-seats. DeJahn took the second seat, and watched as Meralez stopped beside the third. He smiled at her through the dimness, but only for a moment. She only nodded.

He eased the mesh linkcap into place, then settled himself. *Tech deJahn.*

Accepted. Flash background: Snators—bioexplosive. Clutches implanted in five locales, activated at thirty-six minus. Links confirmed. Five targets—all broadband nodecasters. See plots.

The good news was that his targets weren't people, but the bad news was that he was riding herd on reptilian bioexplosives almost as deadly as ultra-ex. He'd need careful timing for the disengagement.

The five plots displayed the snators, all arrayed around Lumut, each less than three thousand yards from the target. Each had been sent in with a biogator weeks or months before, little more than a programmed bioblastula with accelerated growth patterning. That kind of planning was something deJahn didn't want to think about.

Interrogative vector status? snapped DiLayne.

Snators green, standing by for release.

Release at will.

He didn't need any more urging. The first group of snators left wakes, so energetic was their water entry. The odor of decaying meat permeated that link.

No smell through the sensie-links? DeJahn snorted to himself, even as he blocked the decay odor and the snators slowed, their snouts turning from side to side, as if puzzled by the change, but they kept swimming downstream.

The second attack group had begun to slide through the marsh and reeds toward the nodecaster on the low hillock to the south. The last three hundred yards was across what amounted to mowed lawn, and deJahn would have to sacrifice one of the snators to take out the sonic electric gating to the lawn—it might have been a cricket field or pitch, whatever they called it.

Group three had a curving path through the public gardens, exposed most of the way. That worried deJahn. Gatorlike creatures in the gardens would certainly attract some attention, but then, if need be, he could push them into a run, and snators could make speed.

Four and five had near-direct water routes, with only the last few hundred yards exposed, but five had to cross a side road, supposedly with low traffic.

He flicked from image to image, flickering from snator to snator so fast that twice the integrator blanked. The snators' binocular vision was clear, and there wasn't much color. He wanted to get a better and quicker personal sense of locale matched with the plot map, but he forced himself to slow down.

He did have another thirty standard minutes, and the snators were fast.

Group five was running ahead, but deJahn didn't see that it mattered. Better ahead and clear than on sched and facing opposition.

Group three was already on target, less than sixty yards below the nodecaster concealed in an artificial rock cliff slightly north of the center of the gardens.

One of the local patrollers was also there, and she had a stun-rifle out, leveling it at the lead snator. DeJahn dropped the third snator into limited free hunt, because its reactions and impulses were far faster than his through the links.

Her shot went wide. She did not get a second shot.

Someone else did, with a biodetonator.

Electrofire slammed back through the links, and deJahn shuddered, even as he accelerated two of the gators toward the base of the cliff, seeking whatever access points there might be. Neither of the two lagging snators could locate the attacker, even as one registered projectiles screaming past it.

Giving up on locating the attacker, deJahn pressed the laggards after the leaders, strengthening the lure of decaying meat.

A second snator went up, this time with its own bioex, leaving flame in deJahn's eyes. He shook off the pain feedback and checked the closure. The three remaining were close enough. He triggered them, holding the link for the barest moment to make sure the command had gone true, before disengaging.

Even so, the shock rocked him, because some of the snators' death agony washed back over him.

One down, four to go.

Automatics of some sort popped up from the sides of the cricket field right after deJahn detonated and disengaged from the sacrificial snator. Two of the remaining snators were shredded by the autofire, but three others sprinted through the hail of composite to the other side and the base of the nodecaster, surrounded by three yards of impermite. Impermite was weak stuff compared to NorAm bioex.

DeJahn triggered and disengaged.

Pointed iron picks began to chip away at his skull.

Three more . . .

Group four scuttled and splashed through the tanks of a low-tech wetworks to reach the back side of another low hill. A dozen Seasies in dull green uniforms appeared.

DeJahn sent the lead gator toward them, using it—with an early detonation—to clear the way for the others.

Another trigger and disengage.

Now . . . large and ancient cannon were blowing holes in his skull. How it felt, anyway.

Interrogative status?

Three objectives triggered . . . two in progress. His entire body was a mass of fire, pseudo biofeedback fire, but it still the frig hurt.

He struggled to focus on the link to group one. Still short of target.

Five . . . where was five?

Trying to cross the road, and two local patrollers were laying down a fire curtain.

That cost him two snators, but the patrollers and their vehicles went up with the bioex. He just hoped the two remaining snators had enough bioex for the nodecaster as he put them on free search-and-destroy.

Group one.

Just as he linked, he could feel the biofield constrictor sweep across the snators of group one.

He mentally lunged for disengagement . . . *Disengage!*

XI.

Fire! Like being bitten by a thousand scroaches. Light! Brighter than novafly exploding before his eyes.

DeJahn jerked. His eyes were open, saw only purple blackness, link-deep with no link. Every nerve in his body was a line of fire. Where was cool? Darkness?

"Easy . . . easy . . . "

Whose voice? Knew the voice. Couldn't place . . . couldn't find.

"Who?" His voice rasped. Not his voice. Could tell he'd been screaming. Frig! Didn't want to be a screamer.

A hand touched his. Warm, welcome . . . Yet . . . the warmth was fire, knifelike, daggers like the fangs of a chimbat, like the venom of a chimshrew.

"You'll be all right, deJahn . . . be fine. Just disengagement link-shock . . . "

Just disengagement link-shock . . . link-shock . . . Sure, you'll be fine. This time.

"Friggin' . . . disengage . . . "

"You'll be all right." Meralez squeezed his hand once more. This time, there was no pain.

He managed to tighten his fingers around hers for a moment.

He would be fine. He was a tech.

THE WEAPON

William H. Keith

Y^{gal} 20.43

"Come on," the remote descendent of *Homo sapiens* said with something approaching exasperation. "We've known we're due to get clobbered by that thing for, oh, a quarter of a galactic year at the very least. And it's not going to happen for a very long time. What's the big issue?"

The being, which identified herself as Selan Avris, was recognizably human in the shape and expressiveness of her head—large, hairless, and sharp-featured. Her torso was far more flexible than that of ancient gravity-bound forms, however, and long ago her species had exchanged legs for a second pair of long and delicate arms. *Homo extraterrestrialis* was one of some fifteen hundred extant species, all members of a swiftly diversifying genus Homo.

The term *swiftly* was relative, of course. For ephemeral species, the sixty million years since the original genus

Homo had emerged from its gravity-bound cocoon was a very long time indeed.

"But the collision *will* occur," her partner told her, "in another thirteen point seven galactic years. And what will that mean for a nascent K3 civilization?"

The partner was familiarly known as Valova, though it didn't have a name in the traditional sense of the word. It, too, was descended from the original branch of Humanity that had reached beyond the parent world, though it was not, strictly speaking, a member of genus Homo. A fusion of the organic with the machine, it was a true cyborg. All organic components resided safely deep within its smoothly convoluted black-silver shell, a composite material neither plastic nor metal, but something of both.

"Thirteen galyears is seventy-seven percent of the age of the Earth itself," Selan replied with a complex shrug of four shoulders. She reached out with a lower left arm to grasp a convenient handhold and turned to look out into the golden dusting of the Solar Dyson cloud. "None of us will be here to see it. Not even *you*."

"Feeling our mortality, are we?" Valova said, but it included a carefully crafted emotive packet—wry humor and understanding—to rob the words of any sting. "I would think that if Humankind has learned anything, it is the need to take the long view."

"I can't say I'm enthusiastic about this proposed step up to K3 status, is all. What have the Galactics ever done for us?"

"They left us alone," was Valova's reply, "to evolve in our own way."

"Then we should return the favor."

From this particular vantage point, a "spome"—the ancient word referred to a space home—deep within the Dyson cloud, the glow from some billions of habitats all but masked the stars. Humanity's descendents, in many forms, had traveled throughout the Galaxy, encountering and interacting with myriad other minds, but the vast majority remained here, safe within the home system. After all, why venture elsewhere, when the home system of Humankind offered all in the way of comfort, diversity, and diversion any sentient being could ask?

Sixty million years in the distant past, a pre-Civilization scientist named Kardeshev had first suggested a mode for describing extraterrestrial civilizations, should they ever be encountered. A civilization utilizing the energy and material resources of a single world—and generating about 10^{16} watts of power—was designated K1. One that employed the resources of an entire star system, or roughly 10^{26} watts, would be a K2. On that scale, Kardeshev's world might have been rated as a very tentative K0.7; that of Selan and Valova, utilizing some 10^{31} watts, was a solid K2.5.

"Look," Valova said, opening an informational download window within both of their minds. "The Galaxy—the Galaxy as we know it, anyway—is doomed! Andromeda will tear it to shreds."

Within the window, an AI simulation unfolded, revealing the future as determined by cosmology and the laws of physics. Two spiral galaxies, with their attendant satellites, drifted in the Void, the inset scale showing their separation as some two million light-years. Years passed, flickering away at millions per second. The two spirals—the galaxy known as M-31 or the Andromedan galaxy, and the galaxy that was home to Humankind—were on a collision course, the separation between them dwindling.

Less than three billion years into the future, both galaxies began showing marked distortions in the shapes of their spiral arms as they rotated. A few hundred million years later, Andromeda and the smaller home Galaxy of Man plunged through one another, the tidal disruption flinging clouds of stars outward in all directions. Hot, young stars flared into short-lived brilliance as gas clouds interpenetrated and collapsed.

It was not a direct central impact, and both galaxies retained much of their original shapes. Obeying the ancient laws of Newton, however, the two remnant spiral knots slowed, swung about, came together, and collided once again after another billion years. This time, only the much-shrunken remnant of Andromeda survived as anything like a coherent structure, as the larger galactic nucleus devoured the smaller. What remained was a raggedly elliptical mass of newborn suns swarming about a dense double-knot of newborn stars and flaring supernovae.

The majority of stars from both systems were flung outward into the emptiness of intergalactic space.

"So?" Selan asked her partner. "The distances between the stars of both galaxies are so vast there will be few, if any, stellar collisions. Over the course of a billion years or so, tidal interactions will tear both galaxies apart, yes, but that won't affect the individual stellar systems. Civilization—*all* civilizations, I should say—will continue."

"Are you an Isolationist, Selan? You talk as though you are."

"Not at all. I simply see no need to embrace this galactic view so many have been discussing lately. If it's really a problem, why, then, technology will find a way."

"Technology?" Valova could not show emotion through its glittering sensors, but emotive packets revealed both surprise and disdain. "*Technology*? We're talking about diverting an entire *galaxy* here! One twice as large and as massive as our own!"

"So?" Selan held out her upper-left arm, and concentrated for a moment. The habitat's AI picked up the thought, and a vial of nutrient materialized in her hand. She took a dainty sip. "We manipulate matter and energy at a quantum level," she said. "On a small scale, it's true . . . but we pull matter from the chaos of empty vacuum. We manipulate space, and thereby gravity. We can make gravity to order, or abolish it. A billion years from now, what will Mind be capable of? Rather, of what will it *not* be capable?"

"I believe you trust too much in the power of technology," the cyborg replied. "In the long run, overreliance on our own abilities, in isolation from the larger Group Mind beyond, is dangerous. Isolationism is not viable."

"Neither is a superstitious reliance upon the Galactics as some kind of deities, who will solve our problems for us," Selan snapped. "I see no point in continuing this discussion."

"Nor I."

Within the Solar culture of that epoch, "partner" referred to a long-term relationship that had little to do with sex or reproduction, and much to do with philosophical concerns and a symbiosis of avocation and point of view. Their disagreement proved to be the first serious rift between increasingly divergent world views; a few centuries later, Selan and three like-minded partners—all of them *Homo extraterrestrialis*, as it happened—left the partnership. Valova's larger group eventually migrated to the Oort spomeswarm, the still thinly populated fringe of the System, where the view of the Galaxy was unimpeded by Sol or the glow of the Dyson cloud.

Of interest from this new vantage point was the Andromedan galaxy. To the unenhanced vision of *Homo sapiens*, it had long been just visible to the naked eye as a small patch of haze—little more than a faint and fuzzy star—taking its name from a long-vanished constellation. To the optics of beings like Valova, however, it covered an area over six times that of Earth's moon as it had been seen from ancient Earth—before that satellite had been disassembled to fuel the growth of the Dyson cloud. To its eyes, the spiral arms were quite visible. It was easy for Valova to imagine that vast spiral of starlight hurtling down upon it at thirty five kilometers per second.

And epochs passed.

Y^{gal} 24.85

Within the vast and complex tapestry of Galactic history, the history of Humankind was a single, almost microscopic thread. Civilization was not, could not be, a constant. Civilizations rose, matured, aged, fell. Like virtual particles arising from the background foam of the Zero Point Field, unions of thought and world view and purpose came and went, an ephemeral flickering against the Night. More and more often, however, like subatomic particles gathering an illusion of stability, metacivilizations took form, coherent wave forms arising from the background chaos. The Galactics, so disliked by Selan, had been one of these.

But a truly enduring civilization requires a delicate balance between the static and the dynamic. To grow too swiftly means an inevitable collapse into chaos; to remain static is death. The group of cultures inhabiting the Dyson cloud about Sol, like many tens of millions of other civilizations across the Galaxy, found stability in its sheer diversity. Individual civilizations came and went, none enduring more than a few million years, each adding somewhat to the growth and knowledge of the whole before fading and being replaced by a new outlook upon the cosmos.

And slowly, the metacivilization of the Galaxy as a whole took firmer and deeper root. A billion years or so after the time of Selan and Valova, a loose association of very long-lived cultures had emerged as a kind of

Caretaker civilization, though its antecedent cultures had first appeared long before Earth or its sun had emerged from their stellar nursery. Physically located within a swarm of world-sized habitats drawing energy from the black holes, massed suns, and intense radiation fields of the Galactic Core, they were primarily focused on extending and deepening the reach and scope of a genuine K3 civilization, a confederation of Mind known by a symbol that might translate as "the Conclave."

To employ imperfect metaphor, if the Galaxy was the body and the Conclave the brain, Sol and its teeming trillions were a single cell within the body's far-flung nervous system. Sol, by this time, was the heart of a thriving, stable K2.0 civilization; Galactic civilization as a whole, as represented by the myriad worlds of the Core, might have been pegged at K3.1.

Despite advances in physics that would have seemed godlike to ancient Humankind, the speed of light remained the ultimate barrier to communication. A signal sent outward from the Core still required two tenths of a galactic rotation to reach the Outer Rim.

The Caretakers didn't think in terms of galactic years, of course. They tended to measure such relatively brief periods in terms of radioactive decay; Y^{gal} 0.2 was roughly the equivalent of two half-lives of plutonium-239. The concept of a fixed galactic year equal to 225 million years could apply only to the Dyson cloud of Sol and other systems 26,000 light-years out—the length of time it took stars at that distance to orbit the galactic center once.

Still, a tiny fraction of the extremely remote descendents of Humankind had slowly spread throughout the home galaxy. Almost a billion years after Humankind had first ventured from the surface of his world, some hundreds of millions lived on and within a number of artificial worlds and structures scattered along the fringe of the Galactic

Core, and took part in many of the principal deliberations of the Conclave.

"What we need," one of those descendents told the Group Mind, "is a weapon. A very, very *powerful* weapon."

The being was not genus *Homo*—was not, in fact, even remotely organic. The majority of sentient beings throughout the Galaxy—those with a corporeal existence, at any rate—were machines: highly intelligent, long-lived, supremely rational, and capable of taking a very long view of things indeed. Outward form and the physics of reproduction were unimportant; what counted alone was Mind.

"What," another machine mind inquired, "is a *weapon*?"

"A device," the first mind replied. "A tool for applying energy in such a way as to stop or divert a threat. Check your oldest records. Within primitive organic systems, they are used to acquire other organic matter as food, or to acquire political advantage so that one system can impose its will upon another."

"And how does that relate to the threat we face?"

The emotive equivalent of a shrug crossed the light-years. "Our metacivilization faces destruction when the Andromedan galaxy merges with ours some four point three five half-lives of Uranium-235 hence."

"A very long time."

"Not so long. Fewer than ten complete rotations of our Galaxy. And the longer we wait, the more energy we must employ to safely alter Andromeda's vector. In considerably less time than that, a critical point will be reached, after which harmlessly diverting Andromeda will be impossible, and damage—perhaps catastrophic damage—to the metacivilization becomes inevitable."

"I yet fail to see why this is of serious concern," another member of the Conclave put in. Its particular civilization occupied the warm and salty seas beneath the ice crusts of a number of moons circling Jovian-type gas giants, a vantage point less than conducive to an outlook along astronomical scales. "As we understand it, no stars will be harmed by the interpenetration of the galaxies."

"But the component stars of our metacivilization will be so completely scattered," the descendent of Humankind replied, "that communication between the individual systems will become impossibly long. Worse, the collision of gas clouds will initiate a period of intense star formation. The newborn suns will be massive and short-lived, leading to an epoch of supernovae that will flood ambient space in deadly radiation. Many of us can shield our home systems from the high-energy flux, even use it, but countless organic worlds would be rendered sterile."

"Of more serious concern," another Mind said, "is the limiting of available data. We predict that a metacivilization such as ours, in the absence of a viable interstellar data exchange, would inevitably collapse to Type K2.4L within what remains of the galactic cores. Individual star systems flung into the Void could maintain civilizations no higher than approximately K1.9J."

For eons now, the scope and depth of Civilization had been measured by the amount of information it processed and stored. A primitive tribe wandering the surface of a world, with no written language, might process 10^6 bits of data, and be classified as Type A. Each tenfold increase in available data represented another step up the scale. The ancient world of Kardeshev, with all of its books and computer hard drives storing something like 10^{13} bits, would have been classified as a K0.7H. The metacivilization of the Caretakers, with access to the stored data of 10^9 worlds, was currently a Type K3.5Q.

The machine intelligence was pointing out that after the collision with Andromeda, any surviving metaculture would be able to draw upon the massed data of no more than 10^4 worlds, and would therefore be limited to 10^{17} bits—a Type L. Single worlds flung clear of the Galaxy, isolated and alone, would be able to handle no more than the data available to a solitary star system—its data processing capability forever limited to a paltry 10^{15} bits.

The information stunned.

"And the vast and increasing gulf between the individual star systems," the first machine mind continued, "would guarantee that a true metacivilization would *never* reform, that the highest communicative element would be a single star and its population of worlds and habitats. That is the challenge that faces us as Sentient Mind—to prevent the randomization of all we have created, and to ensure our future growth."

The conversation was being carried out across the breadth of the Conclave's environs about the Core, information traveling on the wings of laser, gravitic pulse, and gamma flux emulation. A statement by one member required ten thousand years to reach all of the others, and required a like period for a complete reply. Such was the snail's pace of conversation across the interstellar Void.

For one and a third galactic years, then, as humans might have measured the span, the Conclave deliberated.

And consensus was reached.

In principle, at least, it should be possible to project an induced gravity field in such a way as to deflect M-31, either ripping it apart until it was too diffuse to gravitationally affect the home galaxy's structure, or sending it—more or less intact—off on a different vector entirely, harmlessly into intergalactic space.

By manipulating the Zero Point Field, that subatomic realm of metareality where virtual particles and antiparticles foamed in and out of existence, gravity could be controlled on a scale large enough to redirect the orbits of entire suns. Indeed, the early stages of the Galactic Dyson sphere were already visibly manifest, as neatly ordered rings of stars circled the Core in precise arrays visible from as far out as the Rim. Ordering the stars and their attendant worlds in this way made vastly simpler the task of linking all of the worlds together into a communications web: one that already embraced fifty million worlds, and which one day would link them to all.

And if they could manipulate the paths of individual stars, it was only a matter of scaling up the engineering to manipulate the paths of four hundred billion stars at once.

In Y^{gal} 26.18, work on the Weapon began in earnest.

And the epochs passed.

Y^{gal} 28.95

By the end of the twenty-eighth galactic year after Sol's birth, and some 1.9 billion years after the far-off epoch of Selan and Valova, the two slow-spinning pinwheels of stars had closed the gap between them to something just less than half a million light-years—a mere five times the diameter of the Milky Way, and two and a half times huge Andromeda's breadth. Even to organic eyes—and there yet were many of those even within a metacivilization composed largely of machines or of noncorporeal intelligences resident within the Galaxy's communicative network—the Andromedan spiral now dominated the night skies of appropriately situated worlds, a vast oval of light spanning nearly thirty degrees, or sixty times the size of the long-vanished Moon in Earth's ancient sky. Intrinsically, M-31 was one of the brightest galaxies known—at least among those without a highly active nucleus, and the lanes of dust marking the spiral arms were clearly apparent, as was the brighter bulge of the Core.

Hanging within the emptiness beyond the Rim of the Home Galaxy, a titanic structure was slowly taking shape in the darkness. Within a world-sized construct orbiting the intense gravitational maelstrom of an artificial black hole, two intelligent machines surveyed the huge and pale-glowing spiral of light that was Andromeda.

"I suppose," one machine told the other, "that we could destroy them. That *is* what a weapon does, after all."

"Is it? I thought the purpose of the Weapon was to simply deflect the approaching galaxy. Not to destroy it."

"It is. But it will be powerful enough to destroy. I refer to the Dark Gods."

Over the millennia, repeated attempts had been made to signal any civilizations that might be resident within Andromeda, but, until recently, with no result. Two galactic years before, however, the first fleets of worldships had bridged the Gulf between the galaxies. If a metacivilization existed within Andromeda as well, then perhaps the two could work together, to a common goal.

But sadly, it was not to be. Life was encountered within Andromeda, life as diverse and as stubborn and as swiftly blossoming as that within the home Galaxy, and Civilization as well . . .

But Mind there had taken strange, alarmingly irrational turns, alien from the consensus-Mind of the home Galaxy. There, mind and soul were resources to be harvested, reshaped, enslaved, consumed. Sentience twisted in strange ways, dominated by philosophies bleak and dark, by nihilistic outlooks that made the long-forgotten works of Nietzsche or Camus seem cheerful by comparison. There, civilizations without number, teeming hives of ephemeral organics, fed the godminds of Darkness that, like Kronos, devoured their own children.

Dark Gods. . . .

The first worldship fleets had vanished within Andromeda.

But other fleets followed.

"A whole new metacivilization," one of the machine minds thought aloud, glittering optics staring across the Gulf into the face of Andromeda. "Another . . . what? Ten to the ten, ten to the eleven civilized worlds? Enough, perhaps, to let us advance to K3.6R."

"If what passes for Civilization over there were compatible with our own," the other replied. "What dwells there is not Mind as we know it."

Mind as we know it. The concept, with its corollary—that there were things about Mind that were not, or could not be known—was unsettling.

"The Imperial Network will know what to do."

The social order embracing the home Galaxy had changed with the gigayears. The Conclave had faded into forgetfulness eons ago, replaced by several younger, more vigorous Caretaker metacivilizations—the Syncretium, the Associative, the Commonwealth, the Watchers, and so many thousands of others. For thirty-two and a half million years, work on the Weapon had all but ceased, as the philosophy of the Passive Enlightenment had held sway, dedicated to quiet contemplation of Things as They Are.

But the Enlightenment was short-lived, overthrown by the burst of growth-oriented enthusiasm that followed the application of non-local communications.

Nonlocality, rooted in the ancient dawnings of quantum awareness, proved that the seemingly common-sense concept of space itself was illusory; that what happened *here* could affect things *there* without crossing the seeming emptiness between. Though understood for as long as Mind had understood the weirdness of quantum physics, only now, as an outgrowth of the Weapon's research and engineering, was it applied on a scale that spanned the Galaxy. Using microscopic artificial singularities to reach into and manipulate the Zero Point Field, communication across the vast web of worlds became instantaneous. Within the span of four half-lives of plutonium-239, the time it took for the technology to be physically carried across the Galaxy at the speed of light, every world, every spome, every sentient mind across a hundred billion worlds could link into the Galactic Overmind in realtime. Travel times remained limited by the universal constant of *c*. The transmission of information, however, the only truly viable interstellar commodity, was something else again.

The narrow passivity of the Enlightenment could not long endure what proved to be a true enlightenment, and a burst of creativity on a galactic scale. Ironically, that creativity carried within itself its own set of checks and balances. Attempts to regulate and control the exchange of information resulted in an increased centralization of authority.

It resulted in Empire.

By their nature, galactic imperia tended to be somewhat unstable. The Forty-fifth Empire had arisen from the ashes of the Forty-forth, seized the worlds of the Core, and by virtue of their central position come to dominate most of the Galactic Network. The current emperor, twelfth of its line, had decreed that the Weapon, long neglected, must be completed: swiftly, and with precision.

The Empire's long-term survival depended upon it. After two billion years of sanity, the ancient madness of war had reappeared: this time on an intergalactic scale.

Y^{gal} 29.02

The War of the Galaxies raged for fewer than sixteen million years—a scant one seven-hundredth of a galactic year. For a time, worldfleets spanned the Gulf in both directions, seeking key processing nexi and inducing supernovae to degrade the enemy's capabilities.

Both sides possessed nonlocal communication, so there was no advantage to be won there. But the Home Galaxy also possessed the Weapon, albeit in incomplete form. In

Y^{gal} 29.01, it was triggered for the first time, its first test across intergalactic distances.

The Weapon was comprised of a complex array of over four hundred thousand artificial black holes and their attendant control and guidance facilities, stretching across some two hundred million cubic light-years of space. Interconnected by a complex of microscopic wormholes, the Weapon employed quantum nonlocality to focus titanic Zero Point energies on distant volumes of space.

Aiming the thing, and triggering it, required the massed will and intent of a Group Mind. At the crucial moment, the minds of a hundred billion sentient beings *believed* their intent was manifest, *knew* it to be so.

And it was.

A swarm of Andromedan worldships vaulted into the Gulf at the speed of light, targeting the Galactic Core. Imperial guardians beyond the Rim reported their approach, and coordinated the defense. From the guardian worlds in the Gulf to the orbiting machine-hives feeding the hungry emptiness of the Weapon's singularities to the teeming swarms of Mind encompassing the Galactic Core, messages, commands, *information* flowed.

The command was sent . . . *now.*

Just ahead of and to one side of the enemy worldships, space began to pucker. Titanic energies sprang into being there, bending the quantum substrate of space and time.

The Andromedan worldships, traveling in what seemed a straight line, found themselves *still* traveling a straight line . . . but somehow on a vector 120 degrees off from their original course and millions of years into the future, with the twin spiral galaxies now shrunken, dim and distant in their wakes.

The Enemy dispatched more fleets. These, too, were redirected, as were clouds of asteroid- to planet-sized bodies accelerated to close to the speed of light and hurled at stars and communications nodes within the Home

Galaxy. All of the fleets and most of the deadly relativistic star-killers were safely diverted. The few thousand high-speed rocks that slipped past the Guardians wreaked a horrible slaughter as suns flared into supernovae and Dyson clouds, spheres, and rings were incinerated.

For a few deadly half-lives of plutonium-239, the nonlocal Network was threatened as key communications nodes were vaporized. The original Net, however, remained, taking up the slack between sundered switching points.

Within any dynamic system dependent upon the processing of information, information is power, the *only* power that truly matters. Metacivilizations of Type K3.6Q, with access to some 10^{22} bits of data, the forty-fifth and forty-sixth Empires had little difficulty holding off the Dark Gods. The Andromedan metacivilization complex—totalitarian, inflexible, and unsupportive of truly creative thought—proved to be a less efficient system of Type K3.3P, marshalling only about 10^{21} bits. Despite its losses, the Home Galaxy's victory was certain and absolute.

Two million years after Civilization's final triumph, a Star Lord watched the two galaxies from the vantage point of an artificial world a hundred thousand light years above the Home Galaxy's Core. The Star Lords were composite Minds, heirs of the now vanished galactic empires.

Both galaxies appeared paler now, dimmer than in eons past. The War, in the way of all wars, had drastically thinned both of stars and inhabited worlds. The Home Galaxy had been further dimmed by clouds accumulating about its Core for the past several galactic years—clouds of artificial worlds and titanic structures, orbiting the Core in teeming trillions—the next step in the evolution of a mature K3 metacivilization as the energies of an entire galaxy were harnessed and redirected.

To the inorganic eyes of a Star Lord, however, the Galaxy's face shone more brightly than ever, alive with starlight reradiated in the infrared, with the myriad flickerings and pulses of interstellar lasers, radio, and gravitics, alive with the vivid imprints of Life and Technology.

"The Weapon has proven itself," the Star Lord said. "Employed on a larger scale, it will shield the Home Galaxy from further disruption. We shall survive as a Type 3 metacivilization."

"It may be too late to deflect Andromeda as an intact entity," another Star Lord observed from the communications nexus within a globular star cluster far beyond the Rim. "It will be necessary to completely disrupt and scatter its member suns and dust clouds. Many of its stars may be destroyed in the process." Imagery unfolded within the watching Minds—of the myriad stars of Andromeda channeled by sharply warping space into a thin, tight stream and sprayed out into the intergalactic Void. That channeling would fuse stars and gas clouds into plasma and eject it at close to the speed of light, creating a beam of energy like the polar jets of an exploding galactic core. Suns and worlds by the tens—even by the hundreds of millions—would be annihilated.

"We might yet avoid that necessity," the first Star Lord said. "I hope so. There are still trillions of sentient beings in among the worlds of Andromeda. Communicating with them remains . . . difficult, but it would be a pity to incinerate them all."

"Incineration for them, or the end of K3 metacivilization," another said. "An interesting ethical choice."

"If we act swiftly—within, I estimate, ten half-lives of plutonium-239—few of Andromeda's systems will be destroyed. They will be scattered across the Void, and be unable ever to regain a viable K3-level civilization. But they will survive as independent systems, Type 2."

"Intriguing. That is the same fate we ourselves seek to avoid."

"A question remains," another Star Lord said, this one from a world deep within the Galactic Core itself, "as to whether we can marshal the requisite energy."

"The energy is there," the first Lord said. "We need only tap the Collective Will."

Every alteration of mass or energy—from materializing a cup of nutrient to diverting a galaxy like water sprayed from a hose—required the expenditure of energy. Since the dim prehistory of Galactic Metaculture, that energy had been most efficiently tapped from the Zero Point Field.

Certain philosopher-shamans of the Earth of Kardeshev's day had made the first, crude calculations of the energy resident within so-called empty space. Some had ventured the opinion that a volume of hard vacuum a few centimeters on a side contained energy enough, if released all at once, to destroy the Galaxy. Their peers had refined the figures, and pointed out a slight error in magnitude. The actual energy, they declared, would be something on the order of 10^{100} times *greater.*

Perhaps fortunately, in all of the eons since, only a tiny fraction of that unthinkable torrent of energy could ever be tapped.

The Weapon could not draw upon all available zero-point energy—not yet, at any rate—but it could channel a respectable fraction, and initial estimates suggested that that fraction would be enough, easily, to create a gravity field intense enough to obliterate Andromeda. What was required was the harnessed, ranked, and ordered intent and will of some quintillions of Net-linked minds. During the height of the battle with the Andromedans, a linked and focused array of some twenty to thirty billion minds had been sufficient to redirect the enemy worldfleets and some ninety percent of the incoming relativistic star-killers.

To divert Andromeda would require an effort some nine orders of magnitude greater.

Consensus was reached. The command was given. The Galactic Will would reach forth. . . .

Failure. Cold and stunning failure. The Weapon triggered, but with only a tiny fraction of the necessary power. Some few millions of Andromeda's nearer stars, indeed, were redirected into radically different vectors at a sizeable fraction of *c*, and hundreds of millions more were somewhat shifted in their courses . . . but the vast, spiraling mass of suns continued closing with the Home Galaxy, accelerating now under gravity's inexorable hand as if eager for the final embrace. Both of the Magellanic Clouds, attendant satellites of the Home Galaxy, were devoured by the monster, vanishing like tiny, swallowed morsels into the Andromedan maw.

Through much of Y^{gal} 29, the Star Lords sought desperately to find out what had gone wrong.

The failure, it was soon clear, had been a failure of Will.

And another epoch passed . . .

Y^{gal} 32.54

The Metacivilization of the Star Lords, like all of the Caretaker civilizations that had gone before, was a hierarchical construct: a pyramid with each course dependent for support upon the course beneath. The uppermost levels, drawing upon the energy and the data of the entire Galaxy, now could be classified as K3.8Q. Individual star systems, however, each with its attendant Dyson cloud or pearl-strings of inhabited worlds or rings and shells manufactured from disassembled worlds, drew upon their own energy resources, and none could be said to rate higher than K2.0, with only a few of the larger interstellar associatives weighing in at around K2.5. The transgalactic Net assured access to all available information, however, which was distributed across the Galaxy. The long dreamed-of compendium of all known data, the so-called *Encyclopedia Galactica,* was instantly accessible from nearly every inhabited world or spome—10^{22} bits of information compiled from among 10^{11} worlds. With such a complete distribution of data, a certain amount of homogeneity of culture might be expected, even among a hundred billion worlds.

Such, the Star Lords learned, was not the case.

Unity of culture was a myth. At the level of individual worlds and Dyson clouds—even at the level of individual spomes—Mind delved, pondered, explored, considered, grew, and *changed.* Among hundreds of billions of distinct galactic cultures, though many were similar, no two possessed exactly the same cosmic view or viewpoint.

Well over half of all sentient life within the Galaxy was not even corporeal. It existed within networks of interconnected computers—some widely distributed, most distributed through individual systems. Such beings possessed their own realities, and were barely aware of the material world beyond their ken. From their viewpoint, of course, *theirs* was the reality, where the Cosmos was the shadow.

Of corporeal life, nearly twenty percent was still organic or mostly so. Ephemeral by nature, they looked upon the Cosmos very differently from their long-lived machine partners. Some were long-lived themselves, and many recycled memory, ego, and mind through countless bodies to achieve a kind of immorality, but to beings reliant upon chemical metabolism, even a million years— the blink of a cosmic eye—was a very, *very* long time.

And for the countless immortals, how many different ways, what far-flung diversity of philosophies is necessary to endure the passing eons? Andromeda filled the night skies of billions of worlds now, spectacular, terrible, and beautiful. Among the individual civilizations that comprised Galactic sentience, millions were kallonophiles—devoted to the cultivation and appreciation of beauty. Millions more were armoniaphiles, devoted to the concept of harmony—a harmony that would be sundered by the Weapon. Tens of millions pursued ideals of passivity, peace, and noninterference; like the long vanished Passive Enlightenment, they were devoted to What Is, not to what might be wrested from an uncooperative nature.

A sizeable contingent was comprised of nihilists. For them, ultimately, there *was* no purpose to the universe, or to maintaining the viability of the Metaculture. After all, within a few trillion more years, the last flicker of energy would fade into randomness, and the cosmos itself would suffer the inevitable heat death of a universe doomed from the first instant of its birth.

And an even larger contingent was simply *tired* . . . exhausted by the war, exhausted by the long and ultimately futile striving of Life.

When the Star Lords sought to muster the Collective Will of the Galaxy, they'd succeeded in raising barely twenty-eight percent of what was necessary to trigger the Weapon.

The Star Lords now faced the ultimate paradox. They could muster the requisite will to destroy Andromeda *only* if they adopted the modality of their extinct Enemy—marshaling Mind as they marshaled data. A totalitarian regime might muster the necessary energies. A cooperative association could not.

One Star Lord, occupying a Dyson cloud in one of the Galaxy's spiral arms, asked the necessary question.

"Do we become what we once fought against in order to survive?"

The Overmind of the Star Lords considered the question for a very long time . . . so long that the last possible moment of decision was very nearly upon them. Another few half-lives of plutonium-239, and no amount of energy could safely divert the looming spiral of Andromeda. Already separated by only a couple of hundred thousand light-years, both spirals showed severe distortion, as gravitational tides began to tear them apart. The nearest spiral arms were reaching for one another, as though welcoming that final, deadly embrace.

Consensus was reached at last.

Many Star Lords fled, dissolving their individual partnerships, or escaped entirely, using gravitational anomalies to accelerate themselves into a distant future.

Those who remained would wait, watch . . . and let the cosmic drama play itself out without their interference.

Y^{gal} 34.2

The linked Overmind watched the play's final act. Three billion years after Selan and Valova had argued the point, Andromeda's core punched through the Home Galaxy's disk like a bullet through tissue, flinging stars by the billion into space. The remaining Star Lords did what they could, using the Weapon to divert some stars, some infalling clouds of dust and gas, to ameliorate the worst of the damage . . . continued to do so until gravitational tides disrupted the delicate balance between the individual components of the Weapon.

By Y^{gal} 34.32, the Weapon was no more.

The Andromedan core and the Home Galaxy core separated, slowed, then fell together once more. A billion years after the first impact, and nine tenths of the Home Galaxy had dissolved into hurtling, individual stars. Andromeda's double core melded with the smaller remnant of the Home Galaxy's core: three knots of stars and merging black holes, loosing an intense burst of hard, ionizing radiation.

By that time, however, the Overmind consciousness, its internal communicative network savaged beyond all repair, was fading into oblivion.

Y^{gal} 40.33

Once, eons past, the star had been called Sol. Now over nine billion years old, it had already begun expanding into its red giant phase.

No planets remained. All had been disassembled long ago—even the original birthworld of genus *Homo*—in order to manufacture more and ever more of the spomes and worldlets that comprised the system's Dyson cloud, worldlets now numbering in the tens of trillions.

Upon the surface of the ancient world once known as Earth, civilizations had long since come, flourished, and gone—some of them brilliantly. Vast cities had covered whole continents, and eventually vanished. Mountains had thundered as they reached for the sky, and eventually and silently been worn into sand by the passing eons. Glaciers had come, gone, and come again, the age-old cycle ended at last by only by deliberate adjustments to the planet's orbit. The oceans, eventually, had dried. Earth had lived and passed as had most other worlds throughout the Home Galaxy, eventually providing the raw materials for ten billion new worldlets.

All that Earth had been, however, remained—as galaxies of data stored within the myriad artificial minds on the Dyson cloud.

Now, as Sol grew larger, the Dyson cloud itself was rearranged. Its component orbits changed, moving them further out. Eventually, as Sol collapsed, it would be necessary to follow the warmth inward once more. When Sol was a tiny white dwarf, only a fraction of the habitats would be able to draw upon his dwindled heat. The rest would rely on Zero Point energy—arguably the one inexhaustible resource in a Cosmos grown dark and cold. Cosmologists remained divided over whether vacuum fluctuations might survive the heat death of the universe.

That day remained many galactic years in the future, however. For the moment, the Sol Cloud survived.

The Mind hovered within an individual spome and considered the vast-spread panorama within the hurtling star's wake. Sol had been flung clear of the Home Galaxy by the interpenetration of the galaxies, and now, two billion years later, continued to travel into the Night, eight hundred thousand light-years from the hazy glow of the merged galactic nuclei. The sky was starkly empty; other galaxies shone, dimly, as pale patches of light in the remote distance. The nearest star of this epoch—a sullen ember of a red giant, worldless and sterile—hung in an empty Void almost six hundred light years away.

Worse by far, they no longer had the resources to maintain the nonlocal communicative Net. Once again, the remote descendents of ancient humanity were limited by *c* not only in travel but in communications. The nearest communicative civilization circled the fourth-nearest star . . . over twelve hundred light years away.

For the first time in three billion years, Earth's children were truly alone.

Mind contemplated the Ultimate Night.

"We are not defeated," it said at last.

"We are changed," another said. "Change is not defeat."

A third mind was not so sure. "Our resources are finite. We are changed, yes . . . but for the worse, surely. What hope do we have of reaching our former state?"

All three Minds had been components of the Star Lord that had spoken from one of the Galaxy's spiral arms almost eight galactic years before, the Star Lord associative that had questioned the price of their struggle for mere survival.

There were no other Star Lords within the Sol lifecloud.

But there *was* hope.

"Look there." The first Mind pointed out a distant pinpoint source of x-rays—no, a cluster of sources, tightly grouped. Parallax measurements determined that it lay about five thousand light-years away. "You see it?"

"A fragment of the Weapon," the third Mind said. "Flung clear by the collision. I see another over there."

"And there."

"Resources," the first Mind said.

"To what end?"

"We no longer command a galaxy's trove of data," the first Mind said. "But we know what can be done. We can take energy—a fraction of what is available, true, but enough—from the Zero Point Field. We can divert Sol's Dyson cloud, and Sol itself can voyage to that fragment of the Weapon, and use it to acquire yet more energy. We could return to the Merged Core, if we wished."

"Or not," the second Mind said. "Knowing the possibilities of nonlocal communication, spatial proximity may no longer be necessary. We could form the heart of a new communicative Network, one that ultimately spans a billion galaxies."

"A true Type K4 civilization," the first agreed. "Type 4Z. The Weapon may ultimately help us overcome the Ultimate Night."

That moment in darkness heralded the birth of Universal Mind.

And the epochs passed. . . .

THE LOOKING GLASS WAR

Brendan DuBois

The President of the United States sat before his computer screen, which was still blank, and he sighed in frustration as the damn computer kept on humming at him and doing nothing else. He had switched it on and off three different times, and the screen was still blank. Not a damn thing. He had even gotten on his hands and knees below his desk in the Oval Office—an elaborate carved wood monstrosity that had once belonged to Johnson—and struggled to make sense of the jumbled strands of wire and power cords that were crowded under there, and gave up after a few minutes. Not very presidential but he didn't care. The damn computer was still blank.

He sat back in his custom leather chair, comforted that at least the bearings weren't squeaking any more. At least the chair was now working. It had seemed nothing much else was working this day. Take breakfast, for example. The White House kitchen—which was much improved over the previous administrations, if any of those self-serving memoirs he had read years earlier had been true—had about four or five breakfast choices that they rotated around each successive morning. Breakfast choices, like so many other things, had been settled during the transition period three years ago, and everything should have been fine. Except for this morning, in the private sitting room just off his bedroom, breakfast had been something that he had never liked. Lumpy oatmeal. And cold toast. And no damn *Washington Post* or *New York Times*. He had thought of throwing a hissy fit, start tossing things around and making phone calls to the Head Usher's office, but there had been that embarrassing item in the Style gossip section in the *Post* last month about another incident he was too humiliated to think about, concerning missing toilet paper, so he sat down and ate mechanically, staring at the far wall. Some breakfast, some start to the day. And as he ate, he knew there were many, many things that should be crowding his mind, things to address, things to take care of, but funny, wasn't it, that the only thing on his mind was getting in front of his computer.

That's it. Again, not very presidential, but there you go.

And after his disappointing breakfast, a quick sprint by himself downstairs from the private quarters on the second floor and to the West Wing and his office and then to the computer, and . . . nothing.

A blank screen.

He moved back and forth a bit in the chair, looking out the heavy-set windows in the Oval Office at the best view in town, of the White House private gardens and, there in the distance, the Washington Monument. Since they were bulletproof, the windows had a greenish tinge, and he hated them from day one of his administration, since it felt like he was in the middle of a drained aquarium. But after reading the daily threat assessments against him, he had gotten over his displeasure. Like today. So he turned away from the computer and looked at his desk. There was the leather folder that contained his daily schedule—micromanaged down to fifteen minute chunks—and he opened it up . . .

And slammed it down in frustration. This was too damn much. The damn thing was empty.

He picked up his phone and waited for Mrs. Tompkins or Mrs. Gross to answer, and there was nothing. Just incessant ringing on the other end. Out sick, maybe? Or having a coffee break? He started working his way down the buttons on his phone, trying Rogers, chief of staff; Macomber, his appointments secretary; Gillian, his press secretary, and then through a half-dozen aides and assistants.

No answer.

Nothing.

He slammed the phone back down. Could be a connection with his blank computer screen. He was sure both the phones and the computers worked off of the same type of network system. If one was down, maybe the other was down as well. That thought tickled at his mind, and he remembered a meeting some time ago, when Corcoran, his Joint Chiefs chairman, nice and sharp looking with his Army dress uniform, was waving some length of cable around. Something about a threat. Something to do with computers. Something to do with . . . He couldn't remember.

The President swiveled back in his chair, switched the computer off and on again. It kept on humming along, but the screen was still blank. He could see the reflection of his face in the blank screen, like a mirror, or a . . . looking glass. Right? That was the phrase. Something from Alice in Wonderland, sinking into the blank screen and off he'd go, scurrying along the Internet. He slowly caressed the keys, felt an odd, brass taste in his mouth. Something like the trumpet mouthpiece he had suckled on back in high school in upstate New York, before he joined the debate club and found that secret strength he never knew he had, the power of talking, of words, of being able to link words and sentences into something people cared about.

Another secret he never revealed, even to his wife. It had been . . . well, if not easy, then in some way, predetermined. Law school and private practice and lots of pro bono work, and then assemblyman and state senator and majority leader and then governor, joining the list of Rockefeller and Cuomo and Pataki, but unlike those poor sods, he had gone all the way, from Albany to D.C., like Roosevelt, so very many decades ago. Lots of work and late nights and bad food—once he had gotten here to the White House, he had forbidden chicken to be served in any way at any dinner, private or state-related—but here he was. Top of the heap. Ol' numero uno. POTUS and king of all he surveyed.

And he couldn't get his goddamn computer to work.

He traced the plastic keys one more time, and then shook his head and looked back at his desk. He picked up the phone and this time, no dial tone. Nothing. So there was definitely a problem. A dead phone. Then how come no one had told him? And where was Rogers, his chief of staff? Damn it, the man was sometimes so close to him that the cartoonists—and especially that new bastard at the *Post*—drew cartoons that showed him and Rogers, joined to the hip, moving merrily along. Sometimes the two of them were walking in aimless circles, and other times they were walking over a cliff. He picked up a pen and started doodling aimlessly on a fresh legal pad. One of the perks of office. Fresh legal pads on your desk, every morning. But days like this, he sure could have used some of the old perks. Like the ones R.N. was able to use, back when he and his knuckle-draggers ruled the roost. Ol' Nixon was probably the last one with the cojones to use the FBI and CIA and IRS as his personal Praetorian Guard and enforcers, and he sure could have fun using that kind of power. Have that cartoonist bastard at the *Post* get an audit, go through seven years of his financial records. See if his pen inked so straight after that little adventure.

He put his pen down and leaned back again in his chair. This was too much. Where was everyone? He glanced down at the underside of his desk and the tiny red pressure-plate marked on the side, within easy reach. Just a second of pressure there by his knee and the room would be filled with Secret Service agents. That would sure get someone's attention. The radios would be crackling with code words, saying that he had signaled that he was in danger. Code words. Let's see, Reagan had been Rawhide and Carter had been Deacon. Nice choices. Those SS guys always had a quirky sense of humor. And Bush the Elder and Bush the Younger . . . who the hell knew? His own code name was Tailor. His father had been a tailor and he himself enjoyed fine clothes, and the name was okay. Of course, some of his best critics—like that smarmy economics professor who wrote a column for the *Times*—said his code name often meant that he tailored his opinions and objectives to whichever way the wind was blowing. Which hurt, in a weird way, though he had tried to make up for it lately at . . . what was the place?

Sprat. Something Sprat.

And look where that had gotten him.

He stood up from his desk and paced around the Oval Office, wanting to stretch his legs some. No, he won't be triggering the panic switch. Love to see that incident in the next day's *Post*! He stopped by the fireplace, leaned back on the mantelpiece. The first time he had been here, during some governor's delegation visit to the previous POTUS, he had taken it all in and had come away with two impressions. First, that the Oval Office was a hell of a lot smaller than he had thought. And second, well, he knew it was kind of crazy, but the room sort of spoke to him. In a friendly way. Something like, ol' man, the next time you're in this place, you will be The Man, and it will be yours for four years, eight if you're lucky, and we'll be seeing you. And he had whispered—real crazy times, now—he had whispered, "You bet." And thought with a brief moment of terror that one of the escorting Secret Service guys had heard him, and he giggled with relief later when he realized the agent hadn't.

He looked up at a clock on the fireplace's mantelpiece, a warm gift from the people of some African country that had successfully bamboozled him out of a few million dollars of foreign aid last year in exchange for pretending to cooperate in the latest version of the war on terror. It was a bit ugly but it worked, and it told him that it was 10:30. The morning almost halfway shot, and he hadn't spoken to a single person since getting here! What a waste of a day!

He looked over at his desk, and got a little chill that started at the base of his skull and which dripped down his back. Funny, from here, you could see what it looked like on television. He frowned as he remembered the last time the in-house TV crews had trooped in here and had set up the lights, microphones and TelePrompTer. He was sweating and his legs were trembling under the desk, and had needed a pep talk from Rogers before going on national television. It was the first time since high school—since he was a teenager for God's sake!—that he had actually experienced stage fright. His hands were so moist that they were making wet marks on the paper sheets of his speech, the one on his desk in case the TelePrompTer shit the bed, and he knew that the others in the office could smell the fear about him. Rogers, Gillian and a bunch of aides were all staring at him, and in one corner was an angry-looking Corcoran, head of the Joint Chiefs of Staff, glaring at him with contempt. That look had frightened him. The head of the most mighty military in the world was staring at him with hate, and something else . . . yes, something else. Fear. There had been fear on the face of that old foot soldier, fear that the trillions and trillions spent over the decades, in building up the greatest force the world had ever seen, fear that . . . He shook his head. Refused to think about Corcoran any more.

And what was it that Rogers had said, just before that speech? "They need to be reassured," he had said, almost plaintively, a warm hand on his shoulder, leaning in to whisper in his ear. "They need to see that, sir, in your voice and mannerisms. They need to know everything will work out, that everything will be fine."

There were questions he wanted to ask, more questions, but then the red light over the main television camera went on and he went into autopilot, and said the words written for him as best as he could. He read them and part of him was far away, wishing he was up at Camp David or the summer White House up in the Adirondacks, phones off, television off, everything off, and just getting drunk and sitting around and reading paperback mystery books. That's what he wanted to do, more than anything else in the world, and instead he had been sweating in an office that really didn't belong to him, talking to millions of people who were his countrymen, and lying the best way he knew how.

The President shook his head in distaste at the memory and strolled back to his desk. Again, he switched the computer off and on, and the screen was still blank. Well, time for some action. He went across the office and then stopped, thinking he had seen something. He looked out the murky green windows. There. Just over the trees. Some smoke. Something was burning, and it didn't look like the D.C. fire department had the sucker under control. Of course, anything that the government of D.C. ran was invariably out of control, but that was an opinion he never shared, even with some of his warhorse buddies from New

York State. Votes were votes, and you tried not to screw over those friends of yours when you could.

Out of the office door and into the secretarial area. Nothing. The desks were empty, plastic dust covers over the terminals. His Secret Service detail wasn't here. The military officer with the briefcase that held the launch codes, also known as the football, wasn't sitting at his usual post. Spooky. Could everyone have called in sick today? Was it possible?

Or maybe they were just out of the building. In training or something, or one of those loony empathy or encounter training groups the Department of Labor was pushing, where people had to play role games and be the oppressed or the oppressor or something. God, that was something he would have to put the squeeze on, and soon. Election day was just over a year away, and problems, man, he had problems that he didn't need to add to. He made a mental note to ask his Secretary of Labor to put a halt to some of the more loony programs. He had the loony left on his side. Had to make sure you didn't piss off the muddling middle.

He went to one of the secretary's desks, ran a hand over the smooth plastic. He supposed he could have taken off this dust cover and then sit down and work at this desk. Then he could log on, check his e-mail, check the overnight wire reports, and then do a little . . . Well, just for a while, to relax his mind. His mouth was dry at the thought. Could work now, couldn't it? But as he started tugging off the dust cover, he stopped. That wouldn't do, not at all. The President of the United States couldn't be seen typing at someone else's desk. That was unseemly. He was a bit of the man of people but he also knew what Reagan and his crew had worked with. A little pomp and circumstance was something the people craved. So no saxophone playing, no jogging and no boxers versus briefs for this Chief Executive. And no being alone with any goddamn female interns! And he'd hate to see the kind of gossip that would come around if he had been at this desk, and the entire section trooped back in and saw him here. Nope. Wouldn't do at all. Not very presidential.

He went down the hallway and then slowed and stopped. Damn, it was quiet. No phones were ringing, no voices, nothing. Where was everyone? He was in the southwest corner of the West Wing, known as the Rectangular Office, which belonged to his chief of staff. He poked his head into his chief of staff's office. Empty. Through the windows of the office he could make out the gothic ugliness of the old Executive Office Building. Damn it, if the man had a meeting or was out of town, he should have known about it. This was unseemly.

A few more office checks found the same thing. Empty desks, empty chairs, no lights on at all. That tingling feeling came back to him and, as he rounded into a connecting corridor, he heard voices and started smiling. There, at least someone was here and could tell him what was going on with the phones and the computers, and why in hell the goddamn place was so empty. Another office section and he went in, and three women sat up from their desks and looked over at him. They had the White House passes around their neck and he vaguely recognized their faces, and there was something a bit . . . a bit off as he entered the room.

First of all, they had been staring intently at their computer screens when he had come in, and he had caught a tantalizing glimpse of green and magenta colors on their screens that had made him smile with unexpected pleasure. But like they were part of a drill team, each woman tapped a single key and the colors disappeared, to be replaced by rows of numbers. Second, he didn't know what kind of dress code his administrative folks were enforcing, but these ladies looked . . . well, they looked worn. Jeans and T-shirts. No makeup. No jewelry. Puffy eyes, like they hadn't slept well in the past few days. And their desks were piled with food and water and soft drinks, like they expected a blizzard or something to hole them up here for a week or two.

The closest of the three women said, "Sir?" in a tentative voice, and he put on his best campaign smile and said, "Is there something wrong with the telephone system?"

She slowly nodded. "I believe there is, sir. I mean, I know the phones haven't rung here in a while."

"Then it's been reported?"

She looked to her companions, and then back to him. "Yes, sir, I believe it has."

"And what about the staff?" he asked. "There seems to be a lot of absentees here today."

"Flu," the second woman said, and the third nodded and said, "Training," and the first woman said, "To tell you the truth, sir, I haven't really noticed. We've been busy ever since we've gotten here."

"I see," he said, not liking the expressions in their faces. "Your computers, though."

"Sir?" she said.

"I mean, your computers are working just fine."

"Yes, sir, they are," and the other two women nodded in agreement.

"Ah," he said. "Well, you see, I have a problem. In my office. My own computer isn't working."

The women stared at him, and he saw that their fingers were trembling over the keyboard. He cleared his throat and went on. "I mean to say, would any of you know anything about computers?"

The first women spoke quickly. "No sir, I'm afraid we don't."

"Well, I don't mean the inner workings. I mean just getting the damn thing to work." He tried his smile again. "It's in the Oval Office. You could come by, give it a shot."

They all shook their heads no. He tried to think of something and came up with, "If you come in, I could get one of the White House photographers to stop by and get your picture. Something to show your family."

By now the other two women seemed to be actually sitting on their hands. The first woman shook her head even more firmly and said, "Mister President, I'm sorry, we don't know anything about computers. Not a thing. I'm sorry we can't help you, and we must be getting back to work."

He nodded and moved to leave, and then looked back. Their faces disturbed him. Something was wrong there, and he knew what it was. Nothing was going to get them out of their chairs. Bribes, promises of autographed photos with the president, maybe even threats of dismissal. Nothing. The three women were desperately waiting for him to leave, so they could get back to whatever they were doing, and that something wasn't columns of numbers. It was . . .

Boss key.

Now why in hell did he think of that?

He went down the hallway, past the antiques and the paintings of POTUSes past, and then it came to him. Something he had read somewhere. Boss key. Workers with computers could be playing games, stored or on line, and all you had to do was strike a single key if the boss came by, and the computer screen would instantly show something else. Like a word processing program, or a graphics program.

Or columns of numbers. Boss key. And that's why those three women, that's why their fingers moved in unison when he entered their office. They were up to something and didn't want to have the Boss of Bosses find out what they were doing.

Boss key.

Damn it, he'd have to talk to Rogers today, if that Chief of Staff ever showed up. It wasn't right for the White House staff to be playing games on the taxpayers' dollar. If the Speaker of the House ever heard about that, there'd be hell to pay, above everything else, and he didn't need that. No more aggravations, please. Was it too much to have a working computer so a man could relax for a few minutes?

By now he was in a corridor near the gardens and thought he could use some fresh air. There were glass doors and a man in uniform standing outside, and the man snapped to attention when he went out. A Marine, in dress blues, and the sight of the man standing there was fine indeed. He stood next to the Marine and nodded to him, but the Marine just stared ahead. The President walked out onto the grass and enjoyed the fresh air, and then wrinkled his nose in distaste. Something was burning. A lot of somethings was burning. In fact there was so much smoke that there was a faint haze about the trees.

And another thing. Off in the distance. Popping noises, like firecrackers. He sighed. Gunfire again, in the capitol. No matter whatever they tried, this was always a high-crime district. He remembered as a state senator, hooting with disbelief as Bush the Elder went on national TV to display some crack cocaine that had been seized from a dealer across the street, in Lafayette Park. At the time he thought it was a cheap-ass political trick. Now? Now that he had been living for these years at 1600 Pennsylvania, he realized what a disaster the outer neighborhoods were, some just a handful of blocks away from what was known as the People's House.

The gunfire seemed louder. There were finally some sirens. If the People ever found out what kind of rough neighborhood their House was ever in, they'd demand to move. Maybe to Montana or someplace safer.

Safe. The thought made his head ache. He wished Bush the Elder and his several successors hadn't left him such a mess in D.C., not to mention everywhere else in this quarreling world.

As he went back to the open doors he nodded again to the Marine and said, "How's it going, son?" out of reflex, from nothing else, since all the Marines at the door ever did was to stand there and stare straight ahead.

"Sir?" came the hesitant voice.

He stopped, amazed. The Marine was now looking at him, a slightly scared young man, and he found if he stared at the Marine, the uniform almost disappeared and there was no one standing there but a nervous young boy, about nineteen or twenty. The white hat seemed almost too large for his head, and he saw that the boy had a bit of a complexion problem.

"Yes?" he said, not even guessing what the young man wanted.

"Sir, I'm very sorry to bother you, but I don't know what to do," the Marine said, his voice quavering. "I haven't been paid in over a month, and my wife and kid, well, we're running out of money. They keep on saying it's a computer problem and that it'll straighten out, and well . . . I thought maybe if you knew, well . . . I'm sorry sir, I guess I shouldn't have brought it up."

"No, not at all," he said, standing next to the young Marine, again feeling that little bit of acid guilt at the back of his throat. This man and his friends, they would go places, they could die because of a decision he did or didn't make. Those were the kind of decisions he didn't have back in Albany. Politics was politics, and whether it was scratching backs or calling in favors for a highway bill for a state or a nation wasn't that much different.

But this boy here . . . that was in another universe of difference, and it was those kinds of things that kept him awake nighst. Nothing else. Not the fights with Congress or the media or his own people in the party. That was normal. But this . . . the thought of all those young men and women, ready to risk everything, just because of something he thought was the right thing to do, or something his staff thought was the right thing to do, it really did haunt him.

Especially now.

"I'm sorry, son," the President said. "I'll see what I can do. I'll get ahold of one of my assistants and straighten this right out."

The Marine grinned and nodded. "Thank you, sir, thank you very much. And . . . Mister President?"

He had his hand on the French doors leading back into the White House. "Yes?"

"The *Nimitz*, sir," the Marine said. "You did what you had to do. Just so you know."

Nimitz. Sprat. Boss Key. He felt dizzy, shook his head. "Thank you," he said. "I appreciate that. By the way, do you know anything about computers? I've got a problem with the terminal in my office."

The Marine grinned, no longer so scared of speaking to the POTUS, it seemed like. "No, sir," he said. "Could never figure those suckers out. And with the kids . . . never could really afford one."

The President nodded and went back into the cool interior of the White House, again hearing the faint sound of gunfire. *Nimitz*. Sprat. Something was missing. He tried to think of it and he saw in his mind a series of meetings, and something General Corcoran had said, holding up a piece of cable. A glass war. Fiber optics. Sprat. And no, it wasn't Sprat, that wasn't the whole thing, it was . . .

Boss key.

He stood in the empty corridor. Where was everybody? And his stomach grumbled and he started walking again. It was almost lunch and he was damned if he was going to go back to his empty Oval Office and stare at the blank screen and wait for someone to bring him something to eat. If people were in training or were out sick or taking the damn day off, he'd have to fend for himself, and he walked along, making sure that he would tell his worthless chief of staff that this was unacceptable and that if it ever happened again, that this damn White House ground to a halt again, then he would be out on his ass, scrambling for another job on Wall Street.

A Marine guard! Complaining to him about not being paid!

He went down a series of stairs to the service areas, where the real behind-the-scenes people worked. He had read that some of his predecessors could only find their way from the living quarters to the Oval Office and the Rose Garden and back to the living quarters, but he prided himself on knowing the ins and outs of everything around here. The mail room in the Executive Office Building, which handled the tens of thousands of letters he received each week, and the switchboard, where the staff there could literally connect him to everywhere in the world. Like the Majority Leader, or the President of Russia, or even the First Lady, out on one of her tours of . . .

Marla. He felt a warm flush of shame crawl up his back. He hadn't thought about her all morning. She was out in San Diego doing some military hospital tour, and he knew he would have to try to reach her today, if the damn phones ever started working again. He smiled as he walked, remembering how Marla had stuck with him, through everything, and how she had helped him unwind after a brutal series of meetings or fundraisers. One of the many hazards of politics was the lovely and young talent that got tossed your way, and if you didn't keep your pants buttoned, your career could collapse faster than you could say Gary Hart or Bill Clinton. But Marla had always managed to take the edge off, and he had a particularly fond memory of election night three years ago, when she had taken him to the hotel suite and delighted him with something particularly erotic involving silk scarves and strawberries, and she had nuzzled him later and said, "Get used to it, bud. That's the very first of your Presidential balls." And they had laughed for long, delicious minutes.

Even though the switchboard was having a bad day, he'd still have to try to call her somehow later, and then he went through a series of doors, still marveling at the emptiness of the place. Through an empty and dark dining area, he went through another series of double doors and heard voices, and saw two men inside one of the three White House kitchens. They were talking and packing boxes and if he didn't know better, it looked like they were taking food supplies away from the kitchen. There was an older and a younger man, and the older man seemed in charge. Both were dressed in jeans and gray sweatshirts, and both hadn't noticed when he came into the kitchen.

"So make sure when we get back that your mom's get everything packed, 'cause we got a long drive ahead of us," the older man said. "There won't be time to waste, and I won't relax until we get to the camp. Then we'll lock all the doors and load up the shotguns and wait this out, 'til somebody—"

The President cleared his throat, and both men stared up at him. The older man looked shocked while his son merely glared at him. He looked at them both, standing behind a wooden counter, cardboard boxes about them, with canned goods and boxes of spices and other foods. The older man had a White House pass around his neck, while his son didn't. The kitchen seemed to go on forever—stoves, walk-in refrigerators, pots and pans of every size hanging from overhead—and once he had come here just before a State dinner and was amazed at the organized chaos of the cooks and serving staff moving around in a jumble.

Now it was mostly dark, with only the three of them here. "Sir?" the older man finally said.

"You're on the staff here, aren't you?" he asked.

"One of the chefs," he said, still holding a cardboard box full of canned goods, which he slowly put down.

"Well," the President said. "I was wondering if I could have some lunch."

"Lunch?" he said, surprised. "You want some lunch?"

"Well, it's almost noon, isn't it?"

The man smiled. "I guess it is, sir. Lunch coming right up."

"Dad!" the young man protested. "We don't have time!"

His father started moving around the kitchen with graceful moves, opening a refrigerator door and taking some covered dishes out, and then getting some utensils. "Sure we do, son. We have time to make lunch for the President. Trust me, we do. How does a turkey sandwich sound?"

"That would be fine," he said, and he sat down on a kitchen stool. The older man went to work and the son just stared in anger over the counter at him, making him feel nervous, and the son spoke to his father. "Dad, how can you do this? Cousin Charlie, he was in that task force. How can you sit here and make him lunch?"

The older man gracefully sliced the sandwich in two, placed it on a plain white plate and slid it over. "Because it's my job, that's all. It may be my last day and all, but I'll go out, doing my job. That's what's right. And now, if you excuse us, it's time to leave. Mister President."

"Thank you, thank you very much," he said. He picked up the sandwich and looked at the two men, and even though his stomach was grumbling from hunger and that wretched breakfast he had earlier endured, he put his lunch down. He had to know. Had to.

"Can I ask you something, before you leave?" the President asked. The son was bustling around the kitchen, filling up empty cardboard boxes, stacking up cans of food and even putting some utensils to one side. His father nodded and said, "You may, sir, but we do have to get going. This boy's mom runs a pretty strict ship."

He was ashamed at what he had to say, but it had to be done. "Tell me, where is everybody?"

The man looked shocked. "You mean, you don't know?"

"No, I don't," he said. "I'm sure I must have been briefed but I can't remember. There must be some sort of training going on, right? Something that the entire staff has to attend. Is that right?"

For a moment the President thought something was wrong with the older man, for it seemed his eyes had welled up, but instead the man just quickly nodded and said in a gentle voice, "Yes, sir, you're absolutely right. There's a training session. On the new sexual harassment code."

"And you're here because you already took the training?"

Another quick nod. "That's right, sir. I'm sure everyone will be back here tomorrow. Back where they belong."

The President nodded in return, glad that he was at least getting to what in hell had been going on, and also rehearsing in his mind how he would strip off the outer skin of his chief of staff before this day was over, and he found himself asking another question.

"The food here," he said. "Where are you taking it?"

There was a sharp rattle as the young man dropped a serving spoon, but the older man talked to him in a smooth voice, "We're doing what you've told us to do, sir."

"You are? And what's that?"

"Donations, sir," the man said. "You made it clear in your first month here, that we were to donate extra food items to the Washington soup kitchens. That's just what we're doing here. That's all."

"Oh," he said, remembering that what the cook said was true. "You're absolutely right. Thank you, I'm glad you're doing it. " He picked up his plate and got up from his seat, and then turned and asked the older man one more question.

"Tell me, do you know anything about computers?"

The younger man glared over at him again, but his father was gently wiping down the counter. "No. sir, I'm afraid I don't. I never thought much of them." The man looked up and stared at him with those moist brown eyes of his. "And what I did think was something you couldn't print. They can do a lot of good but I always thought there was something wrong about the millions of the richest and brightest in this country, holing up in front of a screen and staring at nothing else, while their neighborhoods crumbled around them. Seems they didn't care about the streets or jobs or anything else, so long as they could get in front of that screen. It was almost like an addiction. What was on the screen, the blogs, the stories, the games, seemed more real than anything else. But no one ever asked me, and look what happened. So there you go. Sir."

The President nodded. "Well, thanks again for lunch," and he started to walk back to the Oval Office, carrying his lunch in his hands.

Out in the corridors again—what was that phrase, corridors of power?—but there wasn't much power here, just antiques and paintings and old furniture. By the doorway out to the garden the Marine guard was no longer there—probably out to lunch or taking a leak or something—but the three women were still in their office, and as he went by he looked in for a quick second. They were moving in odd fashion, eating with one hand and tapping at the keyboard with the other, and they didn't even look up at him as he paused in the doorway. Strange.

Back in the Oval Office, he put the plate down on his desk and then got a glass of water from the adjoining bathroom. He ate the turkey sandwich in silence—it was quite good—and the water tasted better than he thought, washing it down. He looked out the window. Smoke was getting thicker. He checked the clock. Twelve-fifty. That's it. If the phone didn't ring or if someone didn't come by by one o'clock, then he was going to press the panic button by his desk, and the hell with the *Post* and the consequences.

He went to use the bathroom, and after washing his face and hands, he went back into the office, checked the clock, and stopped.

Voices. Outside.

He smiled. Finally!

He went through the door and into the outer offices, and a group of men were approaching, soldiers it looked like, and he stopped, hand on the doorknob. It must be more serious than he thought.

The soldiers came closer and one saw him and said something to another soldier, and they stopped, staring at him, and the President suddenly felt quite uneasy.

For the soldiers were heavily armed, were wearing unfamiliar uniforms, and they were all Chinese.

An older soldier stepped from the crowd, walking towards him, and the squad followed. The older one looked like an officer, with bright insignia and a holstered sidearm. One of the soldiers had a radio on his back and was talking into a handset. This wasn't right, not at all, and then —

The Boss key quit, and it started to come back, like a little stream, trickling faster and faster, until it became a flood, overflowing the banks with water, overflowing the mind with information, with memories, my God, the memories. Sprat. Spratly Islands. Out in the South China Sea, a God-forsaken bunch of rocks that were claimed by Japan, South Korea, the Philippines and China, and the rocks weren't worth shit except they were over rich deposits of oil, natural gas and other minerals. The

Chinese started building a base there and started sinking fishermen that approached, claiming it was Chinese territorial waters, and Japan, South Korea, the Philippines and *The New York Times* and *Washington Post* started screaming bloody murder, and then . . .

"Mister President?" the Chinese officer asked, his English quite good, only slightly accented.

"Yes?" he said.

Then the pressures started, to do something, anything, and an election year was coming up and this was a good chance to show that no sir, he didn't tailor everything for the polls or public opinion, and a naval task force—the aircraft carrier *Nimitz* and a half-dozen destroyers and cruisers—were sent to the Spratly Islands to show the flag. There were a bunch of scenarios about what might happen—everything from cat-and-mouse games with the task force, to an odd missile or two lobbed into Taiwanese waters, or maybe some dissidents from Hong Kong being shot in the back of the skulls in response to the approach of the task force—but no one had predicted what had actually happened.

The Chinese officer nodded. "That is good, sir. May we see you in your office?"

He couldn't think of a thing to say.

Obliteration. That's had happened. Two Long March missiles fired from Lop Nor and within ten minutes, the task force had been vaporized. The *Nimitz* and her aircraft and her sister ships and thousands of good men and women, turned into radioactive dust and water vapor. Then Japan, South Korea, the Philippines and *The New York Times* and *Washington Post* started screaming again, about losing all those lives and risking a nuclear war over a miserable pile of rocks, and his State Department and others tried to talk to the Chinese, tried to get some sort of agreement, some sort of armistice or arrangement, but the Chinese weren't talking. They were doing. And the last news stories he had read had all said the same thing: the long wait was over. After hundreds of years of humiliation, the Middle Kingdom was re-taking its place in the world.

The President was now back in the Oval Office. He couldn't remember walking inside. The Chinese officer spoke softly to his men and they trooped inside and then he said, "This is nothing personal, you realize."

A lot of questions were bouncing around in his head and were fighting to come clear, but all he could do was nod to the officer. And remember.

A day after the task force disappeared, the computers across the country started failing from types of viruses and bugs that had never been seen before. There was a cabinet meeting with Corcoran and the others, and the general had been waving around that cable, a fiber optic cable. "We're in a war, a looking glass war," he had shouted, "and we're losing!" Then, late at night, in his darkened office and staring at the computer screen, he had found a new game on the White House system. A computer game that involved colors and shapes and manipulating them just so, a game that seemed to suck him right in, and before he knew it, the morning sun was shining through the Oval Office windows.

And all the rest of the day, through meetings after meetings, all he could think about was returning to his screen and seeing which new level he could reach. And from the distant looks of his cabinet officers and others, he knew, in that little last part of him that was aware of what was going on, that so many others were now firmly within that hypnotic grasp.

"Excuse me," he said to the officer.

"Yes?" the officer replied.

"Do any of you know anything about computers?"

The officer rattled off something to his troops and they laughed, and then he spoke to him and said, "A little. What is the problem?"

He gestured to his desk. "I can't get mine to work. The screen's blank."

Another incomprehensible statement to his troops, and one of the soldiers sat at the keyboard, while another went down on his hands and knees underneath the desk, the desk that had once belonged to Johnson, and after a moment or two of adjustments and typing by the soldiers, the screen snapped into focus.

There! He smiled widely and scurried around to his desk, and the soldiers went away and he sat down and he knew there was so much to do, so many questions to ask, but the program was right there on his screen, ready for his fingers to caress the keys and manipulate the shapes, and he couldn't wait. Could not wait at all. He could not remember such desire, such hunger, such thirst . . .

The officer said something sharp again, and the soldiers backed away from the ornate desk. The President triggered the game program and looked over at the officer and asked, "What did you say right then? Why did they move back?"

The officer moved around, his hand at his side. "I told them to give you room. And I told them not to look at your screen."

More questions, much more needed to be asked, but on his screen those wonderful moving and hypnotic shapes returned, the colors of green and magenta quite bright, and he had to get into the game, it had been so long, and he was just touching the keyboard when he dimly heard a sound, like a purse or pouch being snapped open.

And as the President of the United States tried to move up to the next level to the game, he ignored the feeling of something cold and metallic being pressed against the base of his skull.

THE HUMANS CALL IT DUTY

Michael Z. Williamson

Cap slipped through the undergrowth. He was stealthy, for there were things that would kill him if they found him, men and animals both. He surprised rabbits and bouncers and other prey as he appeared like a ghost through the leaves, and they scattered before him, but he was not hunting now.

The sound of Guns had alerted him from his patrol. They came from somewhere near his friend, and he hurried to investigate. Guns were an indication of hunting, and David was alone, with many enemies in the dark woods. He increased his pace, mouth wide to reduce the rasp of his breath, and squeezed between two boles, then under the dead, rotten log he'd passed on the way out. His patrol had only been half done, and he hoped David would understand.

He drew up short. The scents in his nose sorted themselves. That one was Gun smell, and not from David or another friend. That was smell from David's Gun. That was the smell of David, and the smell of blood. Cap dropped flat on the forest floor and eased his way under a brushbush. He gazed deeply into the dappled murk, and widened his ears and nose. The Enemy was not nearby.

He moved quickly, striding forward, dreading what he would find. There was a dip in the ground, leaves hastily tossed to cover it. A few scrapes revealed a hand, then an arm. The sweet-sour smell told him already, but he kept digging until he saw the face, then more. It was David, dead. Cold flowed through him as he stared at the body, ragged holes blown through it by Guns. All David's harness and gear was missing. The thing he called a Comm was gone, and Cap knew that was bad. If an enemy had the Comm, he had to get it back or destroy it. He didn't know why, but that had been one of the things drilled into him from an early age. A Duty, it was called.

He whimpered in pain, for David had been his friend his entire life. Somehow, he had to do what must be done, and return to the fenced Home where David and he lived. He wasn't sure what happened after that, but he knew what he'd been taught, and knew he had to do it. First, he reburied David's body, sad and wishing other humans were here. They knew what to say for the dead, and Cap couldn't say it for them.

Standing and peering around, he spotted the route taken by the Enemy. He would come to that soon enough, but first, he had to do what David called a Datadump. That tree there should work, and he trotted toward it. He scrambled aloft until the branches would barely take his weight, swaying in the late evening breeze. He pressed the broad pad on the shoulder of his harness, and sat patiently. It was a human thing, and he didn't know what it was exactly, only that he was to climb a tall tree and press the pad every day at sunset. That, too, was a Duty. It beeped when it had done what it was supposed to, and he eased back down the limbs and trunk, flowing to the ground like oil.

Now to the hunt.

The path the Enemy left marked them as amateurs. David and his friends left much less sign of their passing, although he could still follow them easily enough. There were some friends, those who David called Black Ops, who were almost as adept as he, and could kill silently and quickly. He wished for their company now. They were hunters as he, even if human, and would understand his feelings. But those fellow hunters were not here, and he must tread carefully. It was his Duty to his friend to continue doing what he was trained to, and to recover the Comm. After that, it would be a pleasure to kill those who had killed David. That was his Duty to himself.

There they were. He dropped into the weeds and became invisible, watching them patiently. There was no hurry, for they could not get away from his keen hunter's skill. He sat and listened, grasping what few words he could, and waiting for the right moment.

"—odd to find one rebel out like this, along our patrol route," said one.

"They're all weird, if you ask me. They don't want law, don't want schools, and don't want support. Why anyone these days would be afraid of the government is beyond me," said another. He felt like a leader, and Cap guessed him to be the Sergeant. There were eight of them, so this was what David called a Squad, and Sergeant was the Squad Leader. They were Enemies. He was sure, because the clothing was wrong, they smelled wrong, and David's people had Squads of twenty.

"It is their planet. Was," said another. He carried a large Gun, the kind for support fire. He was another primary target. "I guess they were happy, but a strange bunch of characters," he agreed.

"Well, we've got a prize, and a confirmed kill, so that should make Huff happy." He was turning the Comm around in his hands. He made a gesture and handed it to another, who stuffed it into his harness. Cap made note of that one's look and smell as Sergeant continued, "He wanted to prove that initiating lethal force was a good idea, and this should help. We'll sweep another few klicks tonight, then pick up again tomorrow. Jansen, take point," Sergeant said.

"Sure thing, Phil," said the first one.

The Squad rose to their feet and trudged away. They might imagine they were stealthy, compared to city people, but Cap easily heard them move out, three person-lengths apart, Jansen first, then Gunner, then Sergeant, then the rest. Cap appeared out of hiding, and followed them, ten person-lengths back. He stayed to the side, under the growth, and avoided the direct path they were taking. The Squad had Guns, and he did not, but he had all the weapons he needed, if he could get close enough.

It was only a short time until one said, "I'll catch up. Pee break."

"Shoulda gone before we left, geek," Sergeant said.

"Sorry. I'll only be a few seconds."

Cap watched as the Enemy stood to the side and relieved himself. He jogged sideways along their path, hidden by leafy undergrowth, and waited until the last man passed by his chosen target. He crouched, braced, and as the man fumbled with his pants, threw himself forward. His victim heard him, and his head snapped up in terror. He was wearing the Goggles people wore to let them see in the dark, but it was too late. Cap swept over him before he could scream, unsheathed, cut, and landed rolling. The body gurgled, dropped, twitched and was still.

One.

Cap slipped quickly away, through more brushbushes, and carefully climbed a tree. He wanted to be high enough to see, but low enough to use the limbs to escape if he had to. He peered through the woods, eyes seeing by the moonlight, and waited for the Enemy to respond.

They weren't a very good Enemy, he thought. They hadn't noticed yet. That was good, he supposed, although a part of him was insulted at the poor competition. He dropped lightly back to the ground and moved back to the kill. Sniffing and listening carefully, he made sure no one was nearby, then hoisted the body up and dragged it carefully off. He buried it under a deadfall, where the ants and flies would take care of it, and erased any sign of his passing. There was no time to rest, but he'd taken a few bites before burying the body. He could go on.

The Enemy had finally figured out that one of theirs was missing. In pairs, they stumbled noisily through the brush, whispering his name, "Misha!" They weren't talking into their magic Comms, yet, that could reach people through the air. They might soon call for others, however, and that made Cap consider things more urgently. From his perch high in a graybark tree, he kept watch over the Enemy's movements. That pair was closer, and separated from the others by a slight ridge. He eased back down and concealed himself under a tangler, where he was unlikely to be seen. They could see heat, but they would not see him. Even faced with Goggles he could be invisible.

They were heading off to the east. Cap followed along behind at a safe distance. Could he take two? Perhaps he should wait. But there was little time, and the Comm had to be found. It had to. He edged closer.

One paused, pulled off his . . . no, her, he smelled . . . Helmet, and drank from a Bottle, leaning against a tree. There was risk from the other, not far away, but Cap took the chance and jumped.

A bite, twist and roll, and her neck was broken. That injury not even people could often fix, and not out here.

He heard a yell and the cough of a Gun firing, and heaved himself up and away, bounding into the heavy darkness, the growth a whisper alongside him as he slipped his feet surely into gaps. No noise from the hunter. That was the way.

"Phil! Guys!" the other yelled. "It's an animal! It got Lisa!"

Two.

Cap shot away under the weeds, found a tree and raced aloft. He could barely see through the tangle of leaves, and was worried about their Goggles. He was hot now, and they had seen him. Did they know what he was?

They were distressed. He knew it from the increasing loudness, the shakes in the voices, the reek of fear from them and their indecision. He would win this yet. He didn't know all of what he heard, but he knew the harness was recording it, and he caught some words he did know.

"—call for evac!" said one.

"We can't!" said Sergeant. "The rebels know we are out here, that's why we walked all this way. We are supposed to find those roving missile teams."

"I know why we're here, goddammit! But that thing killed Lisa and Misha!" one argued.

Sergeant replied, "You're going to call in and abort because of an animal? Any idea how that will sound? And evac is for the wounded."

"It's still out there!"

"So now we know. We shoot it when it comes back, add it to the count," Sergeant said.

"I don't think—"

"I don't care what you think!" Sergeant interrupted. "We'll bivouac here, take a look in daylight if we can, and continue from there. Shoot anything that isn't human. Var, you and Jaime take first watch."

"S-sure, Phil," "Uh-huh," the two replied, not sounding happy. In a short while, the other four tucked cloaks

around themselves and leaned against trees. Var and Jaime walked around the clearing, eyeing each other and the blackness. Cap dropped to the ground and crouched. He meant to kill Jaime if he could, then drag him off.

Jaime had the Comm.

It was halfway until dawn before the chance came. Cap didn't sleep, simply watched and waited, though the day had been draining and disturbing. Patience was a tool of the hunter. The Enemies tossed restlessly before slipping into disturbed slumber. At the darkest, coolest time of night, Var muttered something to Jaime, then sat against a tree, took off his Goggles and rubbed his eyes. That made him almost blind. Cap moved without hesitation.

He leaped over a log, dropped into a slight dip, and exploded out of it. Here is where it was dangerous, if Var was looking. He wasn't.

Jaime was just turning, not from suspicion, but from fear of the woods. Cap caught him on the back of the neck and bit, hard. A swiping pawful of claws tore his throat out and quieted him to a wet, breathy sound, and he dragged the body up the slope and into the dip.

A shout, a cough of a Gun, and a Bullet cracked past his ear, like a rotten bluemaple branch snapping. Cap knew what Bullets were, and flinched. He ran as fast as he could, hampered by the limp weight of his kill, and felt a sting in his tail. There were other shouts and shots, but none came close, and he ran until his legs and lungs were on fire. He crawled under a featherfern and pulled the corpse in with him, then opened his mouth wide to quiet his heaving breaths and listened for pursuit.

Three.

The Enemy was shouting now, scared. They hadn't followed him because they were consumed with their own fear, their fear of him. Cap knew what pleasure was, and that was pleasure. He took a look at his tail, and found some short length had been shot away by the stray Bullet.

It stung badly, and throbbed. He would accept it. He had the Comm, and had done what his friends wanted.

"Jaime has the rebel comm!" one Enemy shouted.

"You make it sound like it chose him on purpose. We'll find it during the day. We have a sensorpack," Sergeant replied.

"I tell you that cat thing is hunting us, and knows exactly what it's doing!" was the response.

"And I tell you it's a dumb animal. It's been hit, look. Here's a blood trail. Grab your gear and we'll follow it."

"*Are you insane?*"

The voices became confused. Cap didn't understand the words, but the fear was clear. They would look for him, but not yet. Not until it was light. Very well. He could hunt in light, too. Rising, he dragged the body further away. They might follow this trail, and he had to confuse it.

The creek was refreshing and cool, and he followed it upstream for some distance, splashing softly in the rippling pebbled shallows. He dragged his burden up a rocky shelf, back into the woods, and found a good spot, near some firethorns. No one went near firethorns. They would spring and sting their prey with a painful bite. He checked again to make sure the Comm was still in Jaime's harness. It was. The fabric was too tough for him to tear, but he yanked at the straps with his fangs until he was able to wiggle it out. He paused, turned to the body and ate noisily and quickly, until he knew to stop. If he filled up, he would be unable to hunt. He tore out a final warm, quivering mouthful of flesh, shredded it with his teeth and tongue, and swallowed. Salty and rich, and he savored it. The taste of his Enemy's death. The rest of the body went into the firethorn bed, where it could fertilize them, and the Comm went several hundred paces away with him. He bit hard, until the case and a tooth cracked, then bashed it against a rock until it was open. It had to be destroyed, and he wasn't sure how good the Enemy's tools were at finding

it. He urinated in the open case, and buried it as deep as he could in a damp depression that was overgrown with weeds.

He was done. The Comm was safe, and he could rest, then transmit his last Datadump and work his weary way back to Home. Hunger and fatigue gnawed at him to do that very thing, but another part was still awake. That part was sad, angry, and mean. It meant to avenge David's death, and it did not want to be ignored.

And there were only five of them left. Rest could wait. The Datadump could wait if need be. Some Duties were more pressing than others.

Dawn was breaking, and Cap was near the Enemy again. They looked ragged, drained, and fearful. He would help them feel that even more. They'd found no sign of either him or the Comm with their tools, and that meant Cap had done well. He felt pleasure, and a hint of satisfaction. They had killed David and taken the Comm, but he had killed three of them already and destroyed it. But it would not bring David back. He whimpered in loneliness.

They were trudging back the way they'd come, and he followed them behind and above, slinking from limb to limb on the overhead path they had yet to suspect. He detoured where the trees thinned, but kept the Enemy always in sight. It was an old game that he knew from instinct and training. When Leopards had been taken from their Old Home to this New Home, they brought their skills with them. The Ripper of the forest might be stronger and faster, but Leopards were better trackers. And Cap, or Capstick, as David had called him since he was paired, was one of the best Leopards in the Military.

Below, Sergeant said, "Look, it's daylight, we should be fine. We'll set mines there," he pointed, "and there. You watch, Cynd, and wake us in two hours. We'll move again, then rest again, okay?"

"I think so," the female Cynd said. Cap watched as the Squad shuffled about the area. They were placing the small boxes he recognized as explosives. He'd seen those in training. They were smaller and different shaped than his people's, but he knew what they were. He paid rapt attention to the placement.

Then the Squad lay down to sleep again, leaving her to stand watch. But she did stand, not sit, and he wasn't sure of his chances.

He watched as she moved around, alert and careful. There was a smell of not quite fear. Eagerness. Worry, that was it. Cap knew how to do this. First, he must move away and out of sight.

Slipping through the growth, padding slowly and cautiously so as not to rustle, he edged around their clearing. There was one box, at the base of a tree, standing on its legs. It took only a moment to bite it gingerly between fangs and turn it the other way. And it was so thoughtful of them to paint the back side yellow.

Another patient turn brought him to two more. The last of the three was stuck in a tree on a spike. It took some figuring on what to do, as it was wedged in tightly. But it shifted a little when he gripped it, and he was able to rotate it around its mount.

After that, it was no trick to get back in the trees, on the high branches. They would take his weight, and afforded him a path to the edge of the clearing. Lower he slipped, quickly and quietly, until he was following a long run over a graybark limb that overhung the area. He crouched on the perch and waited. Whenever she faced away he slipped a few steps closer. Cynd was walking back and forth, and sooner or later would pass under him. The others snored, alertness dulled by fatigue. He would have a few seconds. That would be enough.

Cynd was walking toward him. She would pass underneath . . . now. Reaching down like a stretching spring, Cap got as low as he could. His paws were bare meters above her Helmet visor, unseen in her restricted vision. He let go with his rear claws and dropped, feeling weight pull him down.

She wore Armor and her Helmet, but her face was exposed, and her legs. He knocked her flat under his weight, felt the breath *whuff* out of her, and locked his jaws over her face. She gasped for air, and he knew she was trying to scream in his mouth, as a yearling would. Her hands scrabbled for a weapon, but he pinned her arms down with his paws, letting the claws sink into the flesh and holding them tightly. As her gyrations increased, he unsheathed his rear claws and gouged deeply into her thighs. Hot wetness splashed, and the body underneath thrashed and thumped. He was intent on the kill, but his awareness was still with him, and he heard another voiceless scream of distress and the sound of gear.

With no hesitation, he rolled off Cynd, and charged away, legs pumping and lungs heaving as he drove around the trees in long bounds. Bullets came after him, and he dodged back and forth, stumbling over a rotten stick, rolling through a patch of ground ivy, and away.

Shouts were followed by loud *bangs* as someone detonated the mines. The explosions tugged at him, wind snapping at the leaves. But if they were bad for him . . .

His ears were ringing slightly, but he could hear shrieks and shouts, swearing and confusion. The heavy growth would have stopped most of the metal stings from the mines, but they had to have been disorienting. And frightening. That was what he wanted. He wanted them afraid, wanted them to know, to understand and regret.

This was not their home. This was his. And he would protect it.

There was the sound of pursuit. He listened, head turning, to localize the noise. There was one, that way. He stretched out his hearing again.

Only one, shooting blindly and crying gibberish under his breath. Taken by panic, Cap thought, and the smell agreed. He was coming this way, but only from luck, and there were no others.

He could handle one.

As the Enemy came over the hummock, Cap sprang out of the leaf bed, his deathsnarl tearing the air and terrifying the animals. The Enemy stopped, wide-eyed and color draining from his face. Smell told Cap that Enemy had voided himself, and as he tried to swing his Gun around, Cap took him.

First, he crushed the wrist that held the Gun with his jaws, while scratching for the face to distract him. Bones splintered, the Gun fell, Enemy screamed, and Capstick turned his attention elsewhere. The other hand was bringing up a Knife, and Cap rolled off, pivoted, and leapt back. The blade tore his lip as he hit, but he shattered that arm, also. The Enemy was sheathed in Armor and a Helmet and Boots, but the thighs and the groin were exposed, and Cap sunk his fangs deep into soft, warm flesh. Enemy howled in agony and thrashed, cried and shook, whimpered and twitched, and was still. Cap ate a few more bites to keep his strength up, and trotted off in a circle around the area, ears alert for voices.

Four.

"She has to have a trauma team! Phil! *Abort the goddamn mission!*" Gunner screamed.

"Yes!" Sergeant agreed. "Hold on, okay?" A moment later he continued, "White Mountain, this is Silver Three. Abort! Abort! Abort! Require immediate extraction and medevac." There was another pause, and Cap knew the message was being turned into a squeal before the Comm sent it, so no one would know they were sending it. The magic squeals only other Comms could hear. If he'd only been able to find friends, all these would be dead. Now they would get away. That saddened him. But he might get another yet.

Sergeant spoke again. "Understood, White Mountain. We can make exfil point in thirty minutes." Click. "Okay, let's destroy the excess gear and weapons and bury them . . . Guys, where's Jansen?"

They worked themselves into another panic, and Cap again knew pleasure.

People had good ways to deal with wounds, and Cynd was strapped to a Litter they built. She moaned, and was still alive, but Cap knew he could fix that in a moment's time. All that were left now were Gunner and Sergeant and one called Wes. Wes and Sergeant carried Cynd, and Gunner led the way. They were heading north again, and Cap used the arboreal highway to follow them. Sometimes he led them. He knew where they would go, for a Vertol could best reach them on the Bald Hill.

The three Enemy were jogging quickly through the forest. Cap slipped into the lower branches, flowing along them like an elemental force, silent and determined. They were sweating and gasping for breath, and had taken off their Helmets to get better vision and cooling. That was good. He could see Gunner curve to the right up ahead, and eyes wary, he tensed for action . . . now!

A leap, a tuck, and Wes' head was in his teeth. He somersaulted over, the world twisting, gripping as tight as he could, and felt the neck snap. Sergeant screamed, and Gunner tried to fire, but Sergeant was in the way. He moved to the side, and Cap dodged the other way as Sergeant dropped his end of the litter and tugged at his Gun. Cap tasted brains and sprang away, rolling off the path and into the soft, leafy fronds of a downweed patch, which hid him as he slid down the hill and over the edge of the ravine, roots and tendrils snagging him. Guns sounded again, and he winced at pain in his side. He had been hit, but it wasn't bad. Nor would it matter if it had been bad. He was hunting. He had an Enemy to bring down.

Five.

He circled again, listening.

"—can't leave her here!" Sergeant said.

"Do you want to try getting to a weapon before that *thing* rips your throat out? Mother of God, have they bioengineered those things?"

"I'll carry the back, weapon slung, you do the same up front. Drop her if we have to. At least she'll have a chance!" Sergeant said.

"You didn't hear me, Phil, *I'm not carrying anything!* I'm making that rendezvous, and they are never sending me back without a full platoon. You file any paperwork you want. I'd rather spend the war in jail than have that thing rip me to death. I liked Cynd, but she's not going to make it."

There was the click of a Gun being readied. Sergeant spoke, "Sergeant Second Class Willen Rogers, pick up that litter or I'll shoot you right here!"

"You really are insane, you know that?" Silence. "Alright. Sorry. Nerves. Let's get the hell out of here." The sound of their feet indicated they were carrying the Litter, and Cap felt pleasure again. He would finish this, despite the wound. He might die as he killed them, but David would be avenged.

They were still heading north, and Cap kept back a bit. Sergeant was watching the trees. He was the tricky one, and Cap would save him for last. He wouldn't die quickly, and Gunner might shoot him while he fought with Sergeant.

Ahead was the upper branch of the creek. They would have to cross there, and that's where he'd kill them.

His side hurt severely, and he licked at it, tongue rasping through the fur. It tasted of blood, and the bitter tang of other damage. But he wasn't dead yet, and there were still things that must be done.

He rose and moved. He motion was tight and slower than before, but he ignored the pain and glided along the boughs.

Bald Hill, as the humans called it, was not the highest point around. It wasn't really a hill, just a jutting end of a smooth ridge. The creek flowed past it from the highlands, and Cap would have to be ready, as once they crossed the water they'd be where they could be found, and would have clear space to protect them. He urged himself forward, breath gurgling slightly. The wound in his side had hurt his ribs. No matter. He sprang nimbly from tree to tree, skirting the two Enemy and their burden.

This was good, he thought. They must cross here, with the Litter, as the ground sloped instead of dropping off. He would wait . . . there.

The Enemy was close now. He could hear them muttering to reassure each other, and hear their tortured breaths. They would have few more of those. He waited under the cut bank of the creek, just upstream from the crossing. Their voices resolved through the chuckling sound of the creek.

"—get across and we can rest," Sergeant said.

"Thank God," Gunner heaved out between strangled gasps. His voice was unclear yet. "We'll need . . . ready . . . for when evac arrives. How do we . . . what happened?"

"We tell them exactly what happened," Sergeant said. "There's enough evidence in the monitors."

They stopped at the beach and prepared to cross, and Cap took the moment to swim closer. A projection covered him, and he waited for them to splash into the chill water, the same water that tore painfully at the wound in his side.

Now. Their Guns were slung, they were knee-deep in water, and they couldn't move as quickly as he did. He clambered up the bank, unheard over the water, and sprang, muscles releasing like a tensed spring.

He was on Gunner, and clawed his throat out. Six! Sergeant dropped his end of the Litter, and Cynd tumbled into the water to drown, next to the worms of red leaking up from Gunner's wounds. Seven! Cap turned, and saw Sergeant raising his Gun. He ducked and leapt, using Gunner as a base and felt the burn of a Bullet through his shoulder. It spoiled his attack, but he clawed Sergeant savagely with his right paw, tearing his arm and chest. He tried to force him under water, and Sergeant fired again with his other hand. He missed.

Cap sprang lightly back to his feet in the rocky shallows, sending agony through his side and shoulder. Sergeant was scrabbling for purchase, and wasn't looking as he pounced again. He shoved the man's head under water in the deeper pool, and leaned on it to hold it there. Gurgling sounds came, and he knew death would follow soon. He ignored the pain in his ribs, and the new pains as his Enemy cut him with a Knife. He shrieked, but pressed lower, closing with the blade until it could cut no more.

He fed on the pain, and pressed the attack. He could feel his foe weakening, and knew it would not be long now. Exhaustion was taking a toll, though, and he lacked the strength to attack again. Blood loss was making him weak, and spots before his eyes told him he was fading. But his Enemy was faring no better. He slipped under the water again, and emerged coughing, before falling back once more. Cap crept closer, begging strength from his tortured body.

They clashed again, Cap desperate to finish this, his Enemy desperate to survive. As they wrestled, he felt death hovering nearby. Or was that the sound of a Vertol?

It was a Vertol. Cap snarled in outraged frustration. The Gunners aboard wouldn't shoot yet, but he had to leave or die. He drew back, dragging the limp, almost dead Enemy with him, keeping the man between him and potential Bullets. He slipped under water and headed for a moss-spattered rock, needing to get behind cover. Bullets like a deadly hail stirred the water, and he sank as he'd been taught. There was the cut in the bank, and there was the rocky shelf he'd taken on his way in.

Another burst shredded the growth as he fled, while burning with rage at not killing Sergeant. He could not dwell on that now. He had to escape to make his Datadump, survive to fight again. Let the Enemy keep Sergeant and Cynd alive. They could tell them how the fight would go. Not only the soldiers, but the human settlers and their dogs and even the Leopards would fight.

Cap waited under a featherfern, eyes narrowed to cold slits, and held motionless as the Vertol passed over, then again, then a third time. They knew he was there, but couldn't see him. Cap had played this game before, even though it wasn't a game now. Despite their tools, people couldn't find Leopards. Not one time in a hundred.

The Vertol flew over again, even lower, then the sound of it echoed away across the hills. In moments, the normal sounds of the northern forest returned, and Cap raised himself, all cuts and aches and bruises, to end his mission. It was nearly sunset, and he still had to hurry.

High in a tree, Capstick spent some time recovering from the exertion, feeling his heart thump, sensing his blood boil, hearing his thoughts roar. His injured shoulder was an agony that he would have to accept for now. At Home, it would need Surgery. His ribs might, also, and the wounds to his skin and tail. Then there was the pain within. He was weak, ill, and hot, but he would rest to recoup his strength and press on. The human doctors could heal him, as they had before. People were good at such things. His thoughts were interrupted as his harness clicked and began its Datadump, and he heaved a deep sigh. He knew better than to roar in anger, pain, frustration.

David was dead. He knew other people, but David had been his friend his entire life. He could not yet think of existence without him. Loss . . . emptiness . . . he had no symbols to describe it properly.

Cap still had a purpose, however, and that would give him strength. But fatigue and exertion and his wounds called to him to rest. He would do that now. Tomorrow he would travel gingerly and painfully back to Home. There, he would be paired with a new friend, and he and that friend would hunt the invaders remorselessly. Perhaps the manhunters from Black Ops would join them. If not, he would teach his new friend what loyalty meant and they would hunt as a pair.

The Humans called it duty. To him it was simply the way things were.

CASUALTY

Brian Stableford

Even though it seemed to take every last vestige of her strength to drag herself into the kitchen, Jenny found the impetus to cook breakfast. While she was waiting for the frying pan to do its work, she ate a bowl of bite-sized Shredded Wheat sprinkled with sultanas. Then she ate two fried eggs, two pork sausages, four rashers of bacon, three slices of fried bread and two fried tomatoes. She washed it all down with half a liter of orange and cranberry juice and three cups of coffee with sugar.

There had been a time when she was proudly eating for two, carrying the future of the human race in her abdomen; nowadays she was just ravenous. She had hoped that the food would restore her strength and sense of well-being, but it didn't. She didn't want to vomit, but she still felt utterly drained, hardly capable of movement. She had too much pride actually to crawl back to bed, especially as she had put so much effort into getting dressed, but she collapsed onto the settee like the proverbial ton of bricks.

She called Jackie first, but Jackie was at work and had her mobile switched off. The "Ride of the Valkyries" ran its course and then gave way to voicemail. Jenny cursed, not having realized that it was already after nine. She didn't leave a message. She called the Health Center, where she was due to pick up her Genetic Profile results—and, if necessary, to discuss their implications with Dr. Kitteredge. Her hand was trembling as she held the phone to her ear, although it weighed next to nothing.

"This is Jennifer Loomis," she said, as soon as the receptionist answered. "I have an appointment at eleven, but I can't make it. It's just not physically possible. I know you don't like giving out results over the phone, but could you just tell me whether the baby's Genetic Profile is clear? I think I'm going to have to ask the hospital if they can take me in today—I'm supposed to have three weeks plus to go, but I just can't go on. If I weren't living in a ground floor flat, the stairs would have done for me already."

She felt thoroughly ashamed of herself as she finished the rambling speech. She had always thought of herself as a strong person, capable of heroic effort when the need arose, and she had tried with all her might to believe what the veterans of the prenatal class told her about every first-time mother being taken by surprise by the awfulness of the experience, but she could no longer doubt that something was seriously amiss. It was one thing to be so lethargic that Jackie had to do the shopping for her, but quite another to find it impossible to move from room to room within the flat. She'd got into this mess because she'd heard the famous metaphorical biological clock begin to tick too furiously, but now its tick had been replaced by the knell of doom.

The receptionist seemed to have taken forever to summon her notes to the screen. "It's a good job you rang, Mrs. Loomis," the receptionist said, scrupulously following the rule that required all maternity cases to be addressed as "Mrs." whether they were married or not. "Your appointment this morning has had to be cancelled."

"Well, thanks for letting me know," Jenny said, unable to inject the requisite sarcasm into her tone. "He's all clear genewise, then? Too bloody healthy by half, I dare say. It's me that can't take the strain."

"I'm not able to confirm or deny that, Mrs. Loomis," the receptionist said. "But there is a note here about contacting Dr. Gilfillan. It's marked urgent. Will you call him or shall I?"

"I'm with Dr. Kitteredge," Jenny told her.

"Yes, Mrs. Loomis, of course. Dr. Gilfillan is a consultant. It really would be better if you called him yourself. That way, you can describe your symptoms. His number—"

"Hang on!" Jenny complained. "What *kind* of consultant is he? What's his specialism?"

"I really can't tell you, Mrs. Loomis," the receptionist said, frostily. "All I have here are his qualifications: PhD, RAMC."

"PhD?" Jenny queried. "Isn't it supposed to be MD, if not FRCS? And what the hell's RAMC?"

"Royal Army Medical Corps," the receptionist informed her, with a smugness that reminded Jenny of the general knowledge freak she'd got stuck with the last time Jackie had talked her into going down to the local pub on quiz night.

Awareness of what the voice at the other end of the phone had actually said burst in Jenny's mind like a bomb just as the baby kicked her again, like a kangaroo taking a penalty. "A PhD in the Royal Army Medical Corps?" Jenny repeated, incredulously. "You mean he's some biowarfare boffin from Porton Down? What the hell did that Genetic Profile throw up?"

"I really don't know." The receptionist's disembodied voice suddenly seemed quite unhuman. "I dare say that he'll explain everything when you call him. I'm sure there's nothing to worry about. May I give you the number now?"

You absolute cow! Jenny thought—but all she said was: "Go ahead." She tapped it into the phone's memory as the receptionist read it off, and rang off as soon as she'd strangled a mumbled "thank you," without waiting to be told that she was welcome.

Jenny's hand was really shaking now. She cursed several times. She'd known, of course, that the Genetic Profile wasn't any mere formality—there were horror stories in the papers every day—but she'd had no reason to think that anything serious might be wrong. She had a better than average set of genes herself, and one of the pros of having selected an unwitting member of the armed forces as a potential father was supposed to be the screening that every recruit was put through nowadays. Except, of course, that she *had* had a reason to worry . . .

Jenny hit the speed dial, not to call the mysterious Dr. Gilfillan but to get to Jackie's voicemail. "Something's wrong with the bloody Profile, Jackie," she said, unceremoniously. "Pick up a soldier, you said. Guaranteed A-one physical condition, government screened, guaranteed never to show his pretty face again. The perfect combination of genetic quality and moral irresponsibility. I knew I should have gone for brains instead of brawn. All that stuff about the tactics of biological warfare wasn't bullshit, Jackie. He really did know what he was talking about, the bastard. Something is very, very wrong, and I think I've just become a casualty in Plague War One. Call me when you can."

Then she called the number that the receptionist had given her. She was expecting another receptionist, but the voice that answered on the third ring was male, deep and authoritative.

"Dr. Gilfillan?" she said, querulously.

"Speaking," was the reply.

"My name's Jennifer Loomis . . . ."

"Miss Loomis! Thank god you called. I was beginning to think there'd been some kind of cock-up, or worse—"

Jenny cut him off, brutally. "There *was* some kind of cock-up," she told him, "*and* worse. I just got your message now, when I called the Health Center to tell them I wouldn't be in for my nonexistent appointment because I'm too bloody ill. Now, will you please tell me what's wrong with my kid before I call an ambulance to take me to the hospital?"

"That won't be necessary, Miss Loomis. An ambulance will be on its way within a matter of minutes, and I'll be on board. Keep talking—I'll bring the phone with me."

"No, no, no!" said Jenny, horrified by the fact that her face seemed to be welded to the arm of the settee, so that she was unable to sit up. "You're not shipping me off to bloody Porton Down! Apart from anything else, it must be sixty miles away!"

"I'm not at Porton, Miss Loomis. I'm at a private hospital in South Oxfordshire, no more than twenty miles away. If there are problems, you really would be better off here than your local maternity unit."

"What do you mean, *if*?" Jenny complained. "You know damn well there are problems. What's wrong with me, Dr. Gilfillan, PhD, RAMC? Exactly how did I become a casualty of this month's bioterrorism scare? Because it seems to me that I've been hit by friendly fire, and if that's the case . . ."

"Please don't get carried away, Miss Loomis." The voice didn't sound so authoritative now. Jenny had observed that male voices usually lost their edge when confronted with female hysteria—a serious weakness, she'd always thought. "We'll be with you in less than half an hour. Now, can you tell me . . . ?"

"You're the one who's supposed to be telling me, you bastard!" Jenny screamed, figuring that if hysteria disturbed him she might as well let loose a broadside. "*What's wrong with my baby?*"

She heard him out as far as "I'm not at liberty—" and then she cut him off. She called Jackie's voicemail again.

"They're sending an army ambulance for me," she said, as calmly as she could. "Some hospital in South Oxfordshire—that's as much as he'd say. If it were anything really nasty, like anthrax or Ebola, he'd have sent men in moon suits to storm the flat. Flagging my file with an urgent request to call him is pretty laid back by today's standards, and whatever I'm carrying I've been carrying for the best part of nine months, so the feeling I have that it'll explode any minute, or claw its way out, is probably a trifle exaggerated. That won't stop them invoking the emergency regs, though, so it'll be no phone calls, let alone visitors, once they've got their sticky fingers on me. Don't let me vanish, Jackie. If I'm not in touch soon, start asking questions, and don't stop."

She rang off, and wondered who else she ought to call. The phone rang in her hand, causing her to start, but the hope that it might be Jackie died when she saw Dr. Gilfillan's name in the display. She blocked the call and rang her brother Steve. She figured that there was no point trying anyone at the office, where she'd been out of sight and mind since she started working at home in advance of her official maternity leave, and she hadn't spoken to her father since the funeral. Steve was the only one left who might conceivably give a damn.

Naturally, his phone was off too. "It's Jenny, Steve," she said to his answering machine. "Something's wrong with the baby, and it's nothing ordinary. The army are coming to pick me up. There must have been something wrong with the bloody soldier. I know you blanked it out when I told you about the eating, the kicking and the exhaustion, but it wasn't just feminine frailty. If I don't call you in the next two days, start making enquiries, will you? They say they're taking me to some private place in South Oxfordshire, but they might be lying. This is just a precaution. No need to panic yet."

It wasn't until she'd rung off that she began to think that maybe she was jumping the gun a bit herself, in the matter of panicking. If all this turned out to be a storm in a teacup . . . .

Gilfillan was still trying to get through, so she accepted the call. "Sorry," she said, trying not to sound as if she meant it. "Had to bring a couple of people up to speed. Now, the way I figure it is that the soldier boy who got me pregnant was either a casualty himself or part of some kind of horrible experiment. Either way, I'm carrying some kind of giant mutant that's trying to claw its way out because it knows it won't be able to get out the usual way. Is that about the size of it?"

"You're being ridiculously melodramatic, Miss Loomis," the doctor informed her, reassuringly. "There is nothing wrong with your baby. If anything, he's a little too healthy. If only we'd known about this from the start, instead of having to find out when your Genetic Profile results tripped an alarm, there wouldn't be any problem at all—and the fact that you're as voluble as you are suggests that you're still perfectly able to cope with the stress until we get you into hospital. So please stop trying to make yourself worse by scaring yourself to death."

"So I'm not a casualty, then?" Jenny said, bluntly. "I have your word on that, as an officer and a gentleman?"

"Well," the officer and gentleman procrastinated, "that all depends on exactly what one might mean by *casualty*."

"Exactly what I thought," Jenny said. "Fucked by friendly fire. It's some kind of supersoldier, isn't it? I'm carrying some kind of fast-growing, android, cannon fodder."

"No, Miss Loomis. I promise that I'll explain just as soon as I can, but . . . ."

"I should never have let Jackie talk me into it," Jenny put in, not wanting to listen to a long explanation of why the Frankenstein Corps weren't allowed to talk about their work to mere civilians. Let's sign on for an evening class at the university, I said. Imagine a kid with my head for figures and the instincts of a creative artist. Oh no, she said, your Junoesque body cries out for alliance with Hector or Lysander or the British bloody Grenadiers. Brains are for wimps. I can't believe that I went along with it. It's my baby, when all's said and done. Or is it crown property, given that it must have extra genes cooked up in some secret lab in the wilds of South Oxfordshire? Do you need directions, by the way, or do you *know where I live*?" She tried to lower her voice as she pronounced the last few words, aiming for the customary implication of menace, but it came out all wrong; the hysteria was creeping back.

"We have your address, Miss Loomis," Dr. Gilfillan assured her, trying to sound reassuring. "Our ETA's eight or ten minutes. Please be patient."

"Oh, stick your bedside manner up your jaxy," Jenny said. "I've got to try to get to the loo before you get here, then back again. Wish me luck." She rang off without waiting for a reply.

She did manage to get to the loo, and back again, before the doorbell rang, but it was a close run thing. She even managed to get to the door without having to take a rest en route.

Dr. Gilfillan was very tall and distinguished, and exceedingly well dressed, considering that he might have turned up in a moon suit. In person, he oozed authority, almost to the extent that Jenny might have been inclined to trust him if she hadn't known that he was a slimeball who had dedicated his career to the design and deployment of weapons more insidious than the human imagination had ever been able to dream up before. He had some uniformed chit in tow who didn't look a day over nineteen. The ambulance parked outside her front gate was dark green. Jenny wondered whether it had a red cross on the roof, to warn off enemy aircraft, but she decided that it probably hadn't; warfare had become so unsporting in the last twenty years that today's guerillas used red crosses and red crescents for target practice.

Gilfillan introduced the chit as Sergeant Cray while he looked Jenny carefully up and down, as if trying to figure out how much trouble she might give him.

"Come in for a moment," Jenny said, tiredly. "I think I need to sit down while you try to persuade me that I ought to go with you—because you will have to persuade me."

"I can do that, Miss Loomis," Gilfillan told her, his confidence seemingly renewed now that he had seen her, and the neat little garden fronting her neat little suburban maisonette. "I'm sorry you've been alarmed by your wild guesses. Would it be possible for Sergeant Cray to make us a cup of tea while I try to set your mind at rest, do you think?"

"Kitchen's a mess," Jenny retorted. "Worse state than me. Shall I show you where everything is?"

"I'll work it out," the sergeant assured her.

Gilfillan waited politely for her to sit down when they hit the living room, but Jenny hadn't the strength to make a contest out of it. She slumped down on the settee; he took the armchair. He reached into his jacket and produced a thick sheaf of papers. He peeled off the top half of the stack and held them out to her. "I'm afraid that I'll have to ask you to sign these," he added.

Jenny didn't reach out to take them. "No consent forms," she said, soberly.

"It's not a consent form," he countered. "It's the Official Secrets Act."

"And if I won't?" she said, trying unsuccessfully to sound menacing.

Gilfillan shifted in the chair, arranging his limbs with more civilian fastidiousness than military precision. "Please don't be afraid, Miss Loomis," he said. "I doubt very much that you'll want to publicize your situation, but I can't tell you what your situation is if you don't sign the document, and that's not what either of us wants. Please sign." He offered her a pen.

Jenny understood well enough that if she signed the Official Secrets Act and then blabbed, even to Jackie, she could kiss goodbye to her so-called career—but she believed Gilfillan when he said that if she didn't sign he wouldn't talk.

"And I suppose the others are my conscription papers?" she said, hoping that she might be joking.

"I don't have the authority to conscript you," the RAMC man told her. "You have to volunteer." He put all the papers together and placed them on the coffee table.

Jenny picked them up. She skipped the Official Secrets Act, and found that the other set really was an application form to join the RAMC in the capacity of "civilian aide." Curiosity was burning up calories Jenny couldn't spare, and she really did need to know what was what, for the baby's sake. She signed the top set of papers and gave them back, but left the others where they were.

"I need to confirm the name of the father," Gilfillan told her, now sounding confident that he not only had the upper hand but the full cooperation of his victim.

"He called himself Lieutenant Graham Lunsford," Jenny told him, putting on her best brave face even though she knew that it couldn't be very convincing. "Very tall, not very dark, and extremely handsome. Have I just got him into deep trouble or won him a medal?"

"That's not for me to say. Was it just the fact that he was a soldier that triggered your anxieties, or was there something more?"

"Apart from your attachment to the RAMC and the fact that we haven't had a good bioterrorism scare hereabouts since Wednesday last?" Jenny countered. "Actually, we did have a conversation—Jackie, me, the lieutenant and the lieutenant's friend. Jackie's my friend. She screwed the lieutenant's friend, but she took precautions."

Gilfillan had apparently been doing his homework too. "That would be Mrs. Jacqueline Stephenson," he said. "Lives at number thirty-two. Divorced five years ago, shortly after your mother died." His tone was remarkably even, but what he was telling her was that he had access to all the information he could desire about Jackie—and about her. He probably knew about Jackie's teenage chlamydia and present sterility, let alone the whole sorry saga of her own mother's cancer. He had probably guessed about the biological clock, and the reasons why she'd gone fishing for unattached sperm rather than wait for the kind of miracle that might equip her with a committed partner and full-time father.

"You had a conversation, Miss Loomis?" the biologist prompted, still scrupulously polite.

"A conversation took place," she said, remembering how little she'd contributed to it. "Jackie has theories. She spent a couple of hours telling them both that soldiers like them would be redundant soon, and would be already if our military strategists had any sense at all. She's a great believer in biological warfare. Never mind shooting and bombing the poor buggers, she says—hit them where it *really* hurts. If you want to be slightly subtle, sow the entire Middle East with a virus that sterilizes women. If you want to be very subtle, use one that does what the female hormones in the local water supply are supposed to be doing to our menfolk by accident: feminize them. See how the apprentice martyrs of Global Jihad cope with *that*."

Dr Gilfillan nodded his head, as if he agreed with every word. "And what did Lieutenant Lunsford and his friend have to say in their turn?"

"They said it wasn't that easy, and that she was looking at the problem from the wrong angles—that the biggest problem with biological warfare was delivery, and after that self-defense. They said it's hard to produce designer diseases that are more velvet glove than iron fist. For the time being, they said, the trick is to make the most of the genes that we already have. Expressionism is the way to go, your lieutenant said. His mate added that Abstract Expressionism is best of all—which was obviously some kind of joke. I didn't get it at the time, but I think I do now. The soldier boy meant genetic expression, and it was a joke because the army was abstracting his sperm for in vitro experimentation." Jenny winced as the baby kicked, expressing himself the only way that was currently available to him.

"Actually," Gilfillan told her, "the joke was a bit more convoluted than that. It's an obscure item of rhyming slang." He paused as Sergeant Cray brought in a tray bearing a pot of tea, two cups, a milk jug, a sugar bowl and two spoons.

Jenny usually stuck a bag in a mug and poured the milk from the carton, so this seemed to her to be uncommonly civilized. "Aren't you having any, Sergeant?" she said.

"Sergeant Cray will pack you a bag while I explain," Gilfillan told her.

The sergeant was standing behind the doctor at that point, and Jenny met her eye. The chit favored her with what was presumably supposed to be an expression of sisterly support. It wasn't convincing. Jenny didn't say that she'd far rather do her own packing, because the simple fact was that it would take every last vestige of her strength just to walk up the garden path to the ambulance. Gilfillan took a genteel sip from his unsugared cup, and pretended not to notice the second heaped teaspoonful that Jenny had shovelled into hers.

"Okay," Jenny said. "I'm gagged. Tell me exactly how I've been fucked over."

"All your test results are fine, Miss Loomis. We'll probably have to think in terms of a precautionary Caesarean section, given the size of the fetus, but we don't expect any further problems. If you want to bring the baby home after we've completed our preliminary observations, you can. We'll stay in the background, if you wish—but if you'd like to move into army accommodation, to be with other mothers in the same situation as you, that would probably suit you as well as us. If you want to arrange mainstream schooling for him, that will be okay too—again, we'll be discreet—but again, it might suit everyone better, especially your son, if we were able to keep him in a protected environment."

"So he *is* a supersoldier with artificially boosted genes? Have you got a battalion full of pregnant squaddies, or are you mixing up the fetuses in petri dishes and outsourcing them all to *civilian aides*? Is it a long-range program, or are the little Action Men programmed to continue growing twice as fast as normal once they're out in the open?"

"It *is* a long-range program," Gilfillan said, remaining perfectly calm in the face of the attempted onslaught. "It compares reasonably well with the time it takes to get a new warplane or missile from the drawing board to the battlefield, but that's not the point. The nature of warfare is changing, though not quite in the direction your melodramatic friend imagines—and so is the range of political thinking."

"I know," she told him, intent on making it clear that her brain was still working even though her body had turned traitor. "The Age of Reckless Haste ended the day oil production peaked and the price of energy began its inexorable upward march. Everybody thinks in terms of generations now. I read the papers—and I fiddle company accounts for a living, or did before I decided that it was time to fulfil my destiny as a woman. You'd better get to the bottom line, Dr. Gilfillan, if you expect me to get into that ambulance when Sergeant Cray has packed my nightie and toothbrush."

"Fair enough," Gilfillan said, seemingly quite pleased by the way she was handling herself. "Your lieutenant was right about the difficulties of biological warfare. We don't know exactly how many biological attacks have been mounted in this country during the last twenty years, but the casualty figures have been tiny, even when the agents were supposedly deadly. Even if the flu epidemics were assisted, they've done far less damage than self-inflicted injuries like junk food and cigarettes. The days when biowar enthusiasts thought that it would just be a matter of opening a test tube on a plane or filling a cluster bomb's warheads with contaminated powder are long gone. Biological agents are delicate, and even the most contagious ones don't spread far if the targets have the sense to move back and wash their hands. The cutting edge of research isn't a matter of designing deadlier or cleverer diseases—it's a matter of designing better carriers. Do you know what a perfect carrier is?"

"A Typhoid Mary, in tabloid-speak," Jenny said. "Someone who can infect a lot of other people with a disease without suffering any ill effect himself."

"Actually, it's a Typhoid Mary with the ability to discriminate: to switch his infectiousness on and off, so that he—or she—can target the contagion."

"And that's what I'm carrying—in a slightly different sense of the word."

"I hope so. You asked whether we have a battalion of pregnant squaddies—well, if things had gone the way we hoped, we might have. At present, we've hardly got a platoon. Your country needs you, Miss Loomis. And when you've had a chance to think it over, I'm sure you'll understand that you might very well need us. If this were to leak out to the media—and I'm certainly not trying to threaten you, because we'll move heaven and earth to stop that happening, whether you come aboard or not—you and your baby would be subject to weeks of intense scrutiny and a lifetime of haphazard prying."

If she had had the strength, Jenny would have laughed—not because what he was saying was absurd, but because it was so obviously true. For her child's sake, and her own, she ought to be begging the army to let her in, not to leave her out in the open, where the eagle eyes and sharp beaks of the media might only be one of the threats facing her. The world was, alas, full of people who might find a use for the kind of weapon she was allegedly carrying in her womb—and might not want to wait until he was in long pants before setting him loose.

"Well," she said, softly, "it wasn't rape, and it wasn't an accident. It wasn't even loneliness or desperation. All those years looking after mum while she went through the chemo three times over, and all the transfusions and transplants, took a big bite out of my life, but I was nowhere near the end of my tether. It was a choice. Go for a soldier, Jackie said. Guaranteed A-one condition, and no complications. And I get the joke now, by the way: abstract expressionism, a load of Jackson Pollocks. Would you like another cup of tea while I make a couple of phone calls?"

Gilfillan's hesitation was only momentary. "No thanks," he said. "Feel free." He didn't utter any objection when she hauled herself to her feet and staggered to the bathroom, locking the door behind her.

Jackie's phone was still switched off. "Now I've joined the bloody army, thanks to you," she said. "I'm in the bloody secret service, and I can't ever pour my heart out to you again, even if I want to. I hope you're pleased with yourself. Call me when you can—it looks as if things aren't quite as bad as I feared."

Then she called Steve. "I won't say it's panic over," she told his answerphone, "but it looks as if I'll probably be able to call and let you know I'm okay. They'll have to whip the baby out a bit prematurely, it seems, but that'll probably make me feel a lot more comfortable. Hold tight—I'll get back to you when I can."

She insisted on having lunch before they left, although she had to be content with a couple of microwaved pizzas, a microwaved chocolate sponge pudding, two bananas, an apple, half a bottle of Lucozade and three cups of coffee.

She knew that the ambulance wouldn't have gone unobserved, and that her uncomfortable journey to its interior would probably end up on a couple of DIY DVDs. The neighbours had got out of the habit of talking to one another, except in emergencies, but they filmed everything out of the ordinary just in case. Someone would be sure to show it to Jackie, in the hope of getting an explanation. The exact nature of her relationship with Jackie had probably been a topic of speculation for some time, even though the dull reality was that they were just friends who'd found one another to lean on when Jackie's divorce had matured in parallel with the final phase of Jenny's mother's losing battle against the Evil Empire of Lymphoma.

"Would you like a sedative, Miss Loomis?" Gilfillan inquired. "It shouldn't be a bumpy ride, but if you suffer from travel sickness . . . ."

"No way," Jenny retorted. "I'm keeping my wits about me as long as I can. I need to think about this situation—the upside, not the downside."

Gilfillan looked at her quizzically. Jenny felt a perverse need to prove to him that she really was capable of understanding anything he might care to tell her, in spite of being a mere accountant.

"The way I'm trying to see it," she said, "is that the military application was just a way of getting the funding. With any luck, Junior's utility as a strike force will be obsolete by the time he's in secondary school. Selective contagion is no bloody use at all if everyone has defenses—the city walls will hold off the cannon every time; it's the long sieges that do the damage. The spinoff from better disease carriers will be better immune systems. By the time my boy starts sowing his own seed, we'll be looking forward to a generation fully-armored against all disease, accidental or deliberate."

The doctor hesitated before rising to the bait, but he rose. "I wish it were that easy," he said. "If I were in charge of the biowar to end all biowars I'd be a happy man. The peace dividend isn't to be sneezed at—the probes we're using as targeting aids will be a key phase in the pharmacogenomic revolution, but the trouble with biological engineering—even when it's only tinkering with expression—is that you can never do just one thing. There's always spinoff."

Jenny knew that he was testing her, to find out how much she understood, and hoped that she was equal to the task. Genetic probes were what the NHS doctors used to do the routine Genetic Profile tests to which her baby had recently been subject. Searching out weaknesses with a view to treatment was only a short step away from searching out weaknesses with a view to convenient murder, which was presumably what he meant by "targeting." As long as there were variations in the individual DNA of human beings—and how could the human race be reckoned healthy if there weren't?—then sufficiently clever probes would always be able to identify ways of attacking some people while leaving others untouched, if not with hostile viruses then with tailored cancers and other innate catastrophes. Her boy, she supposed, was destined to carry an armory of probes as well as the strike forces that would pick out the targets whose vulnerabilities the probes had identified: individual targets, in some instances, but more often families, and whole related populations.

All wars, Jenny knew, were matters of economics—and ever since the oil supply had peaked, moving history into an era of permanently dwindling resources, economics had become an anything-but-dismal science. She understood that, because she was a tax accountant. She knew, too, that since her son had no choice but to be born into such a world, he would be better off as a weapon than he would as a mere target. The world was still a thoroughly civilized place, in spite of all the seemingly random biological attacks that always spread far more anxiety than the actual casualty figures warranted; the price of maintaining as much of that civilization as possible for as long as possible was a price worth paying, even if it included the child she'd set out to procure in a race against the biological clock. She had no problem with that.

But Gilfillan had mentioned spinoff . . .

"Where did it go wrong?" Jenny asked, as the ambulance sped towards its unknown destination. "Why do you only have a platoon and not a battalion? It's because the fetuses are so big, isn't it? There's a nasty side effect you hadn't thought of."

Again he hesitated, but eventually he nodded.

"We couldn't do it by transplanting genes," he said. "Transforming sperm isn't that hard, but the new genes have to pair up within the zygote if they're to stand a reasonable chance of expression, and transforming ova is a very different matter. We had to work with the genes that were already in place, working on the expression process itself. Natural carriers aren't so very rare, and they're not exotic mutants. It's just that their genes work differently—

I would say better, but there are costs. Any tinkering with the expression process reduces the probability that a sperm will implant, so we expected the in vitro program to fail, and that a lot of the embryos conceived in the ordinary way would fail within the first trimester, but we hadn't expected the kind of problems that developed thereafter. Your chances of carrying Graham Lunsford's child to this point in the pregnancy were probably more remote than winning the jackpot on the National Lottery."

Jenny was ashamed that first thought was regret that she hadn't miscarried and saved herself the bother. She tried to concentrate on the intellectual labor and the search for the fugitive upside, but she needed help. "Why?" she asked, trying to sound forceful. "Why do they grow so big? Why are they so bloody *demanding*?"

"It's a matter of imprinting," he said, having set aside his hesitations. "Do you know what that is?"

She had to shake her head.

"Some genes," he told her, "are only expressed in a developing fetus if they come from the father's sperm, whereas others are expressed only if they're already present in the egg. Every pregnant woman is engaged in a struggle for resources with her own offspring. Every pregnancy is a battlefield, in which the best interests of the child are served by ruthless parasitism, and those of the mother by the preservation of reserves to serve the potential needs of future children. So, paternally imprinted genes work to assist the fetus in seizing more resources, while maternally-imprinted ones work to make the fetus's demands more discreet. Over the course of our evolution, natural selection has produced a balanced situation, but we had to unbalance it to get the result we needed. Producing the perfect carrier necessitated favoring certain paternally imprinted genes—but we couldn't just favor the ones we wanted. We had to tip the whole balance . . . with the results you've been experiencing. Fortunately, medical science has given us the means to deliver the baby successfully, so we can get a result that natural selection could never have favored."

Jenny had to be quiet then, not only because she needed time to mull over what she'd been told, but also because she was too exhausted to talk—and because the soldier boy in her belly was already practicing his drill.

When the orderlies brought her out of the ambulance on a stretcher Jenny craned her neck to see where she was, and was glad to observe that it seem to be a perfectly ordinary hospital, not a barbed-wire-surrounded camp. The conditions inside were far from Spartan; there was a TV in her tastefully furnished room. When she asked, Gilfillan told her where she was. He advised her against visitors, but assured her that it was perfectly okay for her to use her phone in spite of the equipment.

For once, Jackie answered before the "Ride of the Valkyries" had progressed through half a dozen bars. When Jenny told her where she was, Jackie seemed impressed. "I nearly went there to have my face lifted," she said. "You could get yours done while you're in. Two birds one stone, and all that rot."

"I'm probably in a special wing," Jenny said. "Only under observation, for now. They'll leave it as long as possible to do the Caesarean, but I'm guessing tomorrow, if not tonight. I've told them you're my official birthing partner, and they said that was okay, but you'll probably have to sign the Official Secrets Act. If I start babbling uncontrollably, you might have to join up yourself."

Jackie thought she was joking, and managed to fake a polite laugh. "I can be there in thirty minutes if it's the middle of the night," she said. "Forty-five if it's rush hour. You want me there now?"

"Not yet," Jenny said. "Got to go—it's just coming up to dinner time."

Dinner was roast lamb and mint sauce with new potatoes, green beans and broccoli, followed by lemon sorbet, but the nurse had obviously dealt with cases like hers before, because she was also permitted to order a packet of Garibaldi biscuits, a five-hundred-gram bar of Cadbury's fruit and nut and three bananas, all presumably paid for by the army. She only had mineral water to drink, because the bathroom was down the hall and she didn't want to subject herself to the indignity of calling for bottles at regular intervals.

She refused the sleeping pills she was offered, but began to regret it when she realized that she couldn't find a comfortable position in which to lie for more than three minutes at a time, let alone go to sleep. She tried to tell herself that it didn't matter, because she still had to come to terms with her new situation, and its prospects.

She was still thinking about it three hours later, when the door of her room quietly swung open. There was a nightlight beside the bed, so it wasn't dark, but the glow was too dim to show her anything but the blurred silhouette of the man who came in. For a moment, Jenny couldn't suppress the fear that this was someone come to steal her baby, even though her baby hadn't been born yet and there was no reason in the world why the army would want to steal him, given that it would work out so much cheaper and so much less trouble to let her bring him up. The absurd panic died when she took note of the fact that the man was exceptionally tall, and realized who it must be.

"Hi," said Lieutenant Graham Lunsford, uncomfortably. It was obvious that he hadn't volunteered for *this* mission.

"You utter bastard," she said. "You knew you were shooting killer sperm, and you just went right ahead. Considering that you must have been trying to get soldier girls pregnant week in and week out, I'm surprised you even wanted to."

"You told me you were on the pill," he pointed out, as he came to stand beside the bed. Standing so close wasn't as heroic as it seemed; he knew perfectly well that she had about as much mobility as a beached whale. "And sex isn't as much fun when you're doing it under orders. You have no idea how much I needed one just *for me*."

"So I lied," she said. "It was Jackie's idea. No, it wasn't—it was mine. Jenny Loomis, walking cliché. Alarm on the biological clock about to go off, no reason to saddle oneself with a bloody husband, no reason why a bloody accountant can't work from home, etcetera. Turned out not to be *just for you* after all, didn't it? It's the medal rather than the court martial, I suppose?"

"What the treatment was supposed to do," he told her—and perhaps his naivety was genuine—"was to make sure that any kids I fathered would be better equipped to live in the future we're heading for. Isn't that what you want too?"

"Sure I do," she said. "You and your mate must have had a fine time listening to Jackie ramble on about the tactics of biological warfare. Abstract expressionism—a load of Jackson Pollocks. If you're here because they've ordered you to be a good father, I'd rather you didn't bother. I'd rather stick to plan A, warts and all."

She watched his face carefully, but couldn't judge the exact extent of his relief. The fact that he changed the subject was a bit of a giveaway, though.

"How much did Gilfillan tell you?" he asked, warily.

"Just enough," she replied, confidently. "He told me about imprinting. I'd never heard of that, but it's a neat idea. The womb as an eternal battleground, where every mother and her child are locked into a struggle for resources. Makes all that old kin selection stuff seem quaintly sentimental, doesn't it? At the end of the day, it's all warfare—even motherhood. We all get caught by friendly fire if our defenses get leaky. There's a certain irony in the fact that a perfect carrier is so hard to carry to term . . . but I can see the upside now. You're absolutely right about my kid being better equipped than most to live in the future we're designing. And I can see the next step in the argument, too—the side effect's side effect. I can see the *real* weapons potential."

Lieutenant Lunsford hesitated a lot longer than Dr. Gilfillan had, and when he did speak, all he said was: "Ah."

"Jackie was right, wasn't she?" Jenny said. "Okay, maybe it's not that easy to design, manufacture or spread viruses that will sterilize women or feminize men—but that's not the name of the game, is it? Expressionism is the way to go. You don't have to invent bioweapons when they're already built in, when all you have to do is upset the balance of power. You don't have to sterilize women if you have a means of doing to them what you've done to me . . . or the opposite. It really doesn't matter, weaponwise, whether it's the mother or the fetus that gets the upper hand in the eternal struggle—just so long as natural selection's carefully negotiated balance is upset. Either the kids become too difficult to carry, or they're starved of resources before birth. A lose-lose situation—unless, of course, you're the enemy. Which we will be. After all, we're the ones with the fancy hospitals and the hi-tech medicine. As usual, it'll be the rich that get the pleasure, and the poor that pay the price."

"You're a tax accountant," the lieutenant said, brutally. "Would you want it any other way?"

"Speaking as an early casualty in this particular war," Jenny said, "no. But I still think you're an utter bastard, whether I lied about the pill or not. You can't excuse the casualties of friendly fire by saying that you thought they were wearing flak jackets."

"You're right," he said, although his heart wasn't in it. "But if you need me, I'm around. All you have to do is ask. Your son is my only child, so far, and the way things are going, he might have to wait quite a while for a little brother or sister—so I'm not sorry about what happened, all things considered."

Jenny opened her to mouth to say "I am," but she couldn't shape the words. She was exhausted, she was being kicked black and blue from inside, she was paranoid, and she was probably even a little delirious, but she couldn't quite manage to be sorry. She was a victim of friendly fire, and she was carrying the spawn of Satan, and she was a complete idiot, and she was *extremely* hungry, but she couldn't quite manage to be sorry. After all, her perfect, healthy, glorious baby boy might still grow up to be an actor, or a lawyer, or a brain surgeon, even if he did have to do his national service as a secret weapon . . . and if progress moved on, he had twenty years to become redundant in that capacity.

"You can go now," she said to him, eventually. "I think I might be able to go to sleep now.

For breakfast Jenny had a big bowl of cornflakes sprinkled with sultanas, followed by three croissants with butter and strawberry jam, a bowl of mixed fruits, including slices of melon, pineapple, oranges and kiwifruit, washed down with half a liter of apple and mango juice and a single cup of black coffee without sugar. Then she had a couple of rounds of toast with butter and lime marmalade. She'd never felt so virtuous in all her life, but she would have killed for half a dozen rashers of crispy bacon.

When she'd finished, she called Jackie. Jackie was already at work, but this time she had her mobile switched on. "I'm ready," she said. "Just say the word, and I'll be there before the contractions have got into gear."

"It's not time yet," Jenny assured her. "Any day now, any way now, I *shall* be released—but I'm hoping not before lunchtime."

"You sound a lot saner than you did yesterday," Jackie observed.

"I was always sane," Jenny assured her. "It's the world that's mad. I saw Lieutenant Lunsford again, but he didn't seem to enjoy it. He's glad he's a dad, I think, but that doesn't mean he wants to complete the mission. Isn't it always the way?"

"Great to hear you so cheerful," Jackie said. "Must go now. Get them to call me the minute the dam bursts."

"I will," Jenny assured her. Then she called Steve. Miraculously, he answered too.

"It's okay," she told him. "The kid's healthy, and I'm in safe hands. Expect to be an uncle some time in the next twenty-four hours."

"What the hell was all that stuff about the army picking you up?" Steve wanted to know.

"I've joined up. I can't explain why—it's a need-to-know sort of thing. I'm okay, though. As well as can be expected, and maybe better. I'll call when I can. Bye."

She put the phone under her pillow, wondering how long it would be before they served lunch, and whether they'd let her have elevenses between. She was, after all, eating for two—and there was a war on.